"Who am I?" I asked.

The world answered back...

Because my lawyer makes me...

Crimson Oak Publishing, LLC

Pullman, Wa 99163
Visit our website at www.CrimsonOakPublishing.com

1 2 3 4 5 6 7 8 9

abra ebner

Annabel Lee

1849 – Edgar A. Poe

It was many and many a year ago,
In a kingdom by the sea,
That a maiden there lived whom you may know
By the name of Annabel Lee;-
And this maiden she lived with no other thought
Than to love and be loved by me.
She was a child and I was a child,
In this kingdom by the sea,
But we loved with a love that was more than love-
I and my Annabel Lee-
With a love that the winged seraphs of heaven
Coveted her and me.

And this was the reason that, long ago,
In this kingdom by the sea,
A wind blew out of a cloud by night
Chilling my Annabel Lee;
So that her high-born kinsman came
And bore her away from me,
To shut her up in a sepulchre
In this kingdom by the sea.

The angels, not half so happy in Heaven,
Went envying her and me:-
Yes! that was the reason (as all men know,
In this kingdom by the sea)
That the wind came out of a cloud, chilling
And killing my Annabel Lee.

But our love it was stronger by far than the love
Of those who were older than we-
Of many far wiser than we-
And neither the angels in Heaven above,
Nor the demons down under the sea,
Can ever dissever my soul from the soul
Of the beautiful Annabel Lee:-

For the moon never beams without bringing me dreams
Of the beautiful Annabel Lee;
And the stars never rise but I see the bright eyes
Of the beautiful Annabel Lee;
And so, all the night-tide, I lie down by the side
Of my darling, my darling, my life and my bride,
In her sepulchre there by the sea-
In her tomb by the side of the sea.

1942:

"Max, I'd love a rose."

Avery's voice was distant. I turned to her, wondering what it was she'd said. "Hmm?"

She sighed, pressing her brows together with annoyance. "I said I'd like a *rose*."

I snapped out of my trance. The sensation of her arm hooked with mine flooded back to me, sending a tingle of warmth over my skin. The wind blew, tickling the white fur on her lapel. Her frosty blue eyes shimmered in the moonlight, so full of light and beauty. Taking in surroundings I had all but forgotten, I saw there was a street vendor beside us that I hadn't noticed before. He was selling roses.

"See, aren't they lovely?" Avery insisted.

I glanced at the blue roses, powdered with wintery frost. I felt a pang in my heart. I should want to buy one for her—I should want to shower her with gifts, with love, but something wasn't right.

Avery jerked at my arm, forcing an answer from my lips. I

looked at the vendor. "One, please."

The vendor eyed me with a flash of pity. Avery swooned at my side, happy with the fact she'd coerced me into buying her a rose. Why hadn't I thought to do so myself? Why hadn't I seen the vendor earlier, thinking of nothing but the way Avery's pouty smile would warm my heart with their purchase? But there was nothing. It hadn't even occurred to me to look.

"Max, you're such a wonderful fiancé," she gushed.

Another gust whipped through the streets of Winter Wood, a town so seemingly human, yet locked within a purely magickal world. It was a place our kind came to mingle, to live, and to experience a sense of belonging. Here we could be free—here, we didn't have to hide.

My eyes traced the distant walls of the town that protected us and kept us invisible. The human world outside these walls was tainted with war and destruction. Winter Wood was the only place to escape their horrors and to live as though all that was a simple, yet horrible dream.

"Here you are, Miss." The vendor handed her the rose, swirling his fingers over the petals as the bud opened before her eyes. She gasped, a silly childish gasp that told me she'd seen this trick a hundred times, but she never tired of it.

It tired me.

How long would my life go on? Soon there would be nothing to surprise me, no wonders as there once were. I was only thirty-three, though I didn't look a day past seventeen. How many more years would I live? One hundred? A thousand? The thought alone made my throat tighten. I coughed.

"You're not catching a cold are you?" Avery squeezed my arm, the rose now tucked into her hair, perfectly placed in a way that complimented her eyes. We had walked on past the rose vendor, moving from street light to street light.

I looked at her sideways. "A cold? Really?"

She giggled, looking down at her feet in the snow. "Sometimes it's just fun to ask, even if it's never true. Human novelty, I suppose."

I shook my head, still unable to enjoy her light-hearted chit chat. My attention continued to pull away from her, finding any means of escape. That's when I saw the apothecary up ahead, the windows warm and inviting. "I may not have a cold, but do you mind if we stop in to visit the alchemist?"

I saw the joy on her face fade. She didn't have any interest in alchemy; as an Element Pixie she had no need to. A pixie's powers of alchemy came naturally. Potions were useless trinkets, nothing but clutter to their efficient ways of living. Their powers so far exceeded all others that most of us could not fathom their extent, and yet they did not abuse them; only the Shadow Pixies did.

"Fine," she answered with a sigh and fluffed her long platinum hair, the ringlets spraying a glittery plume into the air behind her—she smelled like cinnamon.

We reached the shop a few paces later, ducking inside and escaping the cold. Avery released my arm, the warmth of her fading to a bitter tingle lingering on my skin. She floated directly to the shelf that contained the perfume, finding it the only thing of interest. She hummed to herself as she began to test each one, her melody as intoxicating as the fumes with which she surrounded herself with.

The alchemist came out from the back room, hearing the ding of the bell on his door. His eyes grew light with joy when he saw me. "Max! Good to see you! How are you doing?" He enveloped me in his arms, clearly not caring about personal space.

I patted him on the back. "Doing well, Patrick."

Patrick pulled me away from him, seeing through my strained happiness. "Something about the way you say that makes me think differently." His hands were firmly latched onto either shoulder, his clear, blue eyes seeing to the very soul of me. He was more of a father to me than my own, helping me acclimate to my new life in this world since my death many years ago. Even before that, he had been a teacher to me, though his magickal secrets had remained hidden because of the affair that my mother and he shared.

I tried to smile, but I was certain that smile gave everything away. Patrick nodded slowly, as though he knew just what I was thinking.

He glanced over my shoulder. *You're engaged to the Crown's daughter. How can you not be happy?* He asked with his thoughts.

I shrugged.

He gave me a pat on the arm. *I look forward to each day I draw closer to death, because each day is a step closer to your mother once again.* His words carried weight, and I instantly knew he was trying to tell me something.

After a moment I nodded, understanding what he was getting at—he referred to true love, not arranged as my real mother and father's marriage had been, as my engagement to Avery felt.

Patrick broke his silent speech. "So, what brings you here? In need of a potion? A remedy perhaps?" He was trying to avoid raising Avery's suspicions, asking me a practical, contrived question.

I looked over my shoulder, reassured to find that Avery was still content with the perfume and not at all sensing my apprehension. I turned back, leaning close to Patrick and whispering in his ear. "Actually, I'm in need of a *spell*."

"A spell!" he laughed loudly.

I frowned at him, encouraging his discretion on the matter.

Patrick settled himself, leaning into me. "Well, then step into my office." He winked.

I turned back to Avery. "Are you okay here for a moment, darling?"

She twisted a piece of perfumed balsa near her nose, looking annoyed that I'd distracted her from the scent. "Of course."

Standing there, I tried not to act irresolute about us. Her eyes narrowed, contrasted only by her smile. From that simple gesture, I knew insecurities were indeed lying behind those eyes. I knew her well enough to see that inside her, but often her tough exterior was too thick. I was naïve to think she couldn't sense the reluctance in my love for her. I couldn't blame her, though. She'd already given me everything of her soul—her light. Changing my mind now meant destroying her and handing her to the shadows.

I forced a reassuring expression. "It'll just be a moment."

She grinned hopelessly. The guilt of it stung.

Patrick led me into his office in the back of the shop, shutting the door behind us. I settled into an oak chair that sat in front of his desk. He rounded in front of me, leaning two hands against the surface, staring down.

"Are you really looking for a spell?" He looked curious with one eye narrowed, suspicious because I had never asked for one before.

I nodded apprehensively. A spell was the only thing I could think of to fix this.

"What kind of spell are you looking for?" He took a seat and his chair groaned.

I leaned forward, folding my hands on the edge of his desk. "I've been thinking about the future, Patrick. I fear what will become of me if I marry Avery. Most of all, I fear that life has already grown old. I want to know if there will be more for me, or if my time here was ill decided." I paused and diverted my gaze. "A part of me questions if I should have passed on when the chance was presented." I was ashamed to admit it. "Is there a spell that can tell me whether I've made the right choice?"

Patrick sighed long and hard. "I have seen a growing darkness in you. I've seen it for the past few years now. I know you long for more from your life—for meaning." He sat up, lifting his hand where a key hung from his wrist. He unlocked the drawer before him, contemplating what he was about to show me. Committing to his task, he reached inside. When he pulled his hand out, I saw that he'd retrieved a simple clump of fabric. He placed it on the desk between us. "I should have destroyed this long ago, but I knew that one day you would come asking me just such a question, because that's what it told me." He pressed the clump of fabric across the desk. "Inside this fabric is a Truth Stone. It cannot tell you the future in detail, but it will tell you the truth of your deepest desires, which in your case may *contain* the future. It's different for everyone, so I can't make any guarantees. Touch it, and I believe you will leave here a happier man."

I gazed upon the fabric with apprehension, noting the delicate way in which he'd handled it, despite is obvious age.

"Have you ever used it yourself?"

Patrick's lip curled, his thoughts wandering to a place where he was happy. "A few times. Yes." His cheeks deepened in color. "There comes a moment in every man's life when the answers we seek are buried deep within, too deep to reach on our own."

I hung on his words, wishing I could read his thoughts, but his mind had been washed by a potion that blocked it long ago. Only the thoughts he wanted me to hear came through—right now, he wanted to hide everything but his emotion.

"Don't be afraid. The truth cannot hurt you," he reassured.

I clenched my jaw and timidly reached forward, clasping my fingers around the cloth. There was an instant tingle emanating from the rough canvas fabric, warming my hand. I wanted to giggle. I wanted to be a child again. It was a feeling I'd almost forgotten—a feeling of life. I was surrounded by a sudden sense of confidence, of reality and truth. I unclothed the stone and saw nothing but a dull grey rock, a fraction of the brilliance I'd expected. I lifted one brow and looked at Patrick.

"I know it doesn't look like much, but trust me." He grinned.

With my other hand, I pulled the cloth out from under the rock, tumbling it onto my palm. The tingle grew intense and shot up my arm, like a surge of electricity. I gasped as a sense of falling caused my whole body to tense.

The room around me went dark, my lips pressed shut as my breathing ceased.

A girl giggled in the darkness.

I blinked, but saw nothing.

She giggled again, the sound growing crisp.

My lips released and I gasped for air, listening to the sounds. "Hello?"

The laughter stopped. "Max!" the girl yelled. "Max, I'm over here!"

The lights suddenly came on. I was no longer in Patrick's office but in a forest, the sun filtering past green leaves.

"Max!" the girl's voice yelled again, this time closer.

I felt soft hands grip my shoulders from behind. I heaved, thrown forward as I tumbled over the forest floor. I felt the girls legs wrap around my middle, her lips against my ear. I landed face first, but my typical instinct to attack didn't take over. Where the need to be defensive should have been, happiness lived instead. A surprising laugh escaped my own lips, ignoring the uncomfortable position I found myself in. Turning over, the girl that had attacked me shifted until she sat straddled on my stomach.

The beauty of her eyes knocked the breath from my lungs. She was about eighteen, her face alive—her life alive within me. She tucked a long strand of dark brown hair behind her ear. "I found you," she breathed hard, her smile never fading.

I was speechless as I stared at her, my senses drinking her in, wanting to be near her. She wore tattered jean shorts and a white top, a bit of mud smeared across one cheek. She wrapped her fingers into my hair, leaning down until her lips grazed my forehead. I breathed deep, smelling rose and tea leaf, riding on air that was warm and refreshing.

"I missed you," she whispered.

Her words were so enticing that it caused me to shudder. I couldn't blink, I couldn't move, the desire to kiss this beautiful being was all I could think of. I clasped her around the waist, my fingers sensing the reality of her within my grasp. This was my future, and she was as real as the fabric of her shirt in my hands.

But the fabric began to unravel.

The dream began to fade.

Just as quickly as the vision had come, it was gone. I was left in the dark grasping nothing.

I had lost her.

~

Everything was black, the tingling in my arms receding. Slowly, the room around me came back into focus, my head tight and pounding. Patrick grinned as he sat across the desk from me.

"Well?"

I found that though my body was taxed and tired beyond reason, I was still smiling. The sweet smell of the girl was lingering in my senses, a smell I would hold close until I found her again.

"It worked, didn't it? I haven't seen you smile like that since you came back from the dead." Patrick was being dramatic.

I nodded, still at a loss for words. "It did work. I—I just…" There were so many new questions. "When? How do I know when this truth will take place?" I gushed.

Patrick smiled, lifting the cloth from the desk and plucking the rock from my hand, careful not to touch it to his skin. He dropped it back into the drawer and locked it away. "That's the beauty, isn't it? You don't know when, you just know that someday, it will."

I grinned wider, finding the mystery of it intriguing.

"I once saw your mother in the truth. I knew then that there was a future for me—a purpose."

I looked at Patrick, tears of happiness and relief threatening to form though they couldn't.

"Go, Max. I think you know what you need to do."

Patrick stood and walked me back toward the front of the shop. Avery spun as she heard us approach, her face alive.

"Oh, Max! Come smell." Avery beckoned me toward her, thrusting a balsa stick under my nose—cinnamon.

I nodded, finding the act of pretending to be cheerful now worthless—she was not my destiny. Though I would destroy her light, I had no choice. I refused to live a false existence.

"Don't you like it?" Her face sank, her comment meaning so much more than she could understand in this moment.

I shrugged, turning my attention toward the shelf. Drawn to a particular vial, I lifted it and read the label. It was perfect. Rotating it in my hand, the anticipation of the smell that was contained behind its glass walls became palpable. I had to smell it once more. Uncorking the top and placing a balsa stick through the neck, my body shook as I brought it to my nose—tea leaf. I exhaled slowly, allowing the scent to sweep over my senses and roll across my tongue. I could almost taste her. Ferociously driven, I reached for another vial, not bothering to smell, already knowing it was exactly what I wanted.

I turned on my heel. "Patrick, I'd like to have a mix of these two, please."

Patrick's lip curled, trying to understand what I'd seen in the truth. "Of course."

"For me?" Avery swooned.

I looked into her beautiful, powdery blue eyes, round and innocent like a doe. The light of her soul was still there, wavering and afraid, though not for long. "Sorry, Avery." I paused, looking down at the bottles in my hand. "But this one's for me."

The light in her eyes leaked away like ink draining from a bottle. The shadows descended in its place.

The game had begun.

1993:

"Daddy!"

I heard a girl's scream through the thick pines of the woods, her voice cutting through the silence. I was tracking Greg, and I knew that at the source of this scream, I'd find him. He'd left a trail of death and blood for the last few months, angry with my return to Glenwood Springs and determined to make things as uncomfortable as possible for me here. Though I'd left Winter Wood for good, I couldn't leave the area. I couldn't risk missing my chance to find her.

"Daddy! No!"

I heard smashing glass echo through the trees, chilling me to the bone. I took to the sky, my wings forcing me closer to the sound of imminent death. There was a break in the trees up ahead—a road. I flew faster, a rush of urgency washing over me like never before. I carelessly dove down toward the road in my hurry, my wing clipping a branch and sending it crashing to the ground beside me as I landed. It skidded to a stop only once it hit the ditch, leaving a trail of debris the width of the highway. Stepping toward Greg, the pavement under my feet crackled from my weight, causing the fresh wreckage of a car to shift and moan. My fingers were clenched and my wings tightly secured behind me in a battle pose. Greg stood triumphantly over the remains of a Subaru Outback. The tires were still spinning, the bittersweet smell of gas polluting the air.

"Gregory..." My voice was thick and low, traveling over the pavement toward him.

His torso twisted and he faced me, already laughing. *"Brother!* I see you've finally caught up with me." He threw his hands in the air, spattered with blood. "Took you long enough." He stepped down from the wreckage as metal bent, revealing two bodies that had been lying behind him. They were half sprawled on the pavement, half still within the car. My chest felt tight as an unexplainable pain pulsed through me. It was a feeling like never before, a feeling that made my gut wrench.

I was too late. There was too much blood.

I approached the wreck, shoving Greg to the side and sending him stumbling into the ditch beside the branch. His cockiness faltered, surprised by my unexpected strength in this moment.

Struggling to regain his composure, he righted and brushed himself off, pleading his side of things. "Come on, Max. You know this is the right thing to do."

It wasn't the right thing, though; it was murder. I leaned over the man's body, his face down against the pavement. I touched him, feeling a faint flicker of life seep up my arm. Leaning back, I glanced, almost nervously, at the other body that was balled under a nearby hunk of the hood. It was unmoving and small—just a child. Unable to stare for too long, I turned my attention back to the man before me. Many of his limbs were visibly broken, blood flowing freely, his life draining. I grasped him under his shoulder and carefully rolled him on his back, surprised to find he was still conscious. Seeing his face, the reason for my pain was affirmed. I knew him. He'd been a member of the Priory. His eyes fluttered hopelessly as he gasped shallowly. I quelled my pain.

"John," I whispered.

"*Maximus.*" John's words were forced.

"You've got to hold on."

He grabbed my arm. "Maximus, *please*... save my daughter."

I was confused. He had never mentioned a daughter before. "You're *daugh—*"

My words stopped when I once again forced myself to look at the small body beside us, heart racing uncontrollably. My body was alive in a way I hadn't felt for years, and something about it made me wish I'd been here sooner. She was wearing a pink jacket, her blue jeans stained with so much blood that I felt my throat tighten. She moved then, slowly twisting her head to face me. Her dark brown hair tumbled from the hood that had been covering it. Long, brown, soft ringlets soaked with blood on the road. My heart stopped as my eyes met hers. A wind tickled through the forest and over us, blowing her scent toward me like a melody. Breathing deep, the tight pain in my chest threatened to crush me. The scent of tea leaf and rose overwhelmed my senses.

"Please," John coughed.

I found it hard to take my eyes off the girl, but I had to look at John.

His breathing was further taxed, blood oozing from his lips. "I won't make it… but *sh*—she has to."

I slid my arm out of John's grasp and looked ever continually back at the girl. Her eyes were beginning to flicker with death, igniting my anxiety. Dark clouds descended over the brown of her eyes, the color in her cheeks almost gone. I'd waited for her for so long that my hopes had sunk as the years passed with no sign, only to be ignited in their full fury now. Never did I think I'd meet her like this. Never did I consider she'd be so young. Rain began to drizzle from the sky, slicking across the cold pavement. John reached his hand out, reaching for the girl.

"I love you, Jane." His words were fading fast, but all I could think of was his daughter's name—*her* name.

Jane.

Jane's eyes fluttered closed and my body surged to life. I left John, rushing to her side. Hooking my hands under her tiny, broken body, I handled her as though she were my whole life.

She was.

I looked back at John in time to see his spirit leave him—his life here was already gone. I pulled the girl to my chest, at last looking at Greg.

Greg appeared amused by the whole thing, humored in a way that told me he'd known who she was to me, knew what it meant to kill her—killing me.

"What?" he played. "Are you going to *save* her?" His mocking tone was so vindictive and premeditated that it made me feel like I didn't know who he was anymore. "Surely you won't save her."

But that was exactly what I was going to do. I pulled her head beside mine, whispering in her ear. "Stay with me. Don't cross. Don't go." Though she was no more than a child, she was still mine. Someday, she would mean everything to me in love—she meant everything already.

Greg's eyes became wide as he saw the determination on my face. "I was joking. You can't seriously be thinking of—"

I didn't bother to let him finish. *"Leave."* My voice was like death itself. The sound of far away sirens filtered over the cement. I couldn't let them see me, but I had to save Jane.

Greg, too, was lingering. This was not something he was about to miss.

"Leave," I hissed again. "Leave me alone!" But before I could finish the statement, he disappeared, a black cloud of smoke dissipated in the air where he once stood. Squeezing my brows together in internal agony, I looked down at Jane. Her life was fighting to leave her body as her breathing became shallow.

"Stay, Jane. Stay with me, Jane." I wanted to say her name a hundred times, hoping it would keep her here. I touched my finger to her brow, feeling her life pulse through my touch. I winced, the warmth of it something I'd long forgotten, but also something stronger than I'd ever felt.

The sirens were about to crest the hill. I had to be quick. Pressing back my trepidation, I begged for her soul to stay locked with her life, in this body. I bundled her as best I could, allowing her warmth to dwell inside us both. Stoking the flame, I felt our lives twine together like a vine. Her damaged soul welded with what was left of mine. Two feeble halves became a whole. It was perfection. An overwhelming shiver trickled from my head to my toe, threatening to knock me to the ground. Her pain had become my own, and I would heal it. I swallowed it down, promising to hold it there as long as she was alive, promising to allow her happiness, love and life. In exchange for her pain, I'd given her my strength. Together we were a full circle, sharing a patchwork soul for the rest of eternity.

I steadied myself and opened my eyes, looking down at her. Jane began to stir, the rose returning to her cheeks. Quickly, I laid her back onto the cement where the paramedics would find her. The sirens were so close now, pressing me away. Though no single part of me wanted to leave her, when I let go I found I didn't have to. Her life continued to pulse through me, telling me all I needed to know about every breath and every heartbeat we would forever share. She would survive, and I would see her again…

…very soon.

WES:

I was tapping my pencil against the old desk my foster father had made in high school. It was small and well loved, but practical all the same, now jammed into the corner of my room. "What's a square root again?"

Emily let a puff of air pass her lips. "Come on, Wes. Don't make me explain it, for like, the *millionth* time."

I glanced at her, feeling bad for asking. Her face was twisted with annoyance, like it always was, and I loved it. I couldn't help but smile, her freckles begging me for a kiss.

Emily's eyes narrowed. "No." She pointed at the paper before me with the eraser end of her pencil. "Concentrate."

I bit my lip, lifting my brows. "Oh, come on, Em. We've been doing this for hours," I whined.

She rolled her eyes, something she was really good at. "It's only been…" she looked at her pink plastic watch. "Thirty-two minutes."

I pretended not to hear her. "I'm thirsty," I challenged, thinking of blood—more specifically, angel blood.

Her glare only got harsher. "Stop it."

I threw my pencil down. "What? I am. I can't help it."

"Then get a Gatorade."

I laughed, but she continued to preach.

"Just think about the principal of it. Angel blood. Blood! It's just gross!" She shuddered, but I could tell it was a fake shudder—she wanted it too. "It's gross," she repeated, as though she was trying to convince herself.

I looked down at her bag which was left open on the floor. "I bet she didn't think it was gross," I pointed to an Anne Rice book on the top of the pile.

"That's different."

I laughed. "How? You shouldn't even be reading that stuff. Isn't that what Max told you?"

There it was again, another eye-roll. "Leave it alone," she snapped. "I read them before, so I can read them now. Besides, I have control."

I snorted. "Yeah. Sure. Now you do," I murmured, intending it to be sarcastic.

"What?" she snapped again. "And that means?"

I shrugged, not upset at all that she'd heard me. "You weren't always in control, is all I'm saying. You're track record for this type of thing sort of sucks." I began listing on my fingers. "Vicoden, alcohol, sleeping aids… the list goes on!"

"Shut up. That's not fair. You know I only did all that stuff because I thought I was alone, because of all I *endured*… because of all I could *hear.* I thought I couldn't survive without it."

I dropped my listing hand. "That's exactly what I'm saying!"

I could tell by the mounting look on Emily's face that her anger was about to peak.

Still, I pressed the point further. "You were stupid to do those things. Just look how great you are without all that." I shook my head. "Besides, it's not like *I* endured anything, or *anything.*"

She growled, leaping off the floor and tackling me from my chair. My head thumped against the carpet, my ears suddenly ringing. "Ouch!"

Emily's legs wrapped around me like a vise. "Stop it. This is your last warning."

My thumb grazed the skin at the bottom hem of her sweater, a part of me missing the way she used to dress, but happy she didn't dress that way at the same time. She smacked my hand away then slapped me across the cheek. It was fluid—*sexy.*

I rubbed my burning skin, grinning. "What was that for?" I slid out from under her.

She stood, collecting her things. "I hate this." Her muscles tensed and flexed as she pushed me away. My animal instincts sensed a fight flaring.

"Hate what? You mean us?" I wished I could read her thoughts, just once, but all I could do was sense her.

Emily stopped, taking a deep breath. "Do you think it's possible to start over?"

I could feel my cheeks turning red, and not just because of the slap. "What do you mean?"

"Start over, you know, like a first date. Forget everything that's happened and just… start over."

I blinked. The idea was appealing to me, but also appalling. "You just want to forget all this?" I spread my arms wide.

She looked flustered, shaking her head. "No! I mean, it was so screwed up. I want a clean start. Do you think we could do that?"

I thought it over. "I suppose." Where was she was going with this?

"I just want to forget the first month of this year because truthfully, it sucked. I want to forget the blood, the death… *Him.*" Her voice got deep and dramatic. "And, yeah, even us. It's all…" She was searching for the right words. "Topsy-turvy."

I just stood there, trying to look like I was listening when really, I was lost.

She leaned forward. "Is that okay?" The expression on her face conveyed that she was waiting for something, but I didn't know what.

"Okay… so what do you want me to do?"

She sighed. "Ask me out," she said bluntly. Her arms were crossed now, her foot tapping.

"Ask you… *out?*"

She snorted, further annoyed. "Yes."

I felt hopeless. She was looking for finesse, but the only thing I lacked more than brains was finesse. *"Uh…"* I was suddenly sweating with nerves. I didn't like to be put on the spot. "You want to go for pizza with me, or something?"

Emily shook her head, her hands waving the air in front of her. "That was lame. Whatever… just forget it."

"What?" I didn't understand what I'd done wrong. "Come on, Em. Give a man a break!"

She turned to leave.

In two quick strides, I had crossed the room, grasping her hand. *"Stop."*

EMILY:

I stopped, hoping he'd come up with something better than pizza. *What was I doing?* I had what I wanted—I had Wes. The problem was, I always wanted more—I always wanted what Jane had, and what she had was a little romance, too.

Wes squeezed my hand. "Emily Marie Taylor, would you like to accompany me to Vicco's for a gourmet burger tonight?" He was standing as straight as his giant body would allow. Despite my annoyance, I couldn't help but smile. I could see the effort in his eyes—his thoughts.

He was cute.

My body relaxed, releasing the tension from my pent up emotions. "Yes, Wes. I'd love to." I loved Vicco's, and it was the perfect first date with a drive-in feel.

Wes leaned in, his golden eyes sparkling. *"Can I still tell you that I love you?"* he whispered.

I laughed out loud. "I suppose that's all right."

He grinned, giving me a soft, almost-kiss on the lips.

I cocked my head back. "What was that?" My lips felt neglected, dissed.

Wes shrugged. "You'll have to earn a better kiss. I just asked you out, remember? I don't want to move *too* fast." He was being a smart-ass.

I frowned. "That's not really what I was trying to say when I said *start over.*"

Wes tilted his head, his lips pressed together before answering. "That's too bad. You should have thought this through. It's a package deal, so what's done is done." He snapped his fingers.

I ground my teeth together.

"Allow me to walk you home, my beautiful." He bowed from the waist like a Shakespearian hero—more like Shakespearian joke.

I faked a gag. *"Bleck!* Don't call me that! That's what Max calls Jane." My brows knitted together, glaring at him.

He chuckled. "That's just the reaction I was looking for."

Wes placed his hand on the small of my back, leading me through the bedroom door and into the hall. He walked me home every day as though he were my personal body guard, afraid I'd be abducted in the yard between my house and his. Once we passed the threshold of any space, it was all business, all brawn and attention to detail. Wes was afraid that *He* would return—though I doubted it. Snake venom tainted my blood, so to *Him,* I was a big, green Mr. Yuck sticker—He wouldn't touch me ever again. He simply couldn't.

We walked down the stairs, Wes's watchful eye already on full alert. Until the day Greg was dead, I knew Wes would never relax. We all knew he was still alive because Max was. The best we could do was to pretend Greg was dead, and for now, that was the only way to get through it. Since the incident, none of us had yet mentioned his name out loud, let alone think it as I was now. Chills ran down my spine at the mere skip around the subject. I trembled.

Wes held onto the pocket of my backpack like a leash, our proximity to the door reason enough to become overly protective. There was a delicate clatter of dishes in the kitchen as we passed. Wes's foster mother caught my eye, leaning over her old olive-colored dishwasher.

"Hello, Emily." Her voice was soft like a whisper.

"Hello, ma'am." I'd been told to address Gladys properly. Wes respected the fact that Gladys and her husband had taken him in, despite the enormous dent in their grocery bill.

She smiled sweetly at Wes, her mind filled with delighted thoughts of me, how I'd changed, and what a relief it was to see us both happy. I laughed to myself, thinking of the days my father spent with Gladys, drinking tea. It comforted me to know that he had endured the same torture of hearing that I had—the same *knowing.*

Since Jane had told me about my father's secret, my whole outlook on life had changed. I was no longer alone. I was no longer afraid of what was happening to me because I finally felt a part of our family—a part of my father. It was normal for me to hear these things, and I was proud of that fact. I'd managed without Vicoden for two weeks now. Drugs had only separated me from the gift my father left me and the giant shoes I was destined to fill. I was embracing what I once loathed. It felt good.

Wes tilted his head and addressed Gladys, a show of respect he used universally. Grasping the handle of the front door, Wes guided me out onto the porch. I wanted so badly to turn and peck him on the cheek, but I refrained, remembering that I'd ruined my ability to do so with my stupid idea of starting over.

A soft chortling sound animated the otherwise silent fall air. Wes and I both looked up at once. I gasped, my hand flying to my mouth.

"What the—" Wes's gruff voice was close to my ear.

"Shhh," I elbowed him in the stomach.

He grunted, doubling over.

Leaves slowly spiraled to the ground, covering the front yard in an organic blanket of oranges and red. Though that sight alone was gorgeous, it was the brown-white owl perched on Wes's car that had taken our breaths away.

"It's not moving," I commented.

Wes was rubbing the spot where I'd elbowed him. "Well, that's obvious."

I swallowed, glaring at Wes over my shoulder before inching forward. My pink Converse slid across the decking, making nothing but a dull shuffling sound. The owl remained perfectly still, unfazed by me, a statue among the falling leaves.

The owl had yellow eyes, its feathers dappled and thick. It watched both of us, a spark of intrigue in its eye. I wanted to get closer to it. I wanted to hear its thoughts. I lowered my foot off the deck, inching onto the pathway. The owl's feathers fluffed, as though annoyed that I'd tried to come closer. I shut my eyes, focusing my attention, trying to hear. At first it was just a whisper, but as I moved my other foot from the deck and stepped down, there was a sudden burst of sound.

Stop!

My eyes flew open, just in time to see the owl take flight, its talons scratching across Wes's hood.

"*Great.*" Wes cursed under his breath. "Thanks a lot."

I spun. "*Wes!*" I scowled at him, making this his fault, not mine.

"What?" He was genuinely confused, wondering what he'd done wrong.

I tried to re-collect my thoughts. Was it me or the owl that I'd heard in my head? Did it tell me to stop? Or did I tell myself?

I grumbled, "Thanks a lot, Mr. Smooth."

Wes's shoulders hunched in his defense. "What did I do?"

I twisted my backpack out of his hands as he continued to stand on the porch, holding me back and looking shell-shocked. "That thing's been here like, everyday this week, Em. Chill out." He jumped off the porch, both feet landing on the pathway with a loud slap.

"What? It has?" I gaped.

Wes walked to his car and I followed after him. He ran his hand over the hood, inspecting the new set of scratches, right next to a number of other, older ones, some already rusting.

"Well…" I tried to make some sense of it. "What does it want?"

I saw Wes's jaw clench. "I don't know. You tell me."

I shrugged. "I didn't hear anything." At least I didn't think I had.

He leaned casually against the car. "So, then who knows?"

JANE:

I ran my fingers down the frets, my hair draped over the neck of the cello. My eyes were shut, feeling the emotion in me swell. A cold hand touched my neck, tracing up to my ear. I opened my eyes, the song breaking as I gave in to a shiver.

"Max," I whispered, only mildly annoyed. "I thought you were going to leave me alone."

He pressed his forehead to mine, his deep blue eyes smiling. "I have something for you."

My lips curled. "You do?"

He stood back, and I saw that one hand was hidden behind him.

"Is it magickal?" I blurted. Max had yet to show me more tricks and objects, though he'd promised.

"Not really."

I frowned.

Max touched my knee, slowly drawing the cello from between my legs, replacing it with his body as he knelt on the ground before me. Max's hand slid from behind his back, a small green bottle cradled in his palm. It was simple, made of a frosty glass that reminded me of the Caribbean ocean.

"What is it?"

I could see the pride in his eyes, a twinkle of life that I wished was his own. "It's perfume."

My chest rose, filled with delight. I clutched the bottle delicately between my fingers, lifting it from his hand. Max reached for the stopper, removing it as a long spear of glass slid out. He dabbed off the excess oil, lifting it to my nose.

"Close your eyes, Jane."

I shut them, the smile still adorning my lips.

"Breathe deep, and tell me what this reminds you of."

I slowly drew in a careful breath, not wanting the unknown fragrance to overwhelm my senses. It was delicate at first, a sharp tingle, lightly coated in a sweet frost. It was summer in a bottle, happiness and life. I opened my eyes, flooding my vision with the ocean of his eyes.

"It reminds me of…" I couldn't decide just what it was, but it felt like home—like me. I caressed the cool glass, wanting to surround myself with the sensation the smell gave me.

"It's rose and tea leaf." He placed the stopper back into the bottle, allowing me to continue to hold it.

"I love it," I declared, and it was the truth.

"I knew you would." His hands crept around my waist, his fingers resting on my spine, pulsing energy into the root of my nerves.

"Where did you get it?" The bottle felt fluid in my hands, refreshing and clean.

Max turned away from me. "In Winter Wood."

"Winter Wood?" I tilted my head, my brows furrowed. "Where's that?"

"It's here, but at the same time it's anywhere but here." There was a sense of longing in his voice, telling me it was a place he hadn't been in a while.

"Here? Where?"

Max ignored my question. "The alchemist had a shop there once. It's where I got this."

I looked back at the bottle. "So it's old?" It sounded like an insult. "I mean, not old, but..."

Max placed his hand over my mouth, urging me to listen, not talk. "Very old, but I got it for you all the same."

I looked at the bottle again. It didn't seem old at all. The scent was still crisp and new, like freshly picked roses and budding tea leaves. I pulled his hand away from my lips. "What do you mean? If it's old, then surely you didn't get it for me."

Max's finger grazed the skin from my mouth to my chin, directing my gaze to look at him instead of the bottle. "I did get it for you."

"How?" I protested. "Explain." I'd grown tired of his vague responses.

Max bit his lip, apprehension in his eyes. "I'm afraid that reason will scare you."

I frowned. "Then why show it to me at all? Why even say that? You had to know I'd ask about it if you say it like that." Annoyance loaded my voice.

His lips cracked and a half smile emerged.

I laughed. "Max, it won't scare me. I love you, remember?"

He lifted his brow. "And I you, but this is... this is just..."

"What?" I pressed.

He cleared his throat. "Obsessive?"

I drew in a long breath, seeing what he meant by the fear

in his eye. The thing about Max was that I knew he loved me, and I knew he obsessed over me, though I didn't want him to necessarily show that, let alone admit to it—that made it more real somehow. My attitude toward the situation changed and I suddenly wasn't sure if I really wanted to know the story at all, but not knowing it would surely eat me alive. How could he start off with a word like that—*obsessive*—and expect me not to want to know the story?

I rolled the options around in my head. "I still want to know." I'd settle for the facts. It was going to come out eventually.

Max stared at me for a long time, weighing his options. He was trying to read my thoughts though I'd learned to guard against his invasion, along with the help of the ring he'd given me. His lips finally parted, and his story took form. "A long time ago, I was severely depressed by my… *condition*." He looked at the tattoos on his arms. "I was walking through Winter Wood, and came across the alchemist's apothecary with the thought heavy on my mind. I told Patrick about my troubles, and well, he gave me a Truth."

"What's a *Truth*?"I said quickly.

He chuckled, disregarding my disruption. "Well, I mean he gave me a rock that told me a Truth," he went on.

I tried again. "What's a Truth?"

He heard me this time, and sighed. "A Truth is a certainty, sort of like seeing your future, though it's more of an answer to your biggest question. A Truth is just simply the truth."

I nodded, wanting to understand, but finding it difficult.

"I took this rock, and something amazing happened. I went to this field, and…" he stopped himself.

His pauses were really getting tiresome. "And… what?" I was

already seeing myself in this field where I was left hanging.

His lip curled, revealing the dimple in his cheek that I loved so much. "I saw you there."

I narrowed my vision, not completely believing him. "Me?"

"You."

My eyes felt heavy. Happiness, excitement, love and desire all streamed through me and into him. He was using up my positive energy telling his story, and exhaustion overwhelmed me.

Max went on as I sat back. "You were there. You were laughing. I was laughing. I hadn't felt that happy in so long, Jane. You have to understand how amazing it felt." His eyes were deep, sucking me into his soul. "I never learned your name in that dream, but I could never forget the way you looked, the way you *smelled.*"

The bottle was still in my hand and I looked at it lazily. I hadn't paid much mind to its subtle details before, but I realized it was only half full.

The way I smelled?

I swallowed, twisting the bottle amongst my fingers. It suddenly felt heavy in my hand, no longer a simple, sweet gift, but a remnant of the pain he had endured, and the longing he'd had for me for so long. This bottle was the one thing he could hold onto in his otherwise dark and unforgiving past. This perfume had been his hope.

Max's weight shifted, and I could tell that he'd seen I'd put the pieces together. "That was all I had to remember you by. The scent was a name to me, in and of itself. It's all I needed to remember that something better was coming, that there would be a light at the end of it all, and you, my best friend and love."

The question I wanted to ask grew thick on my tongue. I felt such pain, such sadness. How long had he waited for me? "How long ago was that, exactly?" I said it simply.

His mouth trembled slightly. "It was 1942." His gaze fell, as though he were about to cry, though he couldn't. That simple gesture was stolen from him, instead only offered through my own tears. I felt him weaken between my knees, a sudden vulnerability released from such a simple gesture.

Sixty years. He had waited for me for *sixty* years.

AVERY:

I smacked my lips and looked at my nails, waiting impatiently. The trees around me were bare, other than the few evergreens that were mixed in. Fall had once again descended on the mountains of Colorado and I realized just how much I'd missed this place. Grasping at the strap of my quiver, I yanked on it, inspecting the gold inlay and following the pattern with the tip of my finger.

I exhaled impatiently. *"Come on, Greg,"* I mumbled, shaking my leg. *"Any day now."*

No sooner did the words fall from my lips that I heard the distant sound of footsteps. They were heavy, clumsy, and outright disturbing. It was definitely him. Greg had finally entered the wood, his arrival expected in a moment's time.

"Finally." I stood tall, flipping my curls and poisoning the air with the smell of cinnamon.

I shut my eyes and envisioned Greg. His form slipped

through the trees, rounding an evergreen about forty feet away. His black leather coat was flashy and a sharp contrast against the rugged beauty of the bark. He hadn't seen me yet, and I delighted in that fact. Opening my eyes, I reached over my back and grasped an arrow from my quiver. The bow was tucked into my belt; I unhooked it and loaded the string. I brought the golden, feathered end of the balanced arrow to eye level, envisioning its directed path, whizzing just past his ear.

I licked my finger and shined the tip before steadying my hand and releasing the string. The arrow split the air, silent to a human's ear, but whistling within my own. The sound alerted me to its exact position, the slightest twist making all the difference. It passed him as expected, slamming into the meat of a tree beside him. Greg halted, twisting his gaze about the forest before looking to the canopy above.

With my bow in hand, I ran to a nearby tree, wrapping my arm around the trunk and flipping my body up until my knees hooked with the first branch. I curled from my torso, continuing to climb with breathless energy. The branches remained still and silent under my delicate weight. I jumped from treetop to treetop until I was no more than ten feet from where Greg stood on the ground below, looking weak and defenseless.

I let out a little sigh, shaking my head as glitter fell from my hair. It rained to the ground in an array of colors. Not to my surprise, Greg didn't notice. I grabbed another arrow, kissing the end and loading the bow. With a grin, I shot again.

It sliced down through the air with more efficiency than the last, barreling along its intended path right past Greg's other ear. To my surprise, he caught it.

I watched as he rolled it in his hand, a grin growing across his face. "*A*-very!"

I giggled to myself, not because he'd remembered me or my arrows, but because it hadn't taken him long to figure it out.

"Avery, stop teasing!" He yelled again.

I tucked the bow into the quiver on my back and leapt to the next tree before swinging down, landing solidly in front of him. I put one hand on my hip, not even breaking a sweat. "Long time no see, *Greg*. I've been expecting you."

He laughed. "Can't say I've been expecting *you*."

I grinned. This was an impromptu meeting.

He stared at me, unconcerned by my presence, eyeing me guardedly. "You missed." He held my arrow teasingly in his hand, just out of my immediate reach.

I hated the smug look on his face, but that was about to change. "Missed?" I reached forward, touching Greg's ear where cool blood dripped from his lobe. Drawing my hand back, fingers stained, I showed him his weakness with a pleasure I found hard to subdue. "I never miss, dear Greg."

He stood his ground, the smug look remaining. "You didn't kill me," he challenged.

I laughed, feeling the plan inside me already unfurl. "Killing you would defeat my purpose," I admitted—*my revenge*—I added to myself.

Greg's lip was permanently arched in amusement. His pale face and stony features were not unlike his brother's—a man I once loved more than myself. "Your purpose?"

I reached forward, grasping the arrow from his still outstretched hand, refusing to delight him with an answer.

Greg had a knowing look on his face. "Are you saying you're finally seeing my side of things?"

I shrugged, keeping my intentions hidden. "Maybe I am."

Greg relaxed, kicking his foot out and propping his hands on his waist. "Max won't like that news."

The mention of his name made jealousy burn in my heart. "*Max?*" I snorted. "You think I still care about him after what he did to me?"

Greg shrugged in a mocking manner. "Some things don't change."

I could tell he didn't want to trust me, but why would he? I'd once been his enemy, but as the years passed, and the bitterness of rejection grew, I'd begun to see his side of this battle.

I narrowed my gaze. "Anyway, the point is that Max doesn't *need* to know." I stood tall, proud. Greg was trying to read my mind, but I refused to let him. I couldn't blame him for distrusting me. I was a pixie, and there was no doubt he questioned my motives. That's what made this fun.

"So, you're saying you want to trick him?"

I didn't move. I didn't reply.

"Have you even seen him since he's been back?"

I felt his remark trying to dig into my emotions, pulling out my real motivation. I turned my gaze to my hands, mindlessly inspecting my nails as I always did. "Unfortunately, I have seen him." I sighed, conveying indifference. "It seems he's found a new pet. I wonder how long that will last." Especially considering how fleeting our own engagement had been and how badly it had ended. He'd tricked me and stolen my light.

Greg snorted, looking to the trees above. "He thinks he loves her."

We laughed together for a moment. Max loving anything was far fetched as it was, let alone a human—a *Seoul.* She was so in love with death, how could she possibly love anything else?

"A Seoul? He loves a *Seoul?* Classic," I mocked out loud.

Greg's laughter faded, his eyes visibly tempted by my story, enough to intrigue him with my plan. "So, then you're on my side?" he pressed. "*Avery, Avery, Avery...* you impress me."

I let my emotions flash for a moment, my cheeks growing hot. "We need to get rid of that little brat. She'll stain his honor." I paused, gritting my teeth. "*My* honor."

Greg laughed at me, the kind of menacing laugh he was known for. "Jealous, are we?"

I allowed my cheeks to remain flushed, adding to Greg's excitement.

"Finally," he leaned toward me, whispering in a harsh tone. "Someone gets it."

I pushed him away with a firm shove, disliking the smell of death on his breath. He grunted, doubling back.

"What was that for?" He steadied himself, looking embarrassed by the fact I'd caught him off guard.

I approached once more, my hips swaying. Leaves barely crunched beneath my feet as I moved. "I do get it, but that doesn't make us close." With an outstretched hand, I tapped Greg on the nose. "I can destroy you," I whispered. "And I don't care about what that does to Max. Not anymore."

Greg stared at me, our faces so close that there was nothing else for him to look at.

I winked. "As you probably know, I like to play with my victims before I kill them, not unlike you. The thing is that I want to see Max sweat, and I want to see his dear little Seoul wither." Leaning away, I yawned dramatically and changed the subject, growing tired of this conversation. "All this sunlight is *exhausting.*"

Greg straightened himself, tugging his long black coat across his chest. "So what's your plan?"

I tapped my fingers against my chin, thinking of what to tell him and what to keep for myself. "I need to befriend his little toy, make her trust me so that I can figure out what makes her tick and why he loves her so. I want to know what will damage the both of them most."

"What if Max smells you out? You know he's a hard man to trick."

I stifled a growl, knowing it wasn't very ladylike. "Max may be hard to trick, but I'm smarter, and that's all that matters. Besides, there are two of us now, you and me. We'll watch each other's backs."

"If you were smart, you wouldn't be in this situation to begin with," he challenged.

I let the growl escape, wanting so badly to crush Greg, and knowing I could. But still, I needed Max alive, at least a little longer.

Greg rolled his eyes. "Whatever."

I crossed my arms against my chest and took a deep breath, leaning all my weight on one foot.

He pushed. "And then what?"

I despised his impatience. "This plan is just blooming." I leaned close once more, grasping his chin in my boney hand. "Patience, my dear. Let's take it one step at a time." I kissed his cheek, leaving a glittery mark. "Trust. Then I'll tell you more." I tossed his chin from my hand, my nail breaking skin. A drop of his blood dripped to the forest floor where it spattered a leaf, the smell of it elating my senses.

MAX:

I felt a sharp scratch of pain draw across my chin. I winced and rubbed it, trying to hide the sudden disruption from Jane. This happened a lot, a harsh reminder of my connection with Greg and the fact that he was still alive. Turning away as I remained straddled between Jane's knees, I continued to stifle the dreaded feeling of my life and Greg's life as one. My body shuddered, and I knew Jane would attribute it to our conversation, though it was no longer about that. Why I could feel pain instead of happiness or life was cruel. Greg had caused me far too much suffering, but what I needed to remember was that it was over—Greg's presence, waiting for Jane, the sorrow—all of it. It was over—at least that's what I was going to believe.

I thought about Avery then, for whatever reason I wasn't sure. Perhaps it was the fact that she was the one part of my past I hadn't gotten the chance to clean from my conscience. I'd taken an Element Pixie's light in order to experience this moment with Jane, and every sweet moment to come. What weighed on me, however, was the fact that Avery was innocent, and yet I'd torn her life apart despite that. What I failed to convince myself of was that it was the right thing to do—for me. Avery was the reason

I'd left the priory, the reason I'd left it all. I was just as ashamed to be here now as I was then, so close to where it all had happened. But what was I to do? Pass up my own dreams and desires? In the end, the hope of Jane was worth the embarrassment and deception.

"So, you knew you'd meet me one day, you just didn't know when?" Jane ran her fingers through my hair, causing me to turn back to her. The sting on my chin had subsided.

I searched her eyes, and then leaned against her chest. I relished her soft touch—her life and our patchwork soul. Her fingers in my hair sent streams of pleasure down my spine to the pit of my stomach where I held my urges at bay.

I cleared my mind. "Yes. When I saw you that first time..." I shook my head. "I can't even describe how that felt. I knew my loneliness was over. I knew you had come to save me."

"Save you? Max, I believe you saved *me*."

I couldn't help but chuckle. "I guess we saved each other. Seems too perfect," I said doubtfully. "I just feel like it was too easy."

Jane tilted my head up so she could look me in the eye. "It wasn't easy. Besides, that's what soul-mates do. We save each other."

I smiled. *Soul-mates*—I liked that.

The pang of desire I was holding in my stomach escaped. The urge to kiss her washed over me, drowning every thought. I leaned up, our eyes level. I wrapped my hand behind her head, pulling her lips against mine. She was sweet, intoxicating, our mouths dancing with young love—something I'd never grow past, at least not anytime soon. I wanted to let go. I wanted to be with her, but I had to control myself.

Jane's fingers arched against my skin, her body heat rising with each beat of her heart. Her legs around me tightened and the chair she was in became an obstacle between us. I wanted to be as close to her as I could, but the dangers it offered played as a reminder.

I forced my lips away from hers. "Jane," I whispered.

She shook her head, her nose resting in the crook of my own. She was not interested in hearing my excuses. Leaning farther into me, she slid from the chair and into my lap.

"Jane," I said her name again, and this time she opened her eyes, gathering herself as she saw the intensity of my gaze. I gathered her in my arms as I had the day I saved her life, brushing the hair from her face. I kissed her nose. "Wait," I pleaded, but I knew that waiting would have to last an eternity, something I was afraid she wouldn't do if she knew why.

Jane sighed and slid from my lap. She moved to the bookshelves of the library, trying to distract herself with Erik's books. My eyes traced the curve of her torso and down her leg, clenching my jaw as the desire to fall into her emotions grew more intoxicating with every touch we shared. I looked into my hands, hating myself for this.

I should've never become her angel when I knew I already loved her, but I had no choice. I couldn't have let her die, and at the time, she was so young. Intimacy wasn't an issue then, nor did I really consider it when I'd been pressed to make the decision to save her. I knew the happiness she was meant to provide me with, but this was a hindrance I hadn't thought out in its entirety. Taking her emotions meant taking her life.

"Tell me more about Winter Wood." Jane turned away from the shelf and back to me.

I hoisted myself off the floor, feeling the want in me weigh on my conscience. I had to distance myself from my yearning thoughts. "It's where the Priory resides, but also the population of magickal beings in this area."

"And it's here, in Glenwood Springs?"

I nodded. "It is."

"What's the Priory all about again?"

I sat on the couch, feeling the heat in my stomach at last fade with the topic at hand. "The Priory gathered here in order to protect the humans in this area from the Black Angels. Glenwood Springs used to be the center of war long ago, but we overcame it. In my world, the Priory acts as the head government, much like Washington D.C.." I corrected myself. "I mean, in *our* world. You're a part of it now."

Jane turned, smiling at how I included her in this. "You used to be a member of it, didn't you?"

I was silent for a moment, thinking of Avery and her father Srixon, the Crown, or president of our world. When I'd ended the engagement, I didn't bother to stick around to see if Srixon would continue to respect me as a member of the council. It was better I leave than face him. I couldn't deal with the shame.

"Max?" Jane broke my thinking, coaxing an answer.

I looked up at her once more, hoping my eyes hid my secret. "I was a member. I held a seat on the council—a rather prestigious seat, too. I was Second Crown." Just saying it I felt disjointed. "The job wasn't for me, though. Government didn't suit my ambitions."

She nodded arbitrarily, and I could tell it was because she couldn't grasp just how important my position had been. She knew nothing of what the Priory did besides protect humans, but in so, we had been a huge part of her life. "You must have seen a lot," she added, trying to seem considerate.

I nodded, remembering all the murders and war. "I did."

Jane's fingers slid from the books as she left the shelves, approaching the couch where she snuggled into the crook of my arm. She let her head rest against my chest, her life filling it with hope and longing. Once again, I was faced with the challenge of stifling my cravings to suck all that in, reminding myself of the consequences. Her hand slid to my neck, fingering my necklace.

"And this? What's the story?" She grinned. "You told me you'd share it."

I gently took the chain from her hand, kissing the top of her head. "It's what keeps me here with you."

"How so?"

"Well, it's a chain, right? In a way, it chains me to this world. When I died, I earned it." I spun the necklace, the individual links grazing my skin. "See, there's no clasp. No end. You can't break it unless you want to break it, unless your business here is finished."

"I was your unfinished business, wasn't I? Why hasn't it broken when you have saved me?"

I laughed, cupping my hand under her chin. "Until you take your last breath, my business is not finished. Your entire life is my job."

Jane frowned, pulling away from me.

"What's wrong?" I let my hand float across her back, conveying protection and comfort.

She snorted, saying something sharp under her breath.

I leaned closer to her. "What?"

Jane huffed once, positioning herself against the arm of the couch. Her other hand reached out toward me, poking me in the chest. "Isn't it obvious?"

I had no clue what she was trying to say. "No?"

She pressed her lips together, her cheeks gently flushed. *"Feels so stupid,"* she murmured.

I narrowed my eyes, at last sensing what she was thinking. "I knew you'd eventually get to this point. Everyone does."

She looked appalled. "Everyone, *who?*"

I backtracked, shaking my hands. "I mean, beings like me and beings like you. Ones that age fast and ones that age slow. It's common in our world."

Her brows relaxed, looking presumably relieved that I hadn't admitted to firsthand experience. "You're ageing at one-*bazillionth* the rate I am. I think you know where it goes from there. I just hate that it's a foregone conclusion."

"What do you mean?"

She sighed. "It's just so typical. Do you know what I mean?" She eyed me. "Obviously you do. You never age. I do. It's like that stupid movie *Highlander,* or something."

I laughed. "So? I liked Highlander."

She rolled her eyes, looking just like her sister.

I touched her face. Her skin was fresh and youthful. Years would pass before any of that would change. "I don't really think you should worry about that. Not yet. Not ever. If you actually paid attention to Highlander, then you'd see that his love for his wife never changed, even when she was old."

Jane bit her lip, looking like she didn't believe a bit of what I was saying. "*Wife*, huh?"

I ignored her last comment. "I'm serious, Jane. Of all the

things to worry about, that should be at the bottom of the barrel."

And it was true. There were bigger things to think of—like the fact we could never be *together*. Then again, she didn't know about that, and it was going to stay that way as long as possible. I'm afraid that if she knew, she wouldn't want to be with me anymore.

A guardian and their guarded walk a fine line of emotional exchange: too much, and the guardian will suck the very life from their guarded's lungs, resulting in death for the both of them. This happens because there has to be something to regulate angels from becoming guardians, and this sharing of emotion, and the danger of it, is it. These outcomes make becoming a guardian no walk in the park. If that were the case, angels would be saving souls left and right, knowing the connection it makes and the power it gives them. The Gods made us this way on purpose. Our bodies cannot support the complete soul of another. It's simply incompatible. Sharing a soul, however, is permissible as long as intentions are true and righteous. It's the way it was meant to be.

The angels that do choose to take on the challenge, like me, often find that it's because they want to save a human loved one, but as I was beginning to see, it was not for the faint of heart. I'd saved Jane because I truly loved her, because the Truth showed me happiness I would one day have with her. That one little aspect of being together didn't need to be a factor in that decision, though now, it seemed rather important when considering Jane's needs and expectations.

"Take me to Winter Wood," she demanded.

I could sense her determination. She was agitated with me

for not indulging her desires. Her yearning for me only made every minute I denied her worse. Her every movement was like a stab to my wavering inhibitions, the desire inside me like a pool in which I was slowly drowning.

I weighed my options. The last thing I wanted to do was return to that place, but going there and indulging her need to see it would delay this newest problem and relax the overall stress on me. I was naïve to think that the Priory wouldn't find out about me soon enough. Given the choices I had, it was better to go to them before they came to me. It was the lesser of two evils.

Jane's eyes narrowed. "I know what you're doing. You're stalling, aren't you?" Suspicion replaced her confident tone.

"No," I denied, but it came across rather vague.

"Why are you trying to avoid it? So what if you left the Priory? It's not like you have to *re*-join."

I drew in a deep breath, steeling my spine.

"What was that for?" She accused, feeling my resistance—an emotion I borrowed from her.

I was beginning to fear that I wasn't going to win this. "I didn't exactly leave on good terms, Jane. I'm not just going to waltz back into Winter Wood and hope for a joyful welcome."

"What do you mean? And who cares? No one ever leaves a job on good terms, or so it seems."

"Just..." I sat up, forcing her to get up as well. "I'll take you there," I had no choice but to agree, but I could still postpone. "Soon enough... but for right now, let me take you home."

WES:

I stared at Emily as she waited for my response to her questions about the owl. I finally gave up. "I don't know what the owl wants, Em. That's your area." My voice held a hint of annoyance.

Emily's features sharpened, the sour smell of displeasure wafting toward me, catching roughly in my nose. "We should ask Max."

I didn't want to ask Max anything.

Emily shook her head at me.

"What? It's not because of Jane, so don't start thinking that. It's purely instinct. I don't trust him," I defended.

She clenched her jaw. "I know that."

But she didn't. I could tell. "Well, *fine*." I tried to flick her nose with my finger but she beat me to it, grabbing my hand and lacing her fingers with mine.

"You're getting faster at that," I remarked, trying to get her to yield her fiery emotions.

Emily stood tall, her chin high. "My hearing *is* getting better, yes." Her assurance confirmed that she was acting cocky now.

Though cockiness didn't suit her, I was glad we'd moved onto a new subject. Confiding in Max was madness, at least in my mind. I grinned.

"No, we haven't moved on," she concluded. "You're going to ask Max, and that's final."

My grin faded and I cursed myself for thinking anything at all, but it was hard to stop thinking. Just try it, *impossible.* Regretfully, I turned my attention back to the owl that had been on my car. What I was finding hard to ignore was the way my heart leapt whenever I saw another animal these days. I was secretly hoping it was my parents, but I admitted that to no one.

"No one but me," Emily chimed in.

Emily was like a hawk within my thoughts, hunting down every secret I held and poaching it. I sighed.

"That's why I'm going to make you talk to Max. Maybe he can find your parents, or at least tell you where to look." We'd come full circle and I was right back on the subject of Max. I suddenly felt exhausted. We reached her front porch and she spun, grasping my shoulders. "Just think! What if that owl is one of your parents? What if that owl was, like, your father!"

A sigh escaped my lips, trying to ignore the fact that Emily was especially cute when she got excited like this. Her red hair matched the falling leaves, her brown eyes bright and unhindered. "I doubt that," I shook my head, not wanting to get my hopes up, though they still did. "It's not my father."

She smirked, knowing I was denying myself the pleasure of hope. "Thanks for walking me home." She finally relented, allowing my thoughts to remain my own.

I smiled. "No problem." I reached up, giving her another barely-kiss. She grumbled when I pulled away, making the smile on my face widen—two could play this game. "Don't forget about tonight. It's our first date." I winked.

She slouched, her expression filled with trepidation. "Yeah, right. See you tonight."

I was oddly satisfied seeing her regret her decision to start over. Seeing her suffer somehow made my suffering over mental privacy seem fair. I watched her walk into the house before turning and making my way back across the lawn. When I felt I was a safe distance away, I let my shoulders relax and my thoughts pull free. I wished there was a way I could hide them from her, and I knew there was, but again that involved talking to Max. I jumped onto my porch, skipping the use of stairs and humming to myself.

"Hey."

An uncontrollable shiver of hate ran down my spine. I stopped, not bothering to turn my head to look at him. "Hi, Max." Freaky coincidence, or not? His timely presence only made my distrust for him grow deeper.

He laughed. "Still not warming to me, are you?"

I pressed my lips together. "You could say that." I shoved my hands deep into the pockets of my jeans, fumbling with the lint that had gathered there. "What do you want?" I scuffed my shoe across the deck.

"To talk. We have a lot to discuss."

I felt myself rope-in every thought I'd previously freed, guarding them harder than ever. "What if I don't want to talk?" I finally forced myself to hold his gaze and observe him.

He was sitting casually on the cedar bench my foster father had made—he made everything in this house, it seemed. "I think Emily wants you to talk with me."

I grumbled and shuffled toward him. "News travels fast."

Max went on. "You've been avoiding me, and I understand, but what you really need to understand is that I can help you."

I sat as far away from him as possible, my nose crinkled as I smelled nothing but ash. "You stink."

Max laughed. "See, even now, you're avoiding the subject at hand, the one occupying a good portion of your mind."

I tried to deter him from this exhausting subject once more. "Where's Jane?"

Max indulged my procrastination this time. "Inside." His eyes motioned across the yard toward her house. "Brought her home just a little while ago."

I wondered what they did with their time together, and if they'd done *that* yet—I couldn't help it. "Jane hasn't figured out how much of a loser you are yet, has she?" I was challenging him, but I couldn't help that, either.

Max tilted his head toward me. A noticeable tension lighted across his features, something that hadn't been there before. "Wes." His voice was commanding, telling me he was done with games and that I'd gone too far.

I sighed, giving in, if for no other reason than to get him off my back.

"Do you want to know about your parents?" he pushed forward.

I thought of the owl then.

Max nodded. "I'm sorry to say, but that owl is not a shifter. I think she just likes you."

"How do you know?"

Max's cool attitude once again returned. "I can hear her, feel her animal instincts—natural instincts. There is no human in her. I can see that because of what I am."

I shook my head. "*Great.* Now I'm attracting animal girlfriends," I muttered.

Max chuckled, and it angered me.

He stopped suddenly, licking his lips before continuing. "I haven't seen your parents in almost seventy years, but I did know them very well, as I said before."

I felt my heart tighten. A part of me had hoped he *still* knew them.

"They were classmates of mine, and like you, their senior year got complicated rather quickly. Just before I died, they'd finally come to terms with what was happening to them and were falling in love."

I was concentrating on my hands, attempting to hide any emotion that might have shown on my face. Just knowing I had parents that could still be out there was shock enough; knowing Max had known them was worse.

"Your foster parents know, Wes. They took you in with the understanding of what you are. They had to."

I swallowed hard, feeling as though a log had landed on me. "What?" I couldn't picture Gladys holding a secret like that at bay. "How?"

Max continued. "After I died and came back, your parents and I left here for Winter Wood."

I interrupted. "What's Winter Wood?"

"It's our side of this town."

"What?"

"I haven't been there in a long time," he added, fulfilling my curiosity as to whether this was a place he still went, and why we hadn't known about it sooner.

"Is that where they are?" A part of me hoped it was that

easy.

"I'm afraid not."

I felt a little angered by his reply. "How would you know if you haven't been there in a while?" I wanted him to get to the point.

Max tilted his head. "It's a good assumption, but..." His voice trailed off.

"*But* what?"

"Your parents are dead, Wes. I'm sorry." His gaze dropped. "I heard word of it long ago. There was a massive reaping in the mountains of Washington where many of your kind had fled for refuge. No one survived."

Just like that, the little hopes I'd had vanished. "Why tell me this?" My voice was raised. "Why lead me to believe they could still be out there?"

Max touched my shoulder, but I jerked away from him.

"I'm sorry. But in my defense, I didn't have the time to tell you before because of what was going on with Greg, and I regret that you assumed otherwise."

I was suddenly angry at Jane and Emily for putting those thoughts in my head. I remembered the day they'd first mentioned it. It was before we had truly learned what Max was, right before Emily had been taken by Greg.

"You were conceived in Winter Wood, but when your mother gave birth to you, they knew you needed to have a human upbringing. Even with both parents being shifters, there was no guarantee that you would be. They wanted to be sure to prepare you for that. If you never developed the gift, they wanted you to remain in the human world, unaware of their trials and tribulations. It was safer this way. Our world was, and is, a dangerous place."

I put my head in my hands, fingers in my hair. "But I'm not human, so now what?"

"You're one of us, and their trials and tribulations are yours as well."

I sat up. "Great. I could have just been with them instead of stuck here."

He ignored my negative comment. "Your foster parents are friendly with the magickal beings here. They're some of the few humans that know about our world and want to help."

"It's like a giant conspiracy," I muttered.

Max stood. "You should tell them what has happened to you. You can confide in them, and they'll want to know that you've made the transition. They've been anxiously waiting to see if you take to the gift or not. They deserve to know that you have. Your parents were good friends with Gladys. I know she has stories she'd love to tell you about them."

He stepped off the porch, not bothering to turn back. I watched him walk across the lawn toward Jane's house. My gaze fell to my feet as the reality sank in. My parents were dead. Dead as dirt. Dead and gone. Once again, I had no one.

I heard the front door open, the hinges whining. "Are you alright, Wes?" Gladys's small eyes peered out. She tilted her head. "I just don't normally see you sit out here, and—"

"I'm fine, ma'am," I interrupted before she could say anything more. I didn't want to talk about my parents, and I didn't want to talk about me. My parents had left me, and I was going to leave them as well. They never existed in my memories so there was no point reliving their life through stories. There was no point in sharing my life with Gladys.

I would not allow any of them to exist or know.

This was my life.

JANE:

"Oh, Jane. Thank you."

I handed my mother a cup of tea as she wiped her nose with a tissue. She was slouched against the counter in the kitchen, watching me as I rushed to make myself breakfast before school.

"I must have caught that flu that Wes and Emily had last week."

I turned away from her in time to hide the smile. What my mother still didn't understand was that what Wes and Emily had was anything but the flu. Thankfully, Max had made sure she thought otherwise. I turned back to her, toast in hand.

"Well, drink that tea and I'm sure you'll feel better." I smiled, but it was quickly washed away as her future death trickled over me. I saw her running, tripping as she stumbled from a cliff. I jolted and gripped the counter, my hand flying to my mouth in order to cover my scream.

"Jane?" My mother reached across the counter with concern. She touched my hand, making the image more vivid—her body hit the rocks.

I shuddered and shut my eyes, a chill icing the room.

"Jane? Are you all right?" she asked again.

I slid my hand from my mouth. "Yeah, *um...* I just remembered I forgot to do an assignment." I looked into my mother's large, almond shaped eyes, the same eyes she shared with Emily. *She's still alive,* I told myself. *It's not real.* "Sorry... *Darn it.* Now I'm going to get a 'B.'" I tried to make the excuse seem relevant. I pounded the counter with my fist, though the image of my mother dead on the rocks still lingered.

"Oh, well. That's all right. Don't be so hard on yourself. You can't win them all." My mother went back to sipping her tea.

I licked my lips and leaned back against the counter. My talent to foresee death had never been so vivid, never so—strung out. I tried to swallow, finding my throat had dried with fear. I felt my cheeks begin to flush from the lingering burst of adrenaline. The scene played over and over, unrelenting. I went to the fridge, retrieving the orange juice and pouring a large glass. I brought the cup to my lips, drinking quickly, hoping the simple act would help bring me back to my senses.

The patio door off the kitchen opened and Wes walked in. "Hey, everyone."

"Hi, Wes." My mother gave him a pathetic wave over her shoulder, conveying her misery. "Think I caught your flu."

Wes looked up at me, lifting one brow in question. "Oh... Mrs. Taylor. That's... That's *horrible.*" He placed a hand on her back and winked at me. "Feel better soon, okay?"

My mother smiled sheepishly, enjoying the attention.

I pushed my mother's death into the depths of my mind, trying to remember that today was Monday—I had bigger problems than harmless visions. I heard the pounding of feet as

Emily bounded down the stairs. Glancing up as she turned the corner, I saw she was wearing a long sweater and jeans, her hair straightened and her make-up light. This was the Emily I loved. The Emily I always imagined she would grow up to be, not the Goth chick of before.

"Hey, Wes." Emily threw her bag on the counter, hooking one arm around Wes's neck and kissing him on the cheek.

Mother tried to pretend she hadn't seen it, but the smirk on her face gave it away. "How was your date last night, you two?"

"Mo-*om*," Emily whined, embarrassed that she'd even mention it. She'd thrown her hands in the air, eyes rolling. Her reaction was a little excessive.

"Okay! *Nevermind.*" My mother stood from the stool, shuffling to the couch in the TV room opposite the kitchen. She sighed and sunk into the oversized cushions. "Have a good day, everyone. I'm going to go ahead and *die* now."

A chill ran down my spine as Mother said it.

Emily gave me a strange look, mouthing a question as to what was going on.

I showed her the images in my mind, then showed her the real fact that Mom was just sick.

Emily glowered at me. "See ya, Mom." Her eyes remained on me as she slid her bag off the counter and grabbed a banana from the basket. Wes followed her.

I kept my gaze on my mother, last out the side door as I locked it behind me. We walked on the path between the houses toward the driveway where Wes's car was already running. Emily opened the Camaro door, pulling the seat forward to access the back. I stood, waiting.

Emily cleared her throat. "After you."

I was momentarily surprised. I had forgotten that I'd been downgraded to the backseat, Emily now upgraded as Wes's girlfriend. I secretly grumbled to myself, disliking the new real-estate as I squeezed in. Emily was taller than me, so I guess it made sense that I should be the one sitting in the back, but that didn't mean I wanted to. I wasn't used to all the changes, but there wasn't much I could do about it.

Wes turned on the music, shifting the car into reverse as Emily rummaged through her bag. She turned to me, a smirk on her face. "Here, want these?" She shoved her hand toward me, a set of ear buds and a pink iPod lying in her hand.

I tilted my head, narrowing my eyes. "No, but thanks."

She gave me a sassy smile, knowing how much I hated this. From now on, Max was picking me up, whether he stayed for class or not. This plain sucked.

"Fine." Emily shrugged with a satisfied glimmer in her eye.

Her shrug sent a sliver of her future death toward me—me strangling her. Grinning with vengeance, I took the image and aimed it back at Emily, knowing her clairvoyance would hone in on the signal.

Her back steeled against the seat in front of me. "Jane! Stop that!" she howled.

Wes put his hand on Emily's knee, his face crinkled with pain caused by the pitch of her voice. He was telling her something with his mind. I could see it in the exchanged glances. Emily gawked at him before letting out a sigh of defeat, and then she smiled bashfully, her cheeks flushed.

I rolled my eyes. Max was definitely on carpool duty from now on. This was worse than death itself.

Finding things to distract me, I began to stew over my

own irritating situation. Max had skipped fifty percent of his classes since his secret came out, leaving me alone. I hated that I had to suffer while he got to float by. The only classes he ever seemed to come to were the ones I was in, so it's not that things really changed all that much, but it was the principal of it. He'd managed to convince a few teachers to allow him to transfer into the ones with me, but it only caused more issues—I didn't want to know just how he convinced them. I only hoped it didn't involve brainwashing, though I suspected otherwise. Mr. Thompson was never the type to give into anything, but he'd been the easiest to convince. That was all the confirmation I needed.

I sank down as far as I could, my knees leaning against the back of Emily's seat. Trying to forget school, Winter Wood came to mind. I began to wonder just where it was. Emily turned then, glaring at both Wes and I.

"What's Winter Wood?"

Wes looked at me inquisitively in the rearview mirror.

I shrugged.

Wes's eyes narrowed. "Jane, you know about Winter Wood?"

Emily looked from Wes to me, awaiting my reply.

"Yeah. Max told me about it yesterday." I felt as though I'd been caught doing something bad.

Emily looked at Wes.

"Yeah, he told me about it, too," Wes replied, looking the same way. "On the porch after he brought you home."

Emily's expression perked toward Wes. "You talked to him?" She looked perplexed but happy. "How did you hide that from me?"

Wes had a proud smirk on his face. "Just because you can

hear what I'm thinking doesn't mean I'm always thinking of things you want to know."

Emily looked discouraged.

"Think of it as a rare surprise, Em. You should be happy," Wes reminded her. "That was what you wanted, remember? You told me to talk to Max, so I did."

Emily laughed, and I could tell she'd caught wind of the truth in his mind by the sudden smugness of her pose. "You mean he approached you, and forced you to talk about it." Her smugness only lasted a moment more, then her expression turned sad. "Wes…" She placed her hand on his as it rested on the shifter. He'd clearly told her something more, something he didn't want me knowing or else he would have said it out loud. "I'm sorry."

I sat forward. "Sorry? What did Max tell you?" I didn't care if he didn't want to tell me, I still wanted to know because it involved Max.

Wes turned away from the both of us, his jaw clenched. "I don't want to talk about it. There was a reason I was trying to hide it." His voice was bitter, and aimed at us, not Max.

Emily let go of his hand, looking hurt.

We drove the rest of the way to school in silence, my mind wondering what it was Wes had learned from Max, and what Emily knew, too. Beneath it all, Winter Wood still lingered, though buried too deep to broach again today.

I hated being out of the loop, but at least they were talking to me again.

EMILY:

At the end of the week, I sat in history class, shaking my leg. To me, history was anything but exciting. This was Jane's area. If there was any history that I'd be interested in, it was the conversation that had conspired between Max and Wes this past weekend, and what Winter Wood was. Despite wanting to find out, the moment or subject hadn't arisen since Monday. Teachers seemed determined to pile on the work as the weeks of school grew deeper into the season, and everyone was simply struggling to survive. Spending time thinking about anything but homework was foolish, if you cared about grades that is. Unfortunately, Wes and Jane did.

Frustrated, I looked down the aisle, seeing Jake Santé. He had been the boy that helped save Wes from class a few weeks ago by lying about taking me to the nurse after my fake seizure. Jake stared at the teacher as though he were the most interesting thing he'd ever seen. I shook my head, finding his stereotypical nerdiness comical—a momentary relief from my boredom.

I stretched my talents until I could hear his thoughts, draped with excitement over each word that passed Mr. Jackson's lips. I began to think about the way Jake often thought of me when I was near him. His thoughts were always… *endearing*, if that's what you'd even call it, but most guys' were. With Wes as my boyfriend now, he no longer showered me with admiration the way he first did when he used to flirt with me from a distance. It was only natural to miss such praise. My indulgence in the thoughts of other men was harmless, let alone unavoidable. The least I could do was enjoy them, right?

I watched Jake lick an excess of saliva from his lips, his massive braces and thick glasses still as detrimental to his popularity as ever. Granted he wasn't the best boy to receive a compliment from, but in retrospect, it was like enjoying art. You had to appreciate the differences, at least in some way.

Drowning myself in the complexity of Jake's world, I began to think about how funny it was that physical objects could determine someone's popularity, as they did for him. I always admired confidence, though, and Jake never cared what anyone said about him. To me, he was free—a rare thing, and something worth taking the time to study.

"Emily..."

I broke away from my staring game, my head snapping forward. Mr. Jackson was glaring at me. "What do *you* think?"

I hadn't heard a thing he'd said, but it didn't take much to hear what he was thinking about what he'd said and what he wanted for an answer. "I think the Conquistador's conquest in the Americas was justified. They wanted to beat the Europeans to the land."

It wasn't the exact answer he was looking for, but I liked to stir controversy.

"And... Jake?" The teacher turned away from me. "What do you think of Emily's view on the conquest?"

Jake sat up, eyeing me and then looking to Mr. Jackson. "I think they should have left the natives alone. They brought disease to the area—small pox, chicken pox and measles, not to mention the widespread outburst of rabies."

Mr. Jackson grinned from ear to ear, content with Jake's perfect answer. I rolled my eyes. Jake looked at me again, smiling smugly with his giant braces exposed. I held back the desire to giggle—or was it gag?—as his endearing thoughts gushed over every curve of my body.

"Great answer, Jake." Mr. Jackson stood tall, looking between the two of us.

I sank in my chair. *No. Please, no!*

"Pair up everyone. We're going to debate these two answers. Jake. Emily. You two will be together on this. I like where the tension is going."

I shut my eyes, despising Mr. Jackson even more than I did the day he challenged me for answers on the renaissance—non-stop—as though he knew I could read his mind and he was testing that hypothesis. The whole class stood, quickly pairing up with best friends. Jake stood, grappling his books and nearly tripping over every one of the three desks between us before reaching me.

"Shall we go to the library?" he asked.

Jake was breathing hard, the wind of it falling against my skin. Swallowing hard, I refused to breathe through my nose. I didn't want to know what his breath smelled like, and though I tried not to, I imagined it to be something resembling last night's macaroni. I shivered, thinking that I needed a shower as soon as I got home.

"*Uh...* Sure," I replied through clenched teeth. At least there would be more clean, fresh air to be shared in the library.

I grabbed my bag off the back of the chair, following him out the door.

He walked beside me down the hall, his stride suddenly more confident. "This assignment should be easy."

I lifted one brow. "You could say that." Easy to him was finding the answer, but to me there was nothing easy about it. It was Jake, and I had to be his partner.

"I'm a Santé," he went on. "My ancestors are from South America. Being a native, we know a lot about the invasion of the Conquistadors." He cleared his throat. "It'll be like talking at a family reunion." His voice had suddenly grown deeper.

I nodded arbitrarily. "Great," My voice was flat, too distracted by my determination not to breathe through my nose and the sudden change in his voice.

Jake snorted, his back no longer hunched over and his movements smooth. "I get it, Emily. I know you're not impressed by me."

I was shocked by his directness, and I suddenly felt bad. "No, it's not…" I clenched my fists. I'd never made fun of him—at least not like other people did.

"I don't have many friends, not here at least."

I wanted to drop dead with guilt, but I couldn't tell if making me feel bad for him was his ploy or not. Searching his mind, it didn't offer any answers. I stared at him boldly, concentrating as hard as I could.

Stop that.

I heard his voice inside my head. My shoulders jerked back and I halted in the hall. "*What?*" I gaped.

Jake turned and looked over his shoulder. "What?" He shrugged. *I know what you're doing.*

There it was again. I blinked, further shocked. "Wait, how

did you..." I stopped myself, not wanting to sound crazy.

Because.

I stood frozen, glaring at his eyes behind his giant black frames. "How did you do that?" I demanded this time, convinced this was real.

He leaned casually against the lockers. "Do what?" *This?*

"Yeah, Jake, *that.* How'd you talk in my head?"

"What are you talking about..." *Crazy?* he challenged.

Half his words were out loud, the other half in my mind, but it was hard to discern which was which. "I'm not *crazy.*" I hated when people called me crazy.

His face was emotionless for a moment, but then a smirk grew across his cheek. "What? You thought you were the only one?"

My brows stitched together. "What do you mean?"

Mind reader?

"I'm not a *mind reader!*" I squealed, my voice trying to remain low.

"Right, so then what was that? How did you hear me? If you weren't a mind reader you wouldn't have heard me."

"Shut up, Jake." I crossed my arms against my chest, turning away from him. I wanted to go back to class and demand I get a new partner.

"Wait," I felt him grab my arm, his touch shockingly *hot.*

I stopped, unable to wriggle free from his burning grasp. "Let go!"

"Just... chill out, okay?" He was leaning close, his voice a whisper.

"It's sorta hard to *chill out* when you feel like fire!" I spat.

"Try." Jake's tone had changed completely. The raspy,

asthmatic breathing was gone.

My chest was heaving, and finding that getting enough oxygen was becoming a problem, I was forced to breathe through my nose. I expected the worst but was surprised to find it was actually pleasant, like warm apple cider. The warmth of his touch and the oddity of his scent began to make me feel strange.

"Let go." I demanded.

Jake let go of my arm, but I could tell he was poised to grab me if I were to run. He stared at me for a long moment, the stupid smirk on his face never fading. "Want to get out of here?"

I clenched my jaw, hopelessly unnerved. "Not with you."

Jake laughed. "Relax. I'm not trying to freak you out. I mean you no harm."

His thoughts once again combed over every curve of my body, but I no longer found it endearing. "Clearly you do," I challenged.

The thoughts stopped. "Sorry. Can't help it." His apology lacked sincerity.

I snorted with disgust.

"You really can't blame a guy for thinking it. But in all seriousness, I mean you no harm. Besides, Wes would kill me. Especially with being what *he* is." He said it with an exasperated sigh.

I ground my teeth together until my gums hurt. "What do you know about Wes?"

He tilted his head. *Enough.* His mind replied for him.

I weighed my options, but what options did I really have? Library, or finding out more about what Jake knew, or rather, what he *was*. I wasn't buying the fact that he was simply a mind reader. Then why the change in tone?

"Come on," he urged. "You can trust me, I swear. I'm no Gregory Gordon."

My eyes narrowed at the mention of that name. "Shut. *Up,*" I seethed. "Shut up!" My reaction came completely from the hip. It was a name I never wanted to hear again.

"Can't believe you didn't see that one coming," he mocked.

I turned away from him, making up my mind to leave.

"Wait, wait, *wait.*" He ran behind me. "I was just kidding! Come on, Emily. Aren't you curious about me? About Winter Wood?"

I froze at the mention of Winter Wood. "Winter Wood?" He'd pinned the tail on the donkey—forget that—he'd *nailed* the darn tail on.

"Yeah, Winter Wood."

I licked my lips, drunken with the idea of this place that no one seemed to want to tell me about. I twisted on my heel, once again facing him.

His brows were raised. "I knew that would make you stop. Come with me and I'll tell you all about it."

Jake sounded like a text book kidnapper, but I reminded myself that this was Jake. I'd known him since kindergarten. I'd practically seen him in diapers. What was the harm? "Fine," I agreed, but I still wasn't sure that was the right answer.

Jake smiled, his thoughts wandering back to my body.

"Jake..." I lifted my finger in warning. "One more thought like that and I'm bailing."

He laughed, his lips pressing against his braces. "Just because Wes would kill me for trying to steal you away, doesn't mean I can't mentally praise the company."

I turned away, disgusted. *"Gross,"* I murmured under my

breath.

He followed after me, hooking his arm with mine.

I flinched, but allowed it.

"Let's go." He swiftly led me down the hall and out the front doors.

A twinge of shame tickled my stomach, but I ignored it. Something about Jake made me curious, and I wanted to know what that thing was. Forget the tickle. This was the most interesting thing that had happened in days.

WES:

I leaned my head against my hand as I propped it on my desk in English, peering out the window at the football field beyond. The book in my other hand lay open, the pages stationary for close to ten minutes now. I was afraid to admit that I was overwhelmed with grief, something that had festered over the past few days. It was a grief I'd already felt for the loss of my parents; a grief I didn't want to feel again. I was trying to forget them.

Why had I let Max's claims to their existence take root in my thoughts? It was wrong of him to lead me on the way he did, and it only made me hate him more. I drew in a deep breath, turning my head and glancing sideways at Jane beside me.

She turned a page, then another. I felt her heart beating, steady and calm.

She rolled something around in her lap. I strained my gaze, trying to see what it was. She was holding a lump of folded paper, her fingers caressing the fibers with loving possession. I knew what it was all too well, having seen any number of them pass hands the last few weeks. It was another note from Max.

I clenched my jaw, looking back at the words in my book as I leaned back to stretch. From the corner of my eye I saw something move outside the window. Glancing back at the field, the owl that had been on my car this past weekend, and all week, was now perched on the fence just outside. She had freshly landed, still adjusting her weight between two feet.

I laughed to myself, shaking my head. Her persistence was admirable. Every day, without fail, I saw her. She had become a source of happiness to me, and seeing her had become something I looked forward to—my secret.

Too burnt out on school to pull myself back, I continued to indulge in her presence. Her eyes were narrow, a bright yellow that pierced right through me. She fluffed her white and grey dappled feathers, tilting her head with interest in her gaze. Something about her relaxed me, as though she had become my silent reminder to stay calm. A muse, I thought, but my thoughts were quickly stolen by intruders in the background.

Two people walked briskly across the parking lot behind the owl. I pressed my brows together, squinting to see who it was. Despite my calm, I felt suddenly tense, and a part of me wished I could acquire a set of eagle eyes just for the moment. I huffed. Eagle eyes or not, my gut still knew. Only one person at this school had hair that was that red.

Emily.

It flowed freely behind her, her arm wrapped with that

of another boy. I found myself anxious, and I certainly didn't recognize the guy she was with. I grew tenser, a million thoughts rushing to mind. *Was he a dealer? Another man?* I released a long hard breath, trying to remain calm as my muscles ached, each fiber winding tight. *It was no one*, I told myself. *He's just a friend from class.* But friends from class didn't lock arms. Friends from class didn't skip school together. I looked back to the owl. Maybe it was someone borrowing a book from her?

I grumbled. Who was I kidding?

My eyes shot to the clock. There were fifteen minutes left of class, and judging by the position of Mrs. West near the door, there was no escape. She scanned the room, her sharp eyes not unlike those of my feathery stalker outside. I began to shake my leg and it clanked lightly against the leg of the desk. Jane shot me a dirty look, urging me to be still.

"Wes, stop that," she hissed under her breath.

My leg stopped shaking, but my palms began to sweat instead. Steam poured across the surface of the resin desktop where they were flushed flat, fingers spread. I looked behind me, seeing that everyone was nose deep in their books and unaware of my building anxiety. The owl outside lifted it's wings, flapping them flagrantly as though to get my attention. I looked back at her and she stopped. I glared, trying to convey an uninterested expression—like she would notice that.

She opened her beak to squawk, but I couldn't hear her call. I saw a red car leaving the lot, my anxiety peaking. I knew that Emily had to be the passenger. I groused under my breath, discreetly pointing at the owl and then the car. The owl watched me with her head tilted, trying to understand.

"Go," I mouthed, my voice barely following in a whisper.

"*Go.*" I flicked my finger.

The owl took off then, her wings flapping wildly as she tilted back and rounded over the parking lot, just as the small sports car turned onto the main road. I watched the owl do as I asked, amazed by her above-average intelligence, and a little shocked she'd actually done what I'd implied.

I guess she really did like me.

JANE:

I rolled the note over and over in my hand under the desk. *I'll be there to pick you up, I promise,* is what it read. I tapped my fingers on the book, rushing through the words in front of me and trying to retain as much information as possible, though my mind was undeniably distracted.

I wanted to know what Winter Wood was, and I wanted Max to quit skipping class and leaving me to fend for myself. His absence was not allowing me the chance to discuss this apparent magickal city with him, as I'm sure he knew. I saw Wes watching me from the corner of my eye. I ignored him. *What had Max said to him? What was it that had Wes so visibly disturbed all week?*

Wes's leg began to shake nervously. I glared at him. "*Wes, stop that,*" I hissed, quickly looking to make sure the teacher hadn't noticed.

Wes's foreseen death invaded my mind, quickly changing from being murdered, to getting hit by lightning, and then to a bout of extreme anxiety ending in a heart attack. He was dramatically freaking out—my attempt at concentration was useless.

Giving up, I let my full attention fall on him. His hand was flicking about, finger dancing in the air. His gaze remained on the field outside. I wanted to laugh, but quelled it, carefully peering over his shoulder instead. To my surprise, there was a large owl perched on the fence. I frowned, watching as it took off and rounded the lot. Wes's attention turned back to the book in front of him, until he noticed me gawking.

"*What was that?*" I mouthed.

He just blinked, at a loss of words, keeping it to himself. I hated when he played dumb.

"Jane. Wes. Please stop talking." Mrs. West's voice was like ice as it ran down my spine.

I blushed, my eyes darting back to the words in the book, trying to act attentive. Wes also went back to reading, and I wished for a moment we could talk telepathically—it didn't happen.

The bell finally rang a few minutes later. Wes shot out of his seat, slamming the book shut and shoving it in his bag. He dashed for the door, not bothering to address me.

Hurrying to keep up, sweat began to form on my brow. I stopped him before he all but darted out of the room, snatching his arm at the last possible second. "Wes, wait. What's going on?"

He didn't want me to stop him, tugging against my restraint. "Do you need a ride?" he blurted, his body practically shaking with anxiety.

I was confused. "*Er...* no. But, what's—"

"I gotta run, Jane. I'm sorry." He slipped out of my grasp, moving for the door.

I scrambled to follow, the door hitting me on my way out. I winced, but shrugged it off. "Wes, what's going on? Just *tell* me." I tried to grab him again, but he shrugged out of my grasp. I had to practically run beside him down the hall, dodging one student after another. "What's up with the owl?" I was breathless.

He looked sideways at me, as though surprised I'd noticed it was there. Anyone with the gumption to glance out the window would have. "Nothing," he mumbled. Wes threw the front doors open, exiting out into the front lot.

I saw Max's car pulled up to the curb. I stopped dead, a small wave of relief rushing over me. Wes slipped away, but I gave up caring. He'd refused to slow down, refused to give me any answers, and at this rate, I knew I wasn't about to get any. I took a moment to catch my breath, rubbing my arm where I'd run into a hundred other students, and the door, in my quest to keep up. Maybe Max could offer me some answers... *finally.*

I strolled down the path toward Max's car. He was already chatting with a football player, his arm hanging out the window. Max laughed at something the player said, and I found my previous distractions fade as I smiled. I loved the sound of Max's laughter. I loved the feeling of that emotion streaming from me to him, like a thread that would always hold us together. It was my happiness he borrowed, my life that pulsed through his blood as well as mine. When he was happy, I felt it as though it were my own happiness. I had noticed this more and more over the past few weeks. Growing up, I had also felt this, but didn't know what it was, or what it meant, and it was never this strong. We were connected like soul-mates. For all I knew, it's what we really were.

I clicked open the passenger door and got in. I heard what the football player was saying now, things about practice and the game last Friday night. It was as though they were best friends.

"Hey, Jane." The football player broke from his discussion to address me.

Shocked, I looked at him with an expression I was certain resembled a deer in the headlights. "*Uh...* hi, Trent." Trent had never said hi to me before, let alone glance at me, even if I were in his direct path.

"Hey," he repeated, grinning before turning his attention back to Max. "Gotta go, Max, but think about it. Next Friday night, it'll be awesome." Trent gave the car door a little pound before turning and walking away.

"See you, Trent." Max's voice was cool, comfortable. He'd managed to blend in more than I had in my four years here, and it had only been a handful of weeks.

I lifted one brow as Max's eyes met mine. "Making friends?"

Max shrugged. "You could say that."

"What's happening next Friday night?" I knew that next week football had a break in their schedule, so it wasn't a game.

He shrugged again. "Halloween party."

I rolled my eyes. I should have known. "Of course," I grumbled.

"It could be fun," Max urged in a sing-song voice. "You could be an angel, and I'll be the devil."

I laughed. "How is that going to work?"

Max's smile never faltered. "Perfectly. Ready for a fun weekend?" He hooked his hand behind my head, pulling me in and giving me a kiss. His lips lingered against mine, laced with a wanting feeling, but a subdued one. He was forcing back emotions. I felt it.

I leaned away. "What was that?"

Max looked confused. "What?"

I crossed my arms. "I can feel your emotion like it's my own, Max."

"It is your own," he corrected.

"I know that," I said, annoyed. "But I feel you're subduing your desires for me, something I didn't feel the first time you kissed me, not even a little bit. Why? What's changing?" I sounded like a crazy girlfriend.

Max started the car, turning away from the curb and slowly rolling through the lot as one student after another waved at us—Max had been working the friend thing pretty hard, just not the going to class thing. "We're waiting, remember? I'm just trying to remain in control, that's all."

My eyes narrowed, finding his words didn't seem one-hundred percent true. "Ri-*ight*," I said, expressing my doubts in the tone of my voice.

Max was playing with the tiny chain around his neck, and it reminded me of the way we were quite literally chained together—so why wait?

"Do you think we're soul-mates, Max? I mean, like real soul-mates, if there even is such a thing."

He smiled. "There is such a thing. Didn't you know that?"

I shrugged. "Well, I guess the term had to come from somewhere, right?"

He nodded matter-of-factly. "Right." He released the chain and it dropped back below the collar of his shirt. "Would you like to hear the real story?"

This new conversation felt better, and both our emotions reflected that—warm and fuzzy. "Sure."

"First I have to ask, are you hungry?"

I concentrated on my stomach for a second—it growled. "Actually, yes."

"Perfect, Vicco's it is." He pressed his foot down on the gas, our destination now in sight.

EMILY:

"So, where are we going?" I tried to make myself feel comfortable in Jake's car, but the edgy design of the Audi made it impossible. I felt out of place, and could only assume—*hope*—I knew where we were going.

Jake started the car by pressing a button on the dash, no key needed.

"How did you do that?" I gushed.

Jake winked and leaned back, revealing a button that had a key symbol on it. "Magick."

A sharp breath escaped my lips. "Whatever."

I would not be lying by saying that this car didn't suit Jake's stereotype, because it didn't. The windows were tinted as dark as was legally allowed, the leather plush and black. Guns and Roses played on his radio, sophistication and class oozing from every fiber of aluminum. I always imagined him driving a mini-van, the cloth seats torn and books crowding the back seats—this was no van, and this was *not* the Jake Santé I thought I knew.

Jake smiled. "Wouldn't be caught dead in a mini-van."

I snorted, forgetting he could read my thoughts as much as I could read his, of which there was nothing. "How do you hide your thoughts like that?"

"Hide my thoughts? It's not that hard." He reached across my lap.

I froze. "What are you doing?" I demanded, scrambling to push myself as far against the seat as possible.

Jake smirked, his mind opening up and releasing as a series of rude images that flooded my mind. He clicked open the glove box. "Getting this." He pulled out a plastic container that was shaped like a half circle.

"You didn't have to lean so *far* into me," I challenged. He knew just what to do to get a rise out of me.

Jake shrugged and winked. "Gotta get it where I can."

My mouth fell open. This was *definitely* not the Jake Santé I'd known since I was little. No more shyness, nerdiness, or even clumsiness—not by a long shot. What was going on? What had made him suddenly, *normal?*

Jake popped open the blue plastic box—it was empty.

"There's nothing in it," I stated the obvious.

Jake looked sideways at me, opening his mouth as he reached for his braces. He gave them a tug and they slid right off, revealing a row of perfect, white and—

"What the...*Hell?*"

"Hell doesn't even begin to describe it," Jake commented quickly.

"I... *What...*" I couldn't finish my thought, staring—*gawking*—at the obvious.

"Cool, huh?" His voice was sharper now, unhindered by the—*whatever it was*—that had previously crowded his mouth.

Jake placed the fake set of braces and teeth into the box and clicked it shut. Smiling wide, he revealed the telltale indicator of what he was. Was it some sort of animal?

"Those things hide what I am, at least part of it." He removed his glasses then, throwing them in the cup holder. Lifting his brow as he looked at me, I saw that his eyes, which were once a calm green, where now as reflective as newly, minted coins. "That's better."

My mouth was still hanging open, watching as Jake became better and better looking by the second—and yes, that thought was impossible *not* to have.

Jake smiled smugly. "I never thought I'd hear you think that." He rolled his eyes.

My lips still refused to move as a million images flooded my mind. "What are you?"

Jake laughed coolly to himself. "I'm a part of the Phyllostomidae family of mammals, descendants of the Desmodus Rotundus."

I really wanted to know what the heck he was saying, but I didn't. "What?"

He held me in suspense, relishing my confusion. "In other words, Emily, I'm a vampire." He said it with trepidation and annoyance, picking fun at the fact that they'd become so *bourgeoisie.* "But not the kind of vampires you think of." He chuckled. "Artistic types..." He murmured. "They have it all wrong." He shook his head.

"Wrong?" I chimed.

Jake backed out of his parking spot. The movement startled me, forcing my gaze away from him. Watching the road move below us, my hands clenched the seat. If I was going to bail, this was my chance, but then again, did I really want to?

I looked between the road outside and Jake, then back again. I was having a hard time believing what I saw. His teeth hadn't been all *that* different, but the two K-9's were noticeably sharper, more like a dog. I'll admit that the term werewolf had also crossed my mind. I would have settled with either explanation. The bottom line was that his teeth were different enough to warrant the fake teeth, at least. His eyes, though, that was the kicker. It was as though I was staring at a cat in the night, the darkness inside the car adding to the effect. If he hadn't used the term *vampire*, I would have perhaps thought of a hundred other things first.

He shifted out of reverse and into drive. I reached for the handle of the door, thinking tuck-and-roll, but my hand went no further.

I knew Jake knew what I was thinking, but he ignored it, trying to act casual instead. "In class today, remember how I mentioned the rabies in South America during the invasion of the Conquistadors?"

I nodded, timidly pulling my hand back and forcing it into my lap.

"That's where this..." he motioned to himself—the teeth, the eyes, "...really comes from."

I swallowed hard, mouth dry. "South America..." I said it

like a statement rather than a question.

"Yep, hence my last name, Santé. It's like saint, but all scrambled up."

I swallowed hard—a saint of *Hell* perhaps.

Jake heard my thoughts and laughed.

I began to think about blood, more specifically *my* blood, and how I wanted to keep it.

Jake bit his lip suggestively. "Go ahead, ask."

I felt so little beside him. "*D*—Do…"

He licked his tongue across his lip. "Go on."

"Do you drink… *blood?*"

He laughed again, so thrown by the delight I was providing him. "I do, but not human blood." He was looking at the white of my hands as I furiously grasped the seat. "So chill out. That stuff is way too salty, not to mention thick, fatty, and just plain gross. Unfortunately, some who get this disease tend to loose their heads, so I can't say there aren't *some* vampires out there that drink human blood. I'm sure there are." He shuddered, noticeably disgusted by the idea.

I thought about my Anne Rice books.

"Think of it this way: you get the rabies and your whole body changes." He was swirling his hand through the air as though he was conducting an orchestra.

"Do you live forever?"

He chuckled. "Definitely not. You've seen me grow up, right? Clearly immortality is not for me. It was books and fantasy that got that rumor started. Dracula's a joke."

"And the eyes?"

"Man's got to hunt."

I kept throwing out questions, surprised to find myself

relaxing now that I knew I wasn't his next meal. "Are you… *dead?* Like Max?"

His laughter once again echoed through the tiny car. "Certainly not. Feel my forehead."

I did as I was told, placing the back of my shaking hand against his forehead—he was burning up, explaining the heat I'd felt when he grabbed me earlier. "You have a fever," I gasped.

He nodded. "*Really?* I didn't notice." He winked.

I huffed angrily.

He went on. "I've been running a temperature of a hundred-and-four since I was a toddler. It's a great way to get out of school when you want to."

I tried to see him as he was in grade school, but all I saw was a wobbly little geek, not the Jake in front of me. "So, how did it happen?"

Jake shrugged. "I was an orphan when I got bit."

"What bit you?"

He gave me a look that suggested he knew I was smarter than that question. "Another vampire. Come on, Emily, you're better than that."

My brows stitched together. "But I thought you said vampires didn't really drink human blood unless they're crazy?"

He scratched his forehead, growing impatient. "They don't. I was groomed to be a vampire—chosen. You see, because of the change in our genetic code, we're sort of like mules—we can't reproduce." He laughed to himself. "My so-called parents decided they wanted a baby, so they went to the orphanage, picked me out, bit me, and viola! They had a child of their own."

I felt a little disturbed. "Isn't that a bit… *odd?*"

Jake shrugged. "It's no different than anything else. I can't remember what it was like before, so it doesn't really matter."

"So a vampire can just go around biting babies and making vampire families?"

He sighed. "No, you have to obtain a license and have the abandoned child approved by the council of vampires. Vampires that go around recruiting humans without a permit are put to death immediately. It's a very tightly supervised operation."

"Weird."

Jake smirked, allowing one sharp, white tooth to show. As hard as I tried not to, I still marveled at his mini-makeover. His olive skin and flashy green eyes complimented each other well. The stereotypical dead, white skin I often associated with the English vampires in my books was clearly not a factor. I suddenly wanted to throw them all away and laugh. His cheeks were rosy, and I saw why it was I always found him to be so sweaty, but in this new light, it was more like he was glistening instead of sweating—it just sounded more attractive, because it suddenly was.

"*Aww...* you flatter," he teased.

I quickly looked away. I wasn't used to people other than Max reading my thoughts.

"It's okay. You can gawk. Really, I'm no threat. I may tease, but I can't be with anyone other than a vampire, anyway. That's another rule. I guess they're afraid we'd accidentally infect someone who isn't meant to *be* a vampire. We're quite infectious in close proximity." He grinned, and I could see how that would be the case. "We're just like vampire bats. Think of me like that. I'm just a big, rabies-laden vampire bat."

"Like a bat?" I gaped, not wanting to see it that way.

He nodded. "Yeah. Sure. Though flying is out of the question.

Our eyesight is about as bad as a bat's in the daylight, too, hence the glasses, but that's where we get the stellar mind reading ability. Bats aren't meant to see at all, so they rely on sonic frequency to show them around. Thoughts carry the same frequency and I hear them. The rest is history."

"So, you're just a bat-man with no wings and a craving for animal blood."

He snapped his fingers, humming the Batman theme song. "Exactly. Desmodus rotundus. Now you're getting a hang of things. You see, by nature, you should be a vegetarian because of your flat, square teeth." He opened his mouth, openly exposing his oddly shaped jaw line, reminding me of the family dog we used to have. "I'm more of a carnivore now." He pulled down the visor and urged me to look at my own teeth in the mirror. "Have you ever seen a carnivore, other than humans, with such blunt teeth?"

I shook my head and shut my mouth. "No."

He shrugged and lifted his hands off the wheel. "See. Human's aren't meant to eat meat."

I re-thought his statement. "So, do you eat meat, or just blood? I ask because you said carnivore." I was trying to get this straight.

"Sure, I'll eat meat, as long as it's raw and covered in blood. Freshness is the key." He grouped his fingers together and kissed them, looking like a Frenchman.

My body shuddered at the thought. "Gross," I murmured.

He slowed down, pulling off the road and parking in front of a large gate with a sign that read 'no trespassing.' He looked down at me, his brows suddenly serious. "How can you say that? I can smell the blood lust inside you. You can't hide it. Got a little taste of your sister's boyfriend, did you?" He nudged me. "Does your sister know about your escapades with her boyfriend? Or is that your dirty little secret?"

A sharp breath escaped my lips. He was insulting.

"Don't act so demure, Emily. You can't lie to me. I've been watching you since we were little, though clearly keeping my distance. I could tell you hadn't accepted what you were. Then there was that *Gregory Gordon* guy..." His eyes narrowed, and I tried to read what he'd meant.

"Yeah, *him*." I rolled my eyes.

"Well, he's dangerous, so then I really didn't want to be near you. No offense or anything."

"Gee, thanks," I murmured under my breath, thinking of the urge in me, the need to taste Greg's blood once more.

Jake's lips curled. "So, it wasn't Max's blood at all, was it? It was *Greg's* blood. I knew it! Rather obvious, really. I just wanted to tease you."

My anger boiled over. "It's none of your business," I snapped.

Jake leaned back dramatically, his hands floating in the air between us, his palm facing me. "Whoa there. Snappy much? Clearly you haven't gotten the forty days of rehab under your belt. I'm just reading the information you're leaving out for me to see."

I glared, looking away from him and out the window. An owl landed on the gate in front of us, catching my attention. It was the same owl I had seen on Wes's car, I was certain of it. My attention perked, my mind flooding with the incident.

Jake laughed. "Here, watch this." He pressed a button on the visor and the gate began to lift.

The owl rode the gate as it lifted straight into the air until it could hold on no more and was forced to fly off. I was amused, realizing it was nothing more than a glorified security gate, meant to keep humans out.

"Where are we going?" I ventured to ask again, no longer within the comfort of the familiar streets of Glenwood.

"Where else? We're going to Winter Wood." Jake winked. "You wouldn't stop thinking about it in class, and I'm one to keep my promises."

WES:

I drove out of the lot, wondering where the owl went and realizing that having my feathery girlfriend follow my real girlfriend around was rather shrewd, not to mention text book soap opera. *How would I find either one of them?* The day was testing me. I picked up my cell, trying to give Emily a call. It felt like ages went by between each ring, then her voicemail. I didn't bother to leave a message.

Where are you?

I hung up and pressed down on the gas, angry with the world. I took off toward the abandoned road I'd found so comforting last quarter, thinking I'd park there and take to the forest on more 'agile' feet.

I put the car in park and stepped out onto the gravel road,

overgrown with weeds. Almost immediately, I heard the cry of an owl. Looking to the sky with hope, my owl spiraled down, her markings like a name, in and of itself. Flapping her wings, she landed on the hood of my car. I winced, the sharp sound of it sending shivers down my spine.

"Would you stop that? You're ruining my car." I pointed to the scratches, but she didn't seem to care, tilting her head at the sound of my voice and finding it more interesting. I shook my head. "Fine, have it your way."

She chortled, hopping toward me across the hood, her every step like fingernails on a chalkboard.

"I'm going to call you *Trouble,*" I added. Lifting one brow and trying to glare. "You're nothing but trouble."

She chortled again.

"Did you see where Emily went?"

Her chortling continued on like a sentence, but it grew deeper in tone.

I laughed. "Jealous much?"

She stopped talking and her feather's fluffed.

"You seem more like a Stella to me. How's that? Do you like Stella? It's a total heart-breaker name." I stopped myself, the mere act of naming my stalker-owl a sure sign that I was officially loosing it.

She did nothing, just watched me.

"Stella it is."

I shed my leather jacket, tossing it onto the front seat of the Camaro before shutting the door and locking it. I took my keys and hooked them under the front right wheel-well.

Stella's yellow eyes blinked and I smiled, finding the fact that she couldn't read my thoughts refreshing, even if she was just a bird. I stepped away from the car.

"If I fly with you, will you take me to Emily?"

Stella blinked a few times, but it seemed she was complying. I don't know how it was she was able to understand me, or I her, but I figured my nearness with the animal kingdom made our body language speak words our mouths couldn't. I studied her, taking in the essence of what she was.

My hands began to sting, the feeling spreading up my arm and moving faster and faster with each change I made. The feeling overwhelmed me as I caught myself mid-air, flapping my wings before I hit the ground. *Whoa.* I hadn't attempted to be a bird since my first change into the raven. It was awkward.

Stella tittered excitedly, dancing across the hood. I squawked at her angrily, trying to get her to leave my car alone. She finally understood, taking flight along beside me, diving close and trying to nip at my feathers—she was *flirting.*

I squawked again, conveying that I also wanted to be left alone—I wanted to find my real girlfriend, and the one I actually had an attraction to. At least the love portion of the animal instinct didn't carry over—I had no primal feelings toward Stella. *Thank God.*

Stella changed course, now seeming to concentrate on the task at hand, and not her crush. She dove sharply, and it took all my skill to follow, my wings shaking and moving rapidly, jostling me about. She was good at this flying stuff, but then again, flying for her was like breathing.

We ducked through a misty cloud, and the forest below us opened to a road. At first the road looked abandoned and useless, but as we followed it, the gravel slowly gave way to pavement and then eventually shrubbery lined sidewalks joined in. I was confused. How did a road go from condemned to gorgeous? It was then that I was further confused by a lavish iron and stone gate, a sight I'd never seen before.

Stella cut down through the air, fluffing her wings as she landed softly on the iron rungs of the gate, at least fifty feet tall. I tried to do the same but overshot, finding myself gripping the gate with one foot while the rest of me spun around and slammed into the planking below. Hanging upside down, I let go, dropping clumsily to the ground with a '*whack*'. My wings were little help when it came to trying to right myself. I cursed under my breath, but it came out as a squeak instead.

Finally finding my footing, I stood, looking up at the gate as Stella flapped her wings and re-settled them against her body. In thick block lettering against the planking, words read, 'Winter Wood.'

Shocked, I stepped back, wanting to take it all in—this place was real. The gate was sturdy, arching cleanly in a half circle. Two giant stone obelisks held the hinges, and a simple latch fastened the gate shut. The sidewalks behind us continued under archways on either side, each fit with a door.

Stella chortled at me, pulling on the gate as though urging me to move onward. She took to the air as I did, following her over the gate where the road continued ahead. We flew low, and soon the trees parted and the road fed down into a giant bowl in the mountain. Timber buildings and small board and baton houses crowded the otherwise forested bowl, about three miles across. The main road we'd followed into the mountains cut right through the middle of the small town, ending with a large building that resembled the capital building in Washington, D.C..

There were perfectly manicured small evergreens lining the road, each sparkling with what looked like small white lights, though upon closer inspection, there was no wire. Windows were frosted with the cool air at this elevation, bodies walking the streets, looking no different than regular humans, at least from this distance. For the most part, the town appeared no different than any other town, but I knew better than to believe that.

How had no one ever seen this before?

We flew down the center of it all, cars bustling below us. I was afraid to look too closely, afraid to see too much too soon. Stella tilted to the side, diving onto a side street and cutting through an alley past a large red dumpster. Up ahead, something red caught my attention. In front of a grey row house with red shutters sat the car I'd seen Emily leave school in.

Stella fanned herself down onto a flowerbox outside one window, its flowers still blooming, also bright red, despite the fall weather. Stella's feathers fluffed and she turned to me, expecting me to land beside her. I held my breath, trying to fan the air and slow down. I reached out for the edge of the box, tripping only slightly and grazing the window with the side of my body—*thump!*

Stella scratched at me, seemingly annoyed. If I could shrug, I would, hoping she'd finally seen me for what I really was—a klutz. Stella's head twisted back to the window. I followed her yellow gaze. It was a kitchen, and in that kitchen sat a table. Emily was perched there, staring at the both of us with her mouth agape. A boy was at the table with her, leaning back, his arms crossed against his chest. The smirk on his face ignited a fire inside me, a feeling deep and untrustworthy. Analyzing him, I found that there was something vaguely familiar about his features, but I couldn't put my finger on it. I knew they had left from school, so, who was he?

Forgetting myself, I tapped my beak frantically against the glass. Emily stood, placing a mug she'd been holding on the counter. She pointed to the left, urging me to follow her direction. Stella shook out her feathers, looking bothered by Emily's presence. I hopped down from the box, making my way to the left where I found a red door.

It swung open.

"*Wes!*" Emily gasped, her cheeks pink with embarrassment.

I couldn't help myself as I let out an angry squawk, forcing back my desire to change into a lion and rip the boy with her into to pieces.

"*What are you doing here?*" she hissed in a hushed tone.

I wanted to ask her the same thing.

MAX:

"Can I get two Buffalo Doubles with Munchers, please?" Max turned to me. "Anything else?"

Just hearing him say the words was bliss enough. "That's not all for me, is it?" I knew Max never really ate, and I didn't want to pig out on two Buffalo Doubles right in front of him.

"Of course not." He smiled and turned away. "That'll be all."

He finished ordering and sat back.

I tilted my head. "So you eat now?"

He shrugged. "Sometimes it sounds good, but it doesn't satisfy anything because I'm not hungry. It's like when you're sick and you don't want to eat, but sometimes you still want to. I'm not dead, Jane, just moving very slowly."

I giggled. "That's so unreal." The car fell silent as my gaze remained on his face. He had a sexy half smile, his eyes looking across the lot and beyond. "What are you thinking about?"

Max's blue eyes washed over me. It was as though an ocean breeze had fallen across my skin, though it was just a look. I shivered.

"I'm thinking about your question about soul-mates."

I remembered then. "Right. You said they were real. What's the story?"

He took a deep breath. "Well, a long time ago there was one being, the first being on Earth, so to speak. It was neither a man nor a woman, it just… *was.* Try to picture that, can you?"

I twisted my imagination, trying to see this combined beast. "Okay?"

Max went on. "According to Aristophanes, this being was strong, confident, agile and—*well*—cocky. Not a big fan of authority, this being tried to lash out against the Greek gods, thinking he could defeat them. The gods were angered by this, but knew that if they destroyed this being the live sacrifices the being had been providing them with would cease."

I laughed. "Ah. *Politics…* always about what you're getting out of the deal."

Max nodded. "Well, the gods had a pow-wow and decided to weaken the being by splitting it apart, thus creating twice the number of beings for sacrifice, while also weakening them by half. This is when man and woman were created, but because of the split, they shared one soul. That's where the term soul-mate comes from. We are destined to roam Earth, searching for our other half in order to feel complete again. Over the centuries, the task has become close to impossible."

I blushed, thinking of us. "Like a puzzle."

Max's eyes skirted away from me and he smirked. "I guess you could say that."

"So, do you think I'm your other half?" I touched his arm, sensing a sweet tingling in the touch. It was that reaction that told me we were soul-mates, but I wanted to know what he thought.

"I do." He caught my eye. "Like I said before, there was something about you that first time I saw you in the Truth, something I couldn't let go of. I knew it before your father ever asked me to save you. I'd known it long before the Truth showed me who you were. In a way, I feel as though deciding to stay behind as an angel was advantageous to my goals of finding you, my soul-mate."

My heart was pounding now.

"We live many lives, Jane, but very rarely do we find our true soul-mates. They say we continue coming back—reincarnating—in order to find each other. We do not really move on to the Ever After until we reach this goal."

My words had been stolen from me. I suddenly felt a purpose, an intense connection to Max in a way I hadn't before. I believed what he said because I felt it. "How do you know we don't truly move on?" I whispered.

He touched my chin. "Peter told me that story soon after I saw you in the Truth. He had researched the validity of it extensively because he believed this was the case between him and my mother."

"Do you think he was right?"

Max shrugged. "Sometimes I see people after they pass, in Seoul, just on the other side of the river that splits the In-between, or Seoul, from the Ever After. They're waiting. Once a soul has met its true mate, it stops reincarnating, and if one life dies, they wait in the first stage of the Ever After until the other can join them. I've never seen Patrick there, though, or my mother. I believe they are no longer waiting and have descended deeper into the Ever After to their final place. I only hope it's because they're together."

It was magick, the very essence of what we were.

EMILY:

I heard Jake approach from the other room. "Hello, Wes." He arrived at my side, looking down at Wes as an owl.

Don't provoke him, Jake, I whispered in my thoughts, as though Wes could hear, but of course he hadn't. "Do you have some clothes he can borrow?"

Jake looked at me with an annoyed expression. *No,* he answered, once again secretly.

Come on, Jake. Please? I begged.

He's a shifter, he protested.

I tilted my head. *Just do it.*

Jake complied as he turned back into the house. I heard him climb the stairs. I stood alone with Wes, our eyes locked, his mind racing with a million questions.

"No, Wes. I'm not cheating on you. And no, he's not hitting on me, either."

Wes looked noticeably fluffed.

"No, Wes! He didn't even touch me, okay? ...*Who* is he?" Wes was flooding my mind with questions. "That's Jake Santé. Can you believe that?"

Wes tilted his feathered head. His eyes were still the same, the very thing that had given him away.

"I know, right? It is crazy!" Wes shifted his weight "*No,* Wes. I'm positive he didn't touch me. Besides, I can see you're with that *owl* we saw on your car. What's that about?"

Wes's eyes narrowed, telling me his answer.

I laughed as hard as I could without alerting the whole neighborhood. "She has a crush on you?" I could tell Wes wasn't too pleased with my mockery. "And you named her?" I tried as hard as I could to stop laughing. "Wes, that's weird!"

Jake returned with a stack of clothes, looking at the both of us strangely before joining in with my laughter, learning all he needed by searching my mind.

Wes hopped into the house between our legs. Jake motioned him in the direction of the powder room, still chuckling. He placed the stack of clothes on the counter and shut Wes inside.

"Jealous boyfriend you've got there." Jake lifted a brow, his suddenly sharp features accentuated in the dim light of the hall. His eyes glimmered with a veiled light as he walked past me, brushing my shoulder just enough to send a tingle down my spine.

I shook it off and slid up to the bathroom door. "Wes?" I tapped with one finger, figuring that by now Wes would be back in his human form.

I heard rustling—a feathery rustling.

"Wes, what are you doing? Hurry up." I pushed my hands into my pockets and leaned against the door, waiting.

A few minutes later there was a gasp as though Wes had just surfaced from water. I could hear him moving about inside the bathroom, human again.

"Wes? Are you alright?" I was trying to read his thoughts, but they were knotted. "*Wes?*"

"*Er…* yeah. I'm fine."

I knew better than to believe him, but I also knew I was on thin ice as it was. Aggravating him at this point was relationship suicide.

WES:

I was sweating, trying to think of a million things other than what had just happened, hoping that it would confuse Emily and leave her unawares. I looked at myself in the mirror.

"Get it together, Wes," I whispered to myself, keeping my thoughts running in a constant stream of mediocrity so that Emily wouldn't sense that something was wrong—*baseball,*

homework, weather.

I heard a murmur from somewhere else in the house, recognizing Jake's voice.

"Yeah, Jake. Be right there!" Emily yelled, still behind the door.

Baseball, homework, weather...

"Hey, Wes? I'll just be in the living room, okay?"

"Sure." I swallowed, trying to gather my voice once more. "Be there in a minute," I forced the words.

"Okay." There was noticeable concern in Emily's voice, but I heard her footsteps walk away despite that.

I turned back to the mirror, leaning my hands on the counter. *Why was it so hard to change?* It was as though a voice was telling me not to. It was begging me like a chant—*Stay. Stay. Stay.*

I took a few more deep breaths. Distracting myself, I unfolded the clothes. As I fished my legs into each pant leg, I already knew they were three inches too short—Great, Capri's. At least the shirt was loose, though clearly not adding to the fact that my ankles were showing like a woman. I grumbled and pulled on the socks, finding one had a hole that was beginning to unravel on the heel.

I began to wonder if Jake had done this on purpose. I bet he'd wanted me to look like an idiot because he was trying to prove a point—he was better for Emily than I was. I was no idiot, though. Now that I knew who the strange looking kid I'd originally seen through the window was, I knew all too well how he gazed upon Emily in Math class. Could I not catch a break? Besides, what was with the makeover? The disguise?

I splashed a little water on my face, trying to make myself look a little less drained. I flicked off the bathroom light and exited into the hall, drawn by the sound of Emily's voice. She laughed, making my muscles tense with jealousy—now I knew how she felt about Jane.

I rounded the corner, walking into a green room, the couches a deep red in contrast.

"There he is!" Jake stood from the couch opposite Emily—at least he wasn't sitting beside her. Maybe he knew better, maybe he wanted to save that insult for later. He walked up to me, his hand outstretched.

I shoved my hands in the pocket of my Capri's, refusing to grant him the courtesy of a hand shake—he'd still stolen my girlfriend.

"Well," Jake dropped his hand. "Sorry to steal Emily away, Wes." He said it as though he'd known I'd thought it. "I just wanted her to know that she wasn't alone. It's good for our kind to stick together."

"*Our* kind?"

He nodded. "Yeah. Me, her…you…"

I stopped him. "She's not alone. And there's no *you* in this equation. She has me." I tried to keep the anger in my voice at bay, but I wasn't succeeding. I didn't stop observing him, seeing the obvious reflection of his eyes, the unnatural peak of his teeth. "And what are you, exactly?"

Jake stood tall. "A vampire."

"You're *joking,*" I was laughing, but the expression on his face suggested that he wasn't kidding.

"I'm not kidding," he answered, repeating it verbatim from my thoughts.

My body steeled, stunned by an imaginary bolt of lightning. "What?" I looked at Emily. She was smiling. *Why are you smiling?*

"It's true, Wes. He's a vampire." She shrugged.

Then why are you with him? He's a vampire!

She just blinked, her smile never fading.

Her naïve sense of trust was obviously skewed after her friendship with Greg. Her being here proved that. How could she think this was okay? I recalled her vampire books, and it all suddenly made sense. Great, more reasons to worry about her.

Emily tilted her head. "Jake's different than what you think. He's not dangerous."

Like that made me feel any better. I glared at him. "So, are you *dead?*" It was the first thing I could think of. My tone was noticeably annoyed and disgusted. I'd dealt with enough dead—or at least dead-*ish*—people lately.

"No," he answered plainly. "I'm more like you than anything else—just another animal."

"How are *you* like me?" I eyed him from head to toe, seeing nothing but a yuppie poser in sheep's clothes.

Jake laughed, leaning against the arm of the couch where Emily sat. "I'm just a hot-blooded carnivore. That's the real definition of a vampire. I drink blood, yes, but not human blood because it's gross. And I can read your thoughts, so..." His voice trailed, meaning that to be a warning.

"Another mind-reader?" I couldn't handle that. For all I knew he was seducing Emily as we spoke, telling her sweet nothings and nasty lies about me.

Jake smiled. "Nothing like that at all. I was showing Emily how to block the thoughts of others, so she doesn't have to hear every little thing, that's all. I can teach you a few things, too. If you like?"

I felt my muscles relax, but only slightly. It was the first useful thing to breach his lips since I got here. The mere mention of the chance to block Emily's spidery intrusions into my mind was reason enough to change my outlook on the situation. I could bear this madness a moment longer.

Jake chuckled, looking over his shoulder at Emily. "Is he always this charming?"

Her lips pressed together and she nodded sarcastically, agreeing with him in a way that looked like they'd suddenly become best buds.

I could feel my fingernails digging into the skin of my palms as my fists tightened. Jake leaned away from the couch, moving to the other where he sat down, knowing his place was not between Emily and me. At least he seemed to respect that to some degree.

Stepping forward, I collapsed onto the couch beside Emily. I felt relieved as she leaned her head against my chest, weaving her hands around my torso. Smugness puffed my ego, and I lifted my chin.

"Alright then, Jake, I'll buy it. So, start talking."

He sat back, his arms resting on the crest of the couch. "First of all, I'm not here to steal Emily away, I swear." He grinned. "I couldn't if I wanted to. She's not a vampire."

I raised my hand, pointer finger extended. "And she's going to stay that way," I added.

Jake nodded. "And she will *stay* that way. It would be illegal for me to turn someone into what I am without the permission of our coven leader."

"Dracula?" I ventured.

Emily elbowed me.

I winced.

Jake didn't indulge my childish remark. "Like I told your girlfriend, my race is very natural, not at all obscene, ghoulish, or horrific as history would imply. I'm simply a creature that likes the blood and meat of a good juicy animal, and humans are anything but good."

I analyzed the look on his face, seeing true disgust as he said it. "So what's the draw? Why help us?"

Jake shrugged. "Because you're classmates, and I'm not ashamed to admit that it'd be nice to have a few more friends at Glenwood High."

I heard the front door open and close, my ears perking. I kept my gaze on Jake, but I was secretly praying it wasn't another vampire. Jake smirked at me, and it filled me with anxiety. Footsteps approached, slow, soft, and normal, but still, I couldn't help but feel on edge. Halting just behind me, the hairs on my neck became erect and tingly.

"Hey, Jake." The voice snaked over my head, a lot more pleasant than I had expected, and also female. "Oh…" she paused.

I turned, my gaze meeting that of a girl about my age. Her eyes were just as reflective as Jake's, her cheeks pink and glowing. She looked like the sweetest person you'd ever meet, her hair in a lose ponytail, a red checkered dress conservatively fitting over her body.

"Jake, you have *friends*," she continued.

I could tell by the way she said it that 'Jake' and 'friends' didn't typically go together. She had a plate in her hand, covered by a film of plastic wrap. It was such a natural image to see, but I knew that whatever was on the plate was anything but normal.

She glanced at me, pursing her lips. “If I'd known you had guests, I would have brought something else home from the bakery.” She looked back at Jake.

“Don't worry about it, Sierra. We'll be fine.”

I turned to Emily. *“The bakery?”* I mouthed.

Emily shrugged.

Sierra put her hands on her hips, her attention turning back to me. “Yeah. The *bakery.* Do you have an issue with that?” she snapped, her animal teeth flashing with a snarl. Her sweet demeanor changed in an instant, and I retracted my previous calculations.

I felt Emily's hand on mine, her nails digging into my skin.

“Calm down, Sierra.” Jake intervened. “They're new here.” He turned to us. “Sierra likes to bake, but she's a little bitter about the fact that she can't really eat most of it.”

Annoyed by Jake's excuse, Sierra threw the plate at him.

He caught it before it tipped over, the plastic holding whatever it was tight. “Except these.” Jake looked down at the food in his hands, as did Emily and I. “Blood pies,” he explained.

I swallowed down the urge to gag, horror striking the once accepting expression on my face.

Jake sassily grinned at Sierra as she stormed from the room.

Her long red hair flipped behind her, her cheeks flushed an even deeper shade of red. “Moron,” she muttered.

Jake set the plate on the cushion beside him. “That's my sister. As you can see, she's a bit moody.”

Emily released the grip on my hand. “Is she your real sister?” Half moon shapes were pressed into my skin where her fingernails once rested.

Jake nodded. "In this case she is, though often they're not. We were orphaned together. In a situation like that, it's law to convert both or none at all."

I lifted my brows. "You sure have a lot of rules."

Jake exhaled long and slow, gaze focusing on a distant, unseen point. "We do."

"So, why doesn't Sierra go to Glenwood High?" I continued.

Jake propped his legs on the table before us and put one hand behind his head. "She doesn't want to. All she wants to do is play Betty Crocker. She's really good at it, too. She owns the bakery in town. I'll have to take you there sometime."

"Perhaps a day she *isn't* working," Emily whispered under her breath, enough that the three of us heard it, but not enough that Sierra would. We all laughed.

Emily shifted away from me a little, feeling more comfortable as I did as well. The truth was, this wasn't really so bad.

MAX:

I winced, a sharp pain digging into my arm. It felt like nails were ripping into my skin, matching the pain I'd felt across my chin a few days ago.

"What's wrong?" Jane took a sip of her soda as we sat at Vicco's, enjoying our afternoon feast—or at least she was; I'd already grown tired of the food.

"Nothing." I fixed my jaw, trying not to show the pain I felt.

Jane plumped out her bottom lip. She turned back to her burger, her appetite changed as she felt my anxiety pull through her. She dropped it into her lap, the foil crunching. She knew better than to believe me.

This sudden pain was happening a lot more than normal. It was something I'd grown used to over the years, but it had never meant as much as it did now. I had something to live for for the first time in my second life, and Greg was becoming a liability to me. His enemies were in turn my predators. Too many people wanted him dead, meaning too many people could also kill me. Never before had the need to separate myself from him been stronger. I had to be here for Jane no matter what. It was my duty, my job, and not to mention, my desire.

What I needed to do was growing obvious, and what I needed was the Priory. They could help separate me from Greg. They could help me stay with Jane, maybe even in the way she wants. I needed them now more than ever and they would undoubtedly come through. For so long, they had been like a family, and family never turned their backs when asked for help, just as I would help Greg if he ever decided to come around. My stomach grumbled, the food now feeling like a rock.

I'd avoided Winter Wood for long enough, and though the memories of that place stung, they would welcome me home as though nothing had ever happened. They accepted anyone willing to join their vendetta against the Black Angels, regardless. Facing the Crown could not possibly be as difficult as I've manifested it to be. The Crown is a man of business; our personal history would remain a moot point—I hoped.

I glanced at Jane, thinking of Avery once again. Avery had

been my attempt to fit in with their world and accept my fate. Jane had been my reason to leave it, and find purpose within my seemingly endless life. Jane's youthful fears of growing old had begun to infect me with uncertainty. How long would I get to keep her? How long before her death would leave me empty handed once more? I forced back such thoughts, reminding myself that in the end, I would choose death to be with her. We were meant to be together, and so we would be together after our death—no matter what the cost.

Jane signed, rubbing her stomach. "So much for dinner. I think this is kind of it for me." She sighed tiredly.

I grinned, wrapping up the rest of my mostly uneaten burger and putting it back in the bag. "Want to walk it off?"

Her head was resting back against the seat. She rolled it to face me. "Where? I'm not in the mood for tourists today." She crinkled her nose.

I lifted one brow. "Then let's go to my town."

She sat up. "You mean Winter Wood?"

I brushed a strand of hair from her face, her cheeks warm and pink and her freckles accentuated in the afternoon light. "Yes."

Her smile sank to a concerned frown. "I really want to go, but I've been thinking a lot about what you said about having not been there in a long time. Will they mind you coming for a visit? I mean, I don't really know what it's going to be like. Is it… *cultish?* Will they have to capture you and probe your mind for secrets, or…?"

I threw my head back and laughed whole-heartedly, feeling her emotion seep from the tips of my fingers to my head, filling it with lucid hope and happiness. "It's not a *cult*, Jane. It's just a town for people like us. We can get the things we need there: potions, special foods, and safe lodging. It's a bit touristy, but not as touristy as here."

She giggled. "You make it sound like a hybrid version of Vail, Colorado."

I pressed my lips together and tilted my head. "That's pretty much what it's like. It looks the same, at least on the surface. Everyone pretends their local, though they're not. It's a vacation spot for some, others it's their home."

Jane had a million questions streaming through her head. "How many people—or rather *beings*—are there?"

I shrugged. "Probably close to ten thousand permanent magickal residents, being that it's the capital."

Jane's eyes grew wide. "Wow, and I thought I was special, one of the few people like me in the area."

I touched her chin, tilting her head to face me. "You are." I leaned forward, bringing her lips to mine, my hand trailing back and hooking behind her neck. I touched her softly, sending a ripple of desire across her skin.

She moaned gently. "That's nice."

I smiled against her lips, breathing in the smell of tea leaf and rose. There was the ever-increasing tug to give in, even in such a location and time as this. Leaning back, I forced myself to start the car instead. "Time for a walk."

She frowned, but it was quickly replaced with her excitement for Winter Wood—my home.

EMILY:

I looked across the coffee table at Jake, listening to the thoughts he was leaving open for me to hear. He was nothing but friendly, nothing but genuine. Lingering views of him flashed across my mind: Him as a child, the fact that I'd never once met his parents, and the way he was always just sort of *there*, but not at the same time. Was this kid I once knew really the kid I saw now?

Jake's silvery green eyes looked at me then, a small smile curving his upper lip. He slowly glanced away. "So, shall we get to business?"

Wes let out a contented sigh, his thoughts edging on acceptance. I nodded delicately. This was nice. Having Jane and Max within our circle of magick was good, but it was good to have more—less *related*—friends as well. Once Wes got past the initial jealousy, I was certain they'd get along. How couldn't they?

"Teach me how to block some stuff, and stuff." Wes's voice was dramatically exasperated, and lacking the finesse I wished he had.

I gave him a playful slap on the arm. "Be a little more *exact*, why don't you. Not to mention the fact that you're making it sound like being with me is exhausting."

Wes sat up straight, remaining dramatic. "It is!" He laughed. "You know everything about me. A guy's got to have a little space."

Jake was nodding in agreement.

I frowned. "Are you saying there are things you want to hide?"

Wes narrowed his eyes, knowing it was a jealous retort. "No, Emily. You've got to see it from my angle. I can't think about anything, not even the fact that I have to use the toilet! I'd gross you out, so I force myself to think of other things."

I crossed my hands against my chest. "Yeah, I know. Like baseball, homework and weather, right?" I challenged him with a lifted brow.

Wes turned to Jake. "See what I mean? She's incorrigible!" He was talking as though I was no longer in the room.

Jake laughed. "Okay, chill out. I'm not here to play therapist, just to teach you a few tricks, got it?"

Wes nodded bitterly. *Was I really so bad? Was I really such a burden on him?* I grunted and shook my head.

You'd think he'd see the bright side! Jake internally sympathized with me.

I know! I replied.

Jake collected himself and turned his attention toward Wes. He took a deep breath and proceeded to explain how the mind worked, showing us that there were places, like rooms, where you could keep your thoughts. He spoke of it like a mansion, each room holding a different thought, while the main room held public thoughts. This was something that seemed so natural to me, as though I should have known it all along. I picked it up fast.

"What about the kitchen?" Wes joked.

Jake played along. "Public domain."

I grinned, enjoying their camaraderie, enjoying the fact that Wes was learning something that made our relationship stronger. Wes grasped my hand, his touch restrained though I knew that with the slightest squeeze, he could break every bone.

Jake finally stopped talking when the room grew dark with the coming twilight. He sighed deeply, stretching his arms. "Feels so much better when the sun goes down."

Wes was visibly more comfortable as well. "So, do you sleep in a coffin in the basement?" he teased.

Jake gave Wes a reproachful glare. "I don't sleep at all, actually. Up all night, all day. The daylight tires me, but only because my eyes have to work extra hard. It's sort of like staring into a flashlight, except its all day. That's why I like to go to Glenwood High, the halls are dark."

I laughed. "You can say that again. That place is like a cave. I swear the teachers are trying to make us to fall asleep so they can all retreat to the teacher's lounge for coffee instead."

"So you never sleep?" Wes scratched his head, pulling the conversation back. "How does that work?"

Jake shrugged. "I guess I don't have to. The disease makes sleeping uncomfortable and hot, and when night comes, I just don't feel like it. Daytime makes me too anxious to sleep because I feel vulnerable, and that edge of sleep never really comes. I can't even remember what it was like to sleep. I was too young." Jake grasped his stomach. "But it does make me hungry to be this lucid for so many hours."

I couldn't help but feel the slightest bit unnerved by his

comment. Jake looked at me, delighted by the way I'd reacted. His gaze lingered as it had before, longer than it should, and I found myself seeing something that I probably shouldn't have. A thin, blue veil of thought hung like a curtain behind his green eyes. It was seemingly hidden, but as the room had grown dark, the intensity of it had matured. Scanning Wes's thoughts, he didn't seem to notice it. It was my veil. A glowing emotion made just for me, warm, inviting, and happy.

Jake's mind offered me no explanation for its existence. I wondered what it meant as I clung to it, wanting to feel it pulse through me. When Jake finally looked away the blue, veiled light faded, leaving me with an unwanted chill and unexplainable anger. A ripple ran down my spine in its absence, my mouth parched of the sweet taste it once offered.

Wes sat back against the cushion and the couch bounced, jostling me out of my own head. He sympathized with Jake. "I'm hungry, too. Do they have restaurants here? Or more specifically, do they have restaurants serving your… um… *faire*, as well as mine?"

Jake's teeth flashed as he nodded. "Of course. What kind of food are you looking for?"

I saw Wes plump out his bottom lip, tasting the desire that sat on his tongue. "Meat."

Jake nodded along with Wes, as men do when they agree on something wonderful—something purely masculine like quenching the endless male craving for danger.

Jake swooned. "*Me too.* You're like the brother I never had."

I snorted, shaking my head, somehow feeling like the third wheel in this blooming *bro*-mance.

They both looked at me, their eyes like bullets. Jake's warm, veiled light washed over me once more, filling my stomach with all the nourishment it desired.

"Emily?" Wes addressed. "You're hungry, right?"

I tried to feign ignorance, not wanting to reveal my growing hunger for this strange light. "Yes, of course."

Jake winked at me, addressing us both. "Let's go to the Corner Café, then. They have everything."

JANE:

We drove down the freeway, pulling off the road and rolling to a stop in front of a gate that read 'no trespassing.' Something about it was all wrong, almost like seeing something that had been over staged or placed juxtaposed to nature.

"Let me guess, this is just for show?"

Max laughed. "Smart girl." He was looking at the gate with an inquisitive glimmer in his eye. "I used to have a trick for this, but I doubt it still works. They change those things periodically."

"A trick?" I gawked. "Your world's excuse for a remote? Yeah, right."

Max looked sideways at me, then got out of the car. I hungered over the movement of his body. Every day he denied me only made my desire to be with him exceedingly unbearable. I wanted to feel his skin against mine; I wanted to feel everything.

I couldn't help but let the trivial thought consume me. It was my challenge, and I craved a good challenge.

I watched him walk up to the gate and rattle it. Nothing happened.

I sighed, growing impatient with so many things. How could I get him to cave in and open up to me? Aside from his chastity, I also still felt like he was hiding things beyond that, especially things about his past that I should know. My own past was extensive, and yet I'd lived but a fraction of the time he had. Who was Max Gordon? And not the Max I saw now, but the Max that had breathed air into human lungs, felt emotion for him alone, and thought of nothing but life, simple and predictable. What was he like before he died? Who was he really?

I began to wonder about old relationships, thinking of the way they define us—Wes and I, Max and… *whomever.* He was a good kisser because he'd had plenty of practice—at least that's what he'd said. There was the ex-girlfriend factor somewhere along the way, but the downside was that I didn't know who any of them where, or what they were, or if they were even *alive*.

Maybe he'd only dated while he was human. If that was so, then they were likely gone from here, but it also meant that there was eighty-one years of solidarity he'd endured in this angel life. As much as I tried, I had a hard time believing that was the case. He was too attractive to squeak by without the occasional female onlooker, especially given his apparently prestigious role in the government. There was baggage, all right, and I wanted to know about it.

Max finally found what looked like a lever on the side of the gate and pulled it. The gate began to lift and my laughter filled the car. It was like a gated community, an exclusive club, and the best part was that it was mine now, too.

Max sauntered back and hopped in. “There. I got it.” He sounded winded, though I knew better than to believe that—breathing was habit, nothing but show.

“So we just go in?”

Max nodded, shifting his car out of park. “Yep.” Apprehension threaded its way through me like a stitch. I knew it wasn’t my trepidation because in all reality, I was more excited than anything else.

“You’re scared,” I stated, forcing my brows together.

A look of alarm struck his face. “No. I’m not.”

Max’s reply wasn’t very convincing as he squirmed. I placed my hand on his arm, feeling the electric pull as our skin grafted together as one. “Wait a minute.”

He jerked away, annoyed that I’d been able to do that. “What?” He protested defensively. “I’m not scared.” His eyes darted about the car, looking everywhere but at me.

“What’s here that’s so frightening to you?” I asked, my voice calm, low… *inviting.*

Max pressed himself against the back of the seat, visibly discomfited by my accusations. I was confused. This was his idea, so why was I feeling guilty as though it had been mine, as though I were forcing him into this?

“If this is so horrible for you, then why did you suggest it?” I pressed harder, testing my boundaries.

Max ignored my question, clearly avoiding the subject. “I want to come here.”

I snorted, another pull of emotion slithering through me. This time, it was dread. “No, you don’t.” I grasped his arm more firmly this time, pinching the skin where half his tattoo was blazoned. "Come on, Max. Tell me."

His blue eyes locked with mine. "It's not that I don't want to come here..."

A new emotion snaked in behind the last, and I finally got it. I sat up, gripping his arm with both hands and allowing our connection to become pure. I could feel his slow, cold pulse of blood speed up ever so gently. "You're nervous." It was such a simple emotion, disguised behind so many unnecessary ones. "How long has it been since you've been here?" I knew the answer because I'd asked the question before, but the situation had changed. I hoped he'd tell me something more.

"Long enough. You know that." He was like a fortress.

I pressed a feeling of calm from my head down my arm and into my hand, hoping he'd take the emotion for himself. He did, sighing as his body melted more comfortably into the seat. I was controlling him, and I was amazed. "Why did you leave, for real?"

Max's sudden feeling of lucidity felt like an opening door. "I left for you. I told you that. I saw you in the Truth and I knew you were my destiny. The Priory was no longer my primary concern."

I nodded. "I get that, but why did you have to leave? That doesn't justify abandoning the life you led outside the government. Whatever role you played for them shouldn't have driven you away from your home." I gave him a warning squeeze. "And don't say it was because of me again. You know how that makes me feel." My eyes narrowed as I held his gaze.

Max licked his lips nervously. "I was a head member, as I said." He was growing frustrated again, and I knew by that reaction that I'd hit on the root of the problem. "I didn't like being a head member, but leaving was more than just what I wanted, but what they wanted as well. Even if it wasn't said out loud, actions were enough. Winter Wood was no longer home to me."

"They rejected you from everything?"

He shrugged. "In a way."

I grew speculative. "What did you do? Tell me."

His shoulders sank and the small lines around his eyes relaxed. I could tell he didn't want to tell me, but knew he had no choice.

"Please, Max."

He placed his other hand over mine, squeezing it. "I'd broken promises in order to pursue the Truth. That's all you need to know. I'd made a vow to the Crown to protect certain, *important* things, a vow I swore to uphold, but didn't. The Crown didn't force me out at knife point or anything like that, though he may as well have. I left on my own accord, but it's not like I had a choice. What I did was shameful, and no one treated me the same way after that. Their judgments made me recede into loneliness. That was my cage, and I had to get out."

I could tell by the tone of his voice that that was all he was going to tell me. I felt a burn rise in my chest, a jealous burn about the fact that he knew almost every inch of my life, every secret and feeling, yet I knew almost nothing of his. I tried once again to control him and open him up, letting the feeling of jealousy overwhelm me.

He didn't budge.

MAX:

I felt so helpless, but I couldn't let her know about Avery. Not now. *Not ever*. Avery was different than any relationship Jane had ever had with another man. She would not understand the true nature of our engagement, but rather linger on the term itself. Avery had been my fiancé, my betrothed, and my future. I'd promised Avery's father to care for her always, but then I broke that promise. The Crown hadn't cared about the breakup in the business realm, but I could see the disappointment he offered me in the personal sphere. Telling Jane I had been forced out was true. I couldn't handle the whole town's judgment.

I felt my walls wavering, and I could feel what Jane was trying to do to me. Her strength was surprising. I reached across the center console, pulling her into me. I brushed my hand across her cheek, tucking her hair behind her ear until her power over me faded. "There are some things about my past I am ashamed of, things that lend no importance to our relationship or our current situation. I want to bury the things that hurt me and try to be happy."

"But I want to know who you are," Jane whispered, sounding

exhausted.

I pressed my lips against her forehead, surrounding her with the only emotion I could offer—security. "And you will. You are. Coming here with me will show you a lot. I promise."

She relaxed within the circle of my arms, but still, her hands gripped my shoulders. She clung to me with desperation, weakness and longing. I wanted to let go of my apprehensions; I wanted to be with her, but the punishment was not worth the crime. I needed to find a way around this last obstacle and prove to Jane that life is about more than just what she's focused on now. I am an old soul and have seen that the worries she faces are not real worries, but distractions from life. I need to remember that it's also not my place to teach her. She has to find it out on her own. This was something The Priory could help me to understand again, as I have forgotten what it means to be young in the world.

I released her as she still held tight. Wedging my hands between us, I urged her to sit back. "Are you ready?"

Jane looked up at me, her grip releasing. "Are you?"

I smiled. She was trying to be strong for me. "With you, Jane, I'm always ready."

She giggled and winked. "Sort of," she teased.

AVERY:

I leaned against the trunk of a tree, thirty feet above their car. The wind was moderate, leaving me swinging in the air, grasping to what bits of conversation it carried. Max loved his pet, this I already knew, but what I'd just learned added to the already smoldering anger I harbored. She'd been the reason for our end.

I ripped the bark off the tree, grinding it in my hands until there was nothing left. How could such a weak being destroy the strength of our once-great connection? We had power, nobility, and respect. This little leech only offered him love, the simplest of emotions.

My plans suddenly changed. This Seoul was no longer just an obstacle in my way, but what I was here to destroy. She was the reason my heart had grown lightless, a Shadow Pixie amongst the glow of others. Max had taken my radiance, my pride, the one thing we pixie's hold dear, and the one thing my kind kept to give only to our truest of partners. Unfortunately my truest of partners had been a ruse. I should have known better than to trust an angel or my father. I should have known better than to believe in love.

I dug my nails into the now exposed meat of the evergreen tree, smelling sap as it bled across my fingers. The tree moaned softly, a moan only my ears could hear, and a moan I dreamed to hear from the girl called Jane.

She would die. She had to.

EMILY:

Walking down the street, I kept an eye on Jake. He was practically glowing in the dim of the evening, his skin holding the daylight inside. I held tight to Wes, his arm around me, anchoring me to his side. I was thankful for that, because if he hadn't been there to do so, I'd already be lost in the blue, veiled light, dancing wildly and basking in the heat it offered. Jake's glow made me want to be near him in a way I'd never wanted to be near anything, and it frightened me. It wasn't attraction, not quite. It was something else, something that sat right at the tip of my tongue. It took all my strength to resist the feeling, hide the feeling, but the darker the sky grew, the more it tested my strength.

There was a group of girls up ahead, and as they approached, Wes and I stared shamelessly. I pressed my fingers firmly against his arm, afraid of what they could be. The notion felt awkward and uncontrollable. Humans were just human, but not here—never before had it been a thing to think of. The girls giggled and whispered amongst themselves as they passed Jake, a flirtatious sight I would have never previously associated with the Jake from class.

"Hi, *Jake*." Their voices chimed in perfect unison, their laughter intoxicatingly sweet.

They swooned in the same manner when their eyes fell on Wes.

I all but growled at them, no longer concerned with what they were, but what I wanted to do to them. They looked at me with narrowed eyes, and I was shocked by the bright blue of them. The glittering hue of their lashes and the shine of their pearlescent hair and skin made me wither in comparison.

They brushed past, leaving Wes and I in a fog of perfumed air—smelling of cinnamon. Jake's gaze never broke away from their many assets, his neck craned with a smirk on his face. "Too bad they're not vampires," he murmured, shaking his head lightly and clicking his tongue.

Squeezing Wes's arm, I moved closer to Jake, dangerously testing the pull of his blue veiled emotion. "What *are* they?" I whispered, feeling in a fog at this proximity.

He sighed longingly. "Element Pixies."

"Element Pixies?"

Jake nodded, his vision finally breaking away from their swaying hips. "Yep. We have a lot here. This is a dominantly pixie community because the Crown here is an Element Pixie as well—not that I mind. They're the most gorgeous creatures in the world. You see, they can convey the seasons. Winter, summer, fall, and spring. They're the prettiest in the spring. Right now they're transitioning from fall to winter, so it's a bit awkward."

"But still gorgeous," Wes snorted.

I clenched my jaw, ignoring him, not finding it hard to do

when surrounded by my own spring of blue light. "Why don't you live in a dominantly vampire community?"

Jake laughed as though the answer was obvious. "Much too savage for my taste. You get enough of my kind together and they lose touch with humanity, manners, social order, and basic community. It's good to live in a pixie community. They're organized, calculated, and best of all, they make the best warriors. This is one of the safest communities on Earth. Black Angels won't bother to come here unless it's the last standing fortress."

Wes snorted. "Yeah, or unless you're Greg."

Jake laughed. "Yeah, exactly. I guess he thinks he's got some power over us because of Max. The Crown has a special friendship with Max, practically *family,* so I know he won't attack Greg unless it's absolutely necessary."

The way he'd explained the Crown and Max pulled me away from the desire to spread my arms and gather up the blue light dancing around me. I gathered myself back to reality. "What do you mean *family?*"

Jake halted on the street, car's I'd been used to seeing around town now driving past us, their magickal secret revealed.

Jake lifted one brow. "The Crown was Max's *father-in-law to-be* until Max called it off, out of the blue. That was the rumor, at least."

I no longer cared about the magickal people in their cars, or even the blue light. "*What?*"

Jake shook his head as he told the unfortunate tale. "Max was betrothed to the Crown's daughter, Avery. It was a big deal a few decades back. It was the closest thing to a royal wedding our kind had ever seen. The whole town was planning it, even my mother. She'd baked the cake for cryin' out loud. That's who Sierra learned to bake from. I wasn't alive then, obviously. It's just a family story."

Wes exchanged a glance with me.

Jake looked perplexed. "What?" he asked. "Max didn't tell you?"

Wes chuckled sarcastically. "Why would he? He loves Jane. I doubt he'd come out and tell us about his failed engagement to an Element Pixie."

I was horrified. "Do you know why the engagement failed?" A blue wisp tickled my nose.

Jake gloated. "All I know is that Max called it off and then left. When he showed up on school grounds at the beginning of this year, it was the first time I'd ever seen the face behind the legend. You see, no one, and I mean *no one*, breaks up with an Element Pixie. When one falls in love with you, they become a part of you. If you break the heart of an Element Pixie, they succumb to shadow. That's no place anyone wants to be. Forget Black Angels; a Shadow Pixie is far worse. Luckily, she disappeared without much to-do over the situation, but that's why the story is legend." He glanced up over my head and squinted. "Max was lucky in that respect." His eyes widened then. "And speaking of the devil."

I spun on my heel, expecting to see this Avery girl, but seeing Max's Defender instead. It was rolling down the street, chromed rims catching under the street lights. Not to my surprise, Jane was in the passenger seat.

"I'm amazed he'd show his face," Jake murmured.

"What are they doing here?" I hissed, turning to Wes and searching his eyes. I was a little jealous, hoping this could be my town, not hers.

Wes just shook his head slowly, struggling to say much of anything.

MAX:

"What are *they* doing here?" Jane's excited expression faded.

I looked in the direction she was, surprised to see Emily and Wes standing on the curb up ahead; that is, until I recognized Jake beside them. He was just as I saw him under all the disguises in class, but it still took a moment to register.

I slowed the car and rolled down Jane's window. Wes strolled up, resting his arm on the frame. "Fancy seeing you here."

Jane scowled. "How did you find it?"

I could tell she was jealous. She'd wanted this to be her discovery.

Wes hooked his thumb over his shoulder, pointing at Jake.

Jane leaned closer, looking past Wes. "And *you* are?"

"Jake Santé."

Jane sat up straighter. "*Jake Santé,* as in Jake Santé from Glenwood High?"

Jake nodded.

Jane looked at me. "*What?*" Her mouth formed the words, her voice nothing but a squeak.

I simply nodded.

Jane sat back, looking again at Jake. "No way."

Jake grinned then, and Jane gasped.

I grabbed her arm, stopping her before the questions began. "He's a vampire, Jane. I'll fill you in later."

She gawked at my lips and the words they'd formed. Her eyes were horrified and her beautiful mouth gaping. "But…"

"He won't hurt anyone, Jane. Just trust me—*later.*" I tried to say it under my breath so that Jake wouldn't hear, though I doubt it worked very well.

Jake approached my car. "Nice to finally meet you up close, Jane." His hand pressed through the open window, offering her a shake.

Still eyeing me, she numbly clasped her fingers around his hand and gave it a single shake before letting go. "Hi." Her voice was curt.

Jake leaned his weight against the door. "I'm glad you finally found your way here."

I disliked the way Jake was staring at Jane, but it was his nature. Vampires were well-known flirts.

We're headed over to the Corner Café." Jake's attention turned to me. "Want to join us?"

"We already ate," Jane interjected before I got the chance to reply.

Jake frowned dramatically. "Oh, come on, Jane. Give it up already. Your pessimism impresses no one."

JANE:

I snorted loudly, crossing my arms and feeling embarrassed. Jake had called me on my greatest flaw, and as much as I wanted to deny it, he was right. I hated change.

My lips remained sealed, trying not to look into Jake's eyes. They were reflective, their almond contour so different from the beady eyes I'd grown used to seeing through the thick glasses he wore at school. I didn't trust him, nor did I want to. The mere existence of Winter Wood hadn't even sunk in just yet, and now this? I felt like I was dreaming.

"Yeah, Jake, We'll come." Max agreed to Jake's invitation, despite my earlier refusal.

I snorted again, my hands bawling into fists in my lap. I didn't care if Jake saw how rude I was acting. I was beyond aggravated by the whole situation.

Jake pointed to a building across the street with a large neon sign that read 'Corner Café'. It was no different than any other molded brick building I'd seen in Glenwood, therefore making it inviting—another thing that annoyed me. I'd expected more from Winter Wood, and though I didn't know just what that was, it certainly wasn't quite this routine. If you grafted main street Winter Wood to main street Glenwood, you'd think it was the exact same town.

Max rolled my window up, pulling to the curb and parking the car. "Is this okay?" He asked apprehensively, already knowing it wasn't.

I reluctantly went through the habit of unbuckling and stepping out. "Yeah, whatever."

He stepped out, looking at me over the hood. "Good." He glanced back at Wes, Emily and Jake across the street. "You go ahead. I'll catch up in a moment, okay?"

My mouth fell open, wanting to protest, wanting to get angry with him. He'd promised me romance, and now he was ditching me as well? I harshly slammed the door shut. Max was already walking away and up the street. "Where are you going?" I caught up to him.

He stopped and turned. His expression was drawn and pained. An odd, vaguely familiar emotion pulled through me.

"I just need to check in on the alchemist's shop." He tipped his chin, motioning me to look ahead and across the street. On the next corner hung an old sign with a mortar and pestle carved into the wood. The windows were dark and deserted.

My hands were resting at my sides, my nails white as I pressed them into my palms. "Okay," I said nervously, not wanting to be left alone with my sister and her new friend.

"Patrick was like a father to me, and I regret that I wasn't there for him in the end. I owe it to him to check in on his things. I owe it to myself to say goodbye. You'll be fine with your sister, won't you?"

I could understand that this was something Max needed to do, regardless of the fact that he didn't want to invite me along, but still, did he have to do it right now?

Max hooked his arms around my waist. "You're allowing your thoughts to trickle through." He whispered. His fingers trailed down my arms until they weaved between my own. "I'm not leaving you alone." He pressed his weight against me until my back was flush against the building beside us. "I know you're frustrated with me. I know how much I'm keeping from you, but you need to understand how hard this is for me. I just need to get back into a groove, and then I'll tell you everything. Jake is safe. I, of all people, should know this."

I frowned. "It's not fair. I want to be a part of your life. I don't doubt your feelings for me because of the sacrifices you've made, but I don't understand why you're being so elusive. You don't want to be with me intimately, you have all these secrets, and I know nothing of your past."

He squeezed my hands. "Jane, I do want to be with you."

My cheeks reddened at the thought, feeling his weight against mine as my mind wandered.

"I'm just not ready yet. Please be patient, and before long, you'll know everything about me."

I couldn't argue with that, and I hated it. I felt like everything was out of my control—my short life, my guardian boyfriend. Nothing was within my power anymore. Nothing ever had been.

His hands brushed my cheeks. "Don't start thinking that way. I told you that you have every choice in this."

"Do I?" I looked into his eyes.

"You're stalling," he replied.

"Hey, Jane! Come on!" Emily had poked her head out the café door.

Max let go of my hands and stepped back. "You've always

been free. Being with me is your choice."

"But you'll always be there, and it will always be that way because it's what you swore to do."

"I can't change that."

I sighed, stepping closer once more. "I do love you. I want to be with you. I just sometimes wish I'd made that choice. I wish I'd fallen in love with you before finding out all I did. Our life just feels so contrived."

"But you did fall in love with me before," he protested, cupping his hand against my cheek. "You just choose to forget that." He grinned. "You're head was filled with admiration for me that first day you noticed me. I remember it. You walked into that hall and saw me, your thoughts overflowing with curiosity, the crush already growing inside."

I blushed again, remembering the first day of this year. "You knew I was there?"

Max laughed. "Jane, I'd waited almost sixty years to be with you, of course I knew you were there."

"But you didn't even look at me."

He nodded. "Because I wanted to make sure you liked me first. You see, I gave you a choice."

"And if I didn't notice you? What would you have done?"

He lifted my hands to his lips, grazing my skin with a kiss. "I would have watched from a distance. You would have never known I was ever there."

His words soothed me. He was right. I'd stared at him as he stood at his locker that day, stared with a feeling of warmth and desire toward a stranger I wanted so badly to know. Every curve of his body was vivid, exact, and well-committed to memory. His current words had gotten me, though frustration still lingered. For whatever reason, the feeling of being caged in this relationship remained in the shadows, not yet ready to give up, but for right now, at least I felt halfway free.

Max kissed me as sweet emotion fed though his lips. I was ravenous to have the boy I'd seen in the hall—this boy. My body grew hot and tingly with the thought. I traced my hands along his torso to his back, tucking them under his belt and pulling him against me. I didn't care who could be watching, this moment was mine alone.

Max pulled away, shaking and visibly dazed with lust. "I'll just be a moment, okay?"

I nodded, removing my hands. "Okay." I was equally shaken by the intensity of my passion.

EMILY:

We took a booth in the corner. Wes sat between Jake and me, not on purpose, but I was happy for it. Jake scratched his head and picked up the menu, flipping it over. I reluctantly reached for a menu as well, scanning the various sections: Vegetarian, Vegan, Carnivore, Venous, Small Plates...

"What's *Venous?*" I blurted.

Jake looked over his menu, the same warm, veiled light causing me to shift uncomfortably. It was easier to handle in the dull lights of the café, but still, it was there.

“That’s my section,” he answered dryly.

I felt my stomach turn, my eyes skirting across the offerings, too craven to read the content.

A waitress approached, her arms covered in swirly green tattoos. Black feathers were tied in a knot on the top of her head like hair. I couldn’t help but stare at her, wondering what she was, and if she could read thoughts or not. She stopped before us, her movements fluid and shadowy, like a dream.

“What can I get y’all?” Her eyes blinked in two different directions. “Jake, the usual?” Her head tilted like a bird watching a worm, a toothpick hanging from her lipstick-red mouth.

Jake pursed his lips as he debated his choices, and then shut the menu abruptly. “Yeah, the uge.”

She jotted something onto the pad of paper in her hand, her hand pecking with determination.

I continued to stare at her until her jet black eyes glanced up and found mine. I quickly looked away, ashamed by my blatant staring. “*Um*… I’ll have…” My face was puckered as I tried to come up with something, wondering what was going to be edible in my terms.

“Give her the Hot Brown,” Jake remarked casually. “She’ll like that.”

My brows creased deeper, not wanting his help, his warmth, or his sugary, blue glow.

Wes didn’t seem to care. “Baby Backs, please.” He handed the waitress the menu, not even phased by her appearance. “Extra sauce.”

The waitress nodded, giving me one last look before walking away.

“Are you guys going to the Halloween party at Trent’s next

Friday?" Wes began. "I guess it's going to be huge this year. Trent's parents are going to Hawaii, so we'll have the whole house. He's got a hot tub, pool…

Wes's voice faded away as the front door swung open and the bell rang. My heart jumped at the sound, relief replacing the fear as Jane entered. She was alone. Looking around, her eyes lingered on the hostess who was also tattooed, though her head was bald. Jane tilted away from her as she asked her something. The hostess pointed to us. Her glazed eyes found mine and a meek smile pulled at her lips. Approaching, she appeared isolated by the whole situation. Her arms were wrapped tight around her, her steps quick and short.

Squeezing into the booth next to me, she sat closer than she really needed to. Her lips leaned close to my ear. "I can see what's different about Winter Wood."

I nodded, my eyes wide. "I *know!* I thought it looked so normal until I stepped in here." I kept my voice low. "Where's Max?" All I could think about was what Jake had said earlier, pertaining to Max's previous relationships.

"Max had to look in on something real quick." She slid her menu off the table, burying her face in it as though ashamed.

"I see," I replied plainly.

"Jane? Are you going to the party?" Wes asked.

Jane peeked over the menu at him, shrugging.

I glanced out the window behind us to the street outside. Knowing Max's dirty past suddenly made me fear for my sister. I could see that she loved Max, and I didn't want her to end up with a broken heart like this Avery girl did. I turned back to her with a frown on my lips. It frustrated me that I could no longer hear most of her thoughts because of the ring Max had given her, but at the same time, it was the way it was supposed to be, I suppose. First Jane, and now Wes. Where was the fun in that?

It was then that I realized I hadn't really heard many thoughts since being *here,* though there were an abundance of beings. Everyone seemed to have a handle on the possibility of mind readers and had thus learned to block us. I smiled to myself, feeling an old relief wash over me, like the way I used to feel after drowning the voices away with a pill.

Jake looked at me, having supplied Wes with an acceptance to his party invitation, only a senior could invite any underclassmen. "It is nice, isn't it?"

I nodded. "It is."

Jane and Wes's attention turned to us.

"What's nice?" Wes accused.

I sighed dramatically. "Not hearing everyone's thoughts," I reassured him.

Wes's jealousy faded. "Oh. I bet that's nice." He was trying to relate.

Wes glanced sideways at Jane, looking as though he'd picked up on her stench of anxiety. "So, where's Max?"

"Running an errand," Jane recited flatly.

Wes bit his lip. "Really? An *errand*...well..."

I elbowed him in the side, hearing where this was going. He stopped talking as he doubled over, forehead on the table and moaning.

"*Well* what?" Jane pressed, looking a little too intrigued.

Wes sat up straight. "Well..." his voice was forced. "Just excited to see him, is all."

Jane stared at Wes for a long moment, a stare that even I was afraid of.

The waitress returned. "Want anything, honey?"

Jane broke her stare and looked at the feather-haired waitress, her eyes growing wide. "Oh…uh, *no*," she stammered, as taken aback by her appearance as I had been.

The waitress rolled her eyes and turned on her heel. She sauntered off, her hips swaying unnaturally.

"What *is* she?" Jane asked under her breath.

We all laughed at the way she'd said it—without guilt for the taunting manner of it.

Jake tapped a fork against the table to silence us. "She's a Faerie."

Jane pressed her hand against her cheek. "Huh." She pondered the thought as I did before she leaned close to me once more. *"You think it's safe to use the bathroom?"* she whispered.

Jake leaned forward, invading our private conversation. "Seriously, could you be any more obvious? You're like tourists."

Jane's cheeks flushed. "Well… I don't know," she whined.

Jake pointed toward the back of the café. "Back there. I assure you it's plenty safe." He sounded exasperated by our childishness—I felt ashamed, as though it meant the warm veiled light would be taken from me as punishment. I wanted to cry because of it, but I found my senses instead.

Jane slid out of the booth, her hands tight at her sides as she walked rigidly to the back of the restaurant, a cocoon of negative energy surrounding her.

MAX:

I urged Jane into the café, watching her as she crossed the street before turning and making my way to the corner where the apothecary sat, dark. I pulled out my wallet as I walked and searched for a key I hadn't removed from its place for many years. I'd received the key in Patrick's will, but I'd never had the guts to come back here to use it.

Reaching the door, the darkened window was an unwelcomed sight. In my mind, I saw the way the apothecary once was—the windows warm, the scent of perfumes seeping into the street—all that was gone now.

Unlocking the door, I slid inside. The shelves were bare and coated with a thin film of age. I drew in a deep breath, trying to find the smell that reminded me of Patrick, of the father figure I'd grown to love after my own father had died, but I didn't. I exhaled, disappointed.

In my head, I had always seen him as a part of my family. He'd loved my mother in a way my real father never could, and though my real father chose to ignore the love they shared and live a lie, I knew it had still left him bitter. I always thought I was strange because none of it ever bothered me, as it should have.

I guess in my defense, I figured there was no way to know when true love would find you. The unfortunate thing in that were those, like my father and Avery, who'd suffered because of it.

Ruining Avery was never my plan. Understandably, Avery hated me for it. As much as I tried to remain here to be supportive, the string of unhappiness my actions caused robbed me of the sanctuary Winter Wood once offered. She'd disappeared soon after my desertion from this place, a thankful thing, and I really couldn't blame her.

I stole to the back room, opening the office door and finding the space untouched. There was a half burned candle on Patrick's desk, the wax frozen in the last moment he'd beckoned it to burn, forever waiting for his return. I moved forward and pulled out the desk chair, the oak creaking as I sat. I sighed, shutting my eyes and remembering the many times I sought council from him in this very room.

I heard the echo of his voice against the walls, the squeak of the chair a trigger for the vision. There was always the smell of lavender in the air. It was my mother's favorite flower. His belongings were, at all times, perfectly placed, perfectly dusted, and well loved—a far cry from the condition I found them in now. Clearly his friends, family, and the government had already searched his belongings, but found seemingly everything useless, except to me.

Opening my eyes, I leaned forward and began to search through the drawers, all except the middle one, which was locked. I bit my lip, remembering what was once there. I took the key I'd used to open the front door and slid it into the lock, surprised to find it fit. It took a little nudging to make it turn and unlock, but when I slid the drawer toward me, I was disappointed to find it was empty. The Truth Stone was gone.

I slowly slid the drawer shut and sighed.

Was that what I had come here for?

I leaned my elbows against the desk.

Why was I looking for the Truth if this life, right now, was supposed to be all I wanted? Was there still more?

I allowed the Truth I'd seen to come back to me, and one thing seemed to resonate—the moment hadn't yet happened. It's true that I'd found Jane, the very same girl from the Truth, but wasn't the Truth supposed to come to pass, like déjà vu?

What did it mean?

Jane was young in the dream, the same age she was now. It had to happen soon. "She'd found me." I whispered, thinking of the words she'd said in the dream. "If she'd found me, then I must have been lost somewhere." I bit my nails.

Lost.

I let the word roll around in my head, hoping to find a place for it, but nothing came without danger first.

JANE:

I ruefully pushed open the restroom door, allowing it to swing shut behind me. The room was long and narrow, mirrors down the left and stalls on the right. A red stripe of tile dissected the room, white above, and white below. I instinctively looked below the stall doors, and from what I could see, it was empty. I chose a booth and did my business, flushing the toilet with my foot before exiting to wash my hands.

With the cold water running over my fingers, I looked at my reflection in the mirror. I stared deep into my eyes, wondering what it was about me that Max found so important. I'd never done anything worth noting, never succeeded at any real magick, nor did I know any besides creating a few sparks, and I'd never inflicted any Earth-altering change. I was just another person, plugging away each new day as I had the last. A strangling pressure occupied my chest at the thought. I wanted to do something amazing. I wanted to inflict change somehow, but how could I prove to the world that I deserve that? I wanted a real dream.

The restroom door swung open beside me, my heart fluttering with the sound. I didn't want to know who or what was sharing this small room with me. My gaze dropped back to my hands, trying to act natural. I was on edge here, and my heart could barely handle it. Watching from the corner of my eye, a girl advanced to the sink beside me. I breathed a sigh of relief—at least this being was visibly identifiable. Her scent wafted in her wake, sweet and innocent, and distinctly cinnamon.

She turned on the faucet and slowly washed her hands, sighing dramatically as she concentrated on the task.

I allowed myself to take advantage of the moment and glance at her more completely. She was blonde, strikingly beautiful, and strikingly *normal*—at least considering the way our waitress looked. Her lashes were icy blue, her cheeks kissed with pink as though she'd just stepped in from a snowy hike. Her skin glistened like plastic, so smooth you wondered if it had ever seen the sun.

She began to hum, and like a thread of smoke riding on the scent of cinnamon, her future death flooded my mind. As I recognized what it was, one thing was obvious—she was not dead, just as Max wasn't dead within his future death. She spun and spun and spun to the sound of her humming in a field so bright with the sun, there was very little contrast.

She shut off the water, breaking the stream of thought. Turning, she looked hopelessly for a towel to dry her dripping hands, but there was none. "*Ugh...* I hate this place." Her voice was like a song, even though she was complaining.

I giggled a little, feeling just as annoyed by the absence of drying implements. I fanned my hands through the air in a failed attempt to substitute.

The girl looked at me, smiling. "You can never trust a grungy café, can you?"

I shook my head. "No. They're always out of either towels or toilet paper." I smiled back. "I guess I'd rather they be out of towels."

The girl's platinum blond hair moved like water, glittering despite the dull neon light. "Yeah," she agreed with wide eyes. "Thank the gods for that."

I was gawking, wondering how she could look so good given the atmospheric circumstances surrounding her. Her glittery eyes never stopped moving, so full of life. My own reflection showed bags under my eyes, and where she was pale in a beautiful porcelain way, I was pale in a sickly way.

Her gaze at last rested on me. "I've never seen you here before. Are you new to town?" the girl added, giving in to shaking her hands as I was.

"I guess you could say that."

She grinned politely. "That's nice. It's good to have you."

"Thanks, it's good to be here." I felt awkward and nervous, while she was teeming with confidence. "I'm Jane, by the way."

"Jane? That's a lovely name, very *human*." The girl cocked her head to the side, inspecting me. "What are you? Alchemist, clairvoyant..."

"Seoul," I finished the rattle of titles for her. "And you?"

She grinned, displaying a row of perfectly straight and perfectly white teeth. "Pixie," she said simply.

Our growing warmth toward each other helped my shoulders to relax. "You have no death, it's nice," I admitted.

The girl giggled. "I bet. I couldn't imagine seeing that all the time." She crinkled her nose, but still, it didn't make her look unattractive. "I'm Navia, by the way."

She'd paused as though she'd forgotten her own name, but it was endearing. "Nice to meet you, Navia." I allowed her name resonate on my tongue. "Neat name." It was admittedly strange to talk so frankly with someone like this—someone so purely *magickal.*

She tilted her head sweetly. "Thanks."

My hands were finally dry so I stopped fanning them, dropping them to my sides. "Well, I better get back. But it was nice to meet you."

Navia was staring at me with admiration, and I found it off-putting given her perfection—someone like her had no need to be amazed by someone as simple as me. "Nice to meet you as well, Jane. I'm sure I'll see you again."

I turned away from her, her cinnamon scent still invading my nostrils. I grasped the door handle and pulled it open.

"Wait, Jane."

I stopped, looking back over my shoulder.

She swiftly closed the distance between us, her hand outstretched, clasping a white slice of paper between her fingers. "Here, this is my number in case you ever want to see Winter Wood through a pixie's eyes." She thrust a thick card toward me. "It is a pixie town, after all."

"So I've heard." I grasped it, seeing blue swirls circle around ten simple black numbers. I laughed to myself, finding it so formal and organized, just as she was. "Thanks."

Navia clasped her hands before her and stood on her toes, looking excited to have found me. "Don't hesitate!"

I turned away from her, tucking the card in my pocket and pushing open the door. "I won't."

Even if I was delighted to meet her, the truth was that I already knew I wouldn't call her. I had enough supernatural friends as it was. Besides, Max had a particular disliking for pixies. There had to be a good reason why.

MAX:

I leaned away from the desk. There was a file cabinet nestled in the corner of the room, boxed in by a pile of old books. Resting on top of the cabinet was a picture of a youthful Patrick standing before the ocean, a smirk on his face. I had never seen the picture there before, so perfectly placed as though on purpose. I stood, drawn to it, drawn to the weather in the sky behind him and the look on his face. I lifted the frame, looking into his blue eyes. He was maybe in his early twenties, his dark hair lush and covering the whole of his head. His glasses were tucked into the pocket of his simple plaid shirt. I could almost hear the roar of the waves behind him, the rush of the clean sea air.

I flipped the frame over, surprised to see that there was a note written on the back:

Patrick,

Thank you for a wonderful weekend. I'm happy I found you, happy for the time we've spent together. I hope to see you again, very soon.

-A

It was dated 1909. Curiosity sparked my interest.

'A'...

For Annette? My mother?

Why else would he keep it? It had to be her, but it was too early. I thought back, tried to recall my past life, though that was eighty-one years ago. The affair was exposed not long before Gregory murdered us, in 1928. Had Patrick and my mother really known each other for close to twenty years prior to that? I thought about my youth, remembering Patrick. Together, we spent days fishing and boxing, and as I grew older, he helped me discover simple tricks which became helpful when magick grew amongst the human world.

I flipped it over and looked into the alchemist's eyes once more. Extending my arms, I placed the photo back on the cabinet, at a loss of what to make of it. I stood with my head bowed, my mind beginning to tingle with a growing notion. Fleeing back to the desk, I opened the drawers for a second time and searched with refined determination. Love letters from my mother—I had seen them in his drawers a hundred times, though Patrick never knew that I'd seen them at all. I pilfered through the piles of crumpled papers, prescriptions and potion recipes. Finally, the familiar and worn red ribbon snaked its way through the rubbish.

I hooked my finger through the loop of the bow and brought the bundle onto his desk. I untied it, letters sliding out across the battered surface. There were hundreds of letters, each organized by date. I sifted through them like a deck of cards. 1923… 1919…1913…1909…

1909…

I flipped open the carefully tucked flap of the linen envelope.

Patrick,

I refuse to forget the time we spent at the ocean, or the things you told me. You've enchanted me, stolen my heart in a way I thought was forgotten to me. You asked me to forget about us, but Patrick, I can't…

-A

I looked back at the pile, finding the next letter.

Patrick,

You ask me to remain with Henry, but why? He is but a friend to me, an arranged marriage where the love has long since gone. You alone are my true love. I understand your concerns for involving me in your world, but I would do anything to be near you and live a true life as your wife. What grows inside my belly is not Henry's, and I refuse to see it otherwise. I refuse to live the lie...

-A

I swallowed hard, multiple times, each time not able to accomplish breathing. I was about to choke, but there was nothing I could do to take back what I'd read, and what suddenly made so much sense. I placed the letter slowly on the desk, bowing my head into my hands as the sting of emotion tried to stir and spin my world. What grows inside her? I wanted to believe it was love that was growing inside her, but I cursed myself for being so naïve. I looked up at the picture on the file cabinet once more. Why hadn't I seen it before? The clear blue eyes of the Alchemist; the same clear blue eyes *I* possessed.

"He was my... *father?*" I spoke aloud, wanting to hear myself test the term—it felt wrong, and yet so right.

My brows pressed together as my hands attacked the pile of letters once again. 1912...1915...1918...

Patrick,

Our children grow, my love. Our boys are just like you, and I wish you were here to be a part of it. Maximus reminds me of you, outgoing and bright, while Gregory seems reserved—thoughtful. Though I may not have you, I am thankful for the gifts you've given me…

-A

I threw the letter back on the desk—feeling lied to, like I'd been cheated time from my father—my real father. My eyes were then drawn to a letter written in Patrick's hand. I picked it up, tracing the ink of the envelope, feeling the ridges where he'd forced his hand. *1927…*

Annette,

I am pleased to send message that Maximus and our youngest, Erik, show promising signs of magick, but I've come to believe that Gregory lacks the gene. Max must have stolen the gift in the womb. Being twins will do that. My teachings frustrate Gregory, and I fear there is a darkness growing because of this. As much as I try to be neutral about their teachings, Gregory is beginning to notice that he is different. He's too in tune with his brother for us to try and hide Max's gift. I must tell Gregory. We must keep a close eye on our son; even the Element Pixies warn me of the things they've seen in the light of his soul...

-P

Overwhelmed with shock, I allowed myself to pull the emotion from Jane against my fears of allowing her to know. My eyes filled with her sweet tears. I clenched my jaw, the letter inside balled in my fist. Gregory had been lied to, and because of that lie, he'd cracked.

The following year Greg had killed us all. The timing seemed too perfect. He must have found out about my magick and Patrick's true relation to us. *Why hadn't Greg told me?* Of all people, I, as his brother, could have helped him. Greg didn't deserve to handle this alone. He didn't deserve to hear that he was different and his whole world was a lie. I would have given anything to change that, to give him what I'd apparently had all along.

JANE:

As I walked back to the table at the café, I stopped abruptly in my tracks. My heart ached like never before as an overwhelming feeling of loss and betrayal washed over me. *What was Max up to?*

I blinked a few times, feeling my eyes go dry, my own tears being sucked from me. I wanted to cry from the sting of it, but I couldn't. Whatever Max was doing was hurting him—and me. Never before had he taken so much emotion like this. All I wanted was to run to him, comfort him. I forced my feet to move, making my way back to the table instead, caught in a foggy battle as to what was the right thing to do. Wes, Emily and Jake were deep in conversation, their hands animated.

"I think I should go check on Max," I blurted.

Emily stopped talking, her eyes wide. "You're sweating like a *pig.* Is everything alright?" She leaned toward me. "Why are your eyes so red?"

I nodded, wiping my brow. "Yeah, it's just that Max is over at the Alchemist's place, and…" I let my voice trail. My thoughts were thick, my mouth rambling.

Wes nodded with understanding, the first compassionate look I'd gotten from him in a while. That look alone relaxed me a little, making me feel as though there was hope for our friendship. The relief was quickly washed away as another wave of deep sadness fell over me, knocking the very breath from my lungs. I brought my hand to my neck, rubbing it.

"I'll be back, okay?" The words were hard to say, my stomach knotted with anxiety.

"Want me to go with you?" Wes made a move to get up.

My hands flew out. "*No.* No. I'm fine."

Wes slowly sat back down. Emily and Jake nodded.

I pushed away from the table and hobbled to the door, finding Max's sadness had become so deep, so self-damaging, that he'd nearly taken the very fight from my soul. Looking like a crazy person, I flew out of the café and made my way across the street. Guided street light to street light, I staggered until the sign with the mortar and pestle hung over my head.

I burst into the dark shop. "Max?" My voice was shaky and weak.

I heard nothing. Roaming the room, I searched frantically behind the front desk. No one was there. Bracing myself against an old stool, I saw a narrow hallway that led deeper into the shop. I staggered along, hands gripping the wall for support. I was too exhausted to stand on my own, almost too exhausted to go any further. There was a door about five feet ahead of me that had been left ajar. A warm light glowed from inside, followed by the sound of sobs.

Letting all my weight transfer from the wall to the door handle, I burst into the room, swinging on the door as it braced me.

Max looked up with alarm. "Jane." His face was so aggrieved that I forgot my own suffering.

"Max," I whispered, making my way toward him. Exhausted, I laid my body against his, his body hunched against a large desk. Paper and envelopes had been thrown all over the room—freshly disturbed.

Max said nothing as he stroked my arm, his face strained with emotion I'd never seen from him before.

"What's going on?" I whispered, once some of my strength had returned.

I felt his passion as he looked into my eyes, as he saw what he was doing to me. "I'm sorry. I couldn't help it." He'd managed to gather himself, hiding the signs of his internal struggle.

My head slowly stopped spinning, and I glanced around the room. Bookshelves lined the walls, as well as glass beakers, pictures, and paper. I grasped onto Max's shoulders and moved further onto his lap, needing to be near him in order to remain strong. He was holding something in his hand—a picture frame. I pried it from his grasp and turned it to face me. There was a figure within the frame. I was overwhelmed with the many elements of the figure that seemed familiar to me, though I'd never met the man.

"Is this the Alchemist?" My eyes washed over and over his features, the very breath knocked from my lungs when the blue of his eyes cut right through me. There was an ocean inside the alchemist's gaze, an ocean I'd seen many times before. *"Max,"* I whispered, able to put the pieces of emotion and visual evidence together.

"He's my father," he muttered, refusing to meet my gaze.

"Yeah, I..." To me it seemed so obvious, but to Max it clearly hadn't. "You never knew this?" I asked carefully.

He shook his head. "Why would I? I was told otherwise, made to think of Henry as my father since the moment I was born. If that's all you ever know, why question it? Patrick was a man I didn't meet until I was a young boy. I simply didn't see it because when you're young, your brain doesn't work like that."

"Oh, Max." I placed the picture on the desk and wrapped my arms around his neck.

Max leaned his head against mine. "What I really don't understand is that Greg found out about it, yet never told me."

I pressed my lips against his neck, his minty musk invading my nostrils and claiming my senses. "Of course he wouldn't. Greg is a liar."

I felt Max shake his head. "No, I don't think that's it. I think he was protecting us—Erik and I. I don't think he wanted us to find out and feel betrayed as he did. I actually think it was an act of love, not hate."

I sat up straight. "Then why did he try to kill you?" I protested.

Max shook his head. “I don’t know. I just know that when he set the library on fire he didn’t expect Erik and I would be there, but we were. At that point I think he figured there was nothing he could do. Perhaps he thought that by killing us we’d never have to find out.” I felt his grip on me tighten, a thread of grief pulling from inside as it reeled toward Max.

Max caught me as the feeling shook my bones. With his hand on my chin, he tilted my head up. Looking into his eyes, my lips lacked any sign of a smile.

“I think…” I wanted to tell him he was being naïve, but I could tell it wasn’t what he wanted to hear. He was going to validate this in any way that he could. The thread of grief slackened, and the weakness once again washed away.

Max brushed a strand of hair from my face. “But it makes sense. I’ve spent a lot of time wondering how a simple affair could drive my brother to such extremes. It didn’t seem to justify the crime. Knowing who Patrick really was to us changes things. Even I feel anger toward my mother… my father. They lied to us.”

I had to be the voice of reason. “I’m sure your mother and Patrick did it to protect you,” I assured, my blood pumping with a flight of fear for challenging him.

“I had *magick*, Jane. I wasn’t a simple human, but Greg was. Not only did he have to find out that his life was a lie, but he had to find out that he was different than me as well. It must have been crushing.”

My neck steeled—my eyes wide. “You inherited magick? You’re a natural?”

Max nodded. “Here, look for yourself.”

He handed me a letter and I read it, my eyes scanning

and rescanning the words. When the truth had finally set in, I brought myself to speak.

"Perhaps Patrick lied to you, hoping you and Greg would both dodge magick? If that was the case, then believing your father was Henry begins to make a lot of sense. You would have been spared from the magickal world all together. You would have been *safe*."

"But we *weren't*." I felt him push me away from him, irritated that I refused to allow him to settle on a negative notion. "I would have wanted to know the truth. I would have wanted to love Patrick like a father."

I looked around the room, my teeth clenched with determination. "But you *do*. You did." From what Max had told me, Patrick always loved him this way, even if to Max, he was just a teacher. "If he didn't love you, he wouldn't have taken in Erik after the deaths. And he left you all this." I swept my hand about the room. "When all was said and done, Patrick did what he could for you, given the circumstances. It just took you a while to put the pieces together."

Max nodded, but I wasn't sure if he was doing it to get me to stop justifying, or if he really understood and saw my side of it. I looked back to the desk where the image of Patrick lay. Max had the same jaw line, the same eyes. It was so obvious to me, and I didn't understand how Max hadn't seen it sooner.

"I will move here," Max added with determination. "I belong here."

I nodded, seeing his mind was made up.

"I always felt like this wasn't my place, but now I see that being human wasn't my place." He invited me back into the crook of his arm, squeezing me tight. "I really am home."

WES:

I mindlessly tapped my finger on the table, my head resting in my free hand. Jake and Emily were talking to each other as though I wasn't even here, though I sat right between them. I would have joined in with the conversation, but it was boring mind reader stuff. My mind began to wander on its own.

Where had Jane gone? Though I was over all that had happened in the past, I still wanted to make sure she was okay. We were slowly becoming friends again, and I was happy to see that. I flicked away a crumb that had been on the table when we sat down. The look on Jane's face had been unmistakably distressed just a moment ago, and all day, really. I'd felt anxious because of it, and I felt some reservations about letting her go find Max alone. My instincts had grown stronger as I allowed the thing I was to consume me, as it nearly had this afternoon.

Why was it that I'd had such a hard time changing back? I looked at my hand, wiggling my fingers and thinking how uncomfortable I felt in my own skin. Before I knew I was a shifter, I often felt out of place. Knowing what I was now made me want to stay animal all the time. *What if I did?* Would I forget about my human world as I had before? Would I really forget Emily so easily?

The faerie returned with our food, her hands full. As she set each plate down, it crowded the table.

"Anything else?" She looked less than enthusiastic to take another order, simply asking because she had to. Her eyes stopped when they reached mine. She looked at me inquisitively, as though I were the spectacle of the two of us.

"Looks great," Jake replied.

The faerie sighed and looked away, flipping her feathers as she turned and strolled back to the depths of the kitchen.

I looked sideways at Jake's food, surprised that it looked more appetizing than I'd expected. Sure, there was blood, and a lot of it, but it was dark crimson and coagulated like a spicy steak sauce, drizzled over a raw looking piece of meat. To me, it looked like an afternoon kill, something I had an increased hankering for lately.

Glancing back at my own food, I noticed Emily staring at the same thing I had from the corner of my eye. Her face was creased and pale, her reaction a far cry from what mine had been.

"Doing all right?" I asked, giving her a nudge, a smirk dancing upon my lips.

Emily nodded, but it didn't hide the nauseated glaze of her eyes.

The door to the café opened, letting in the sound of street traffic outside. I looked up, anxiously hoping it would be Jane. A crowd of people blocked my view, but even if I couldn't see her, I still sensed her. At last it was confirmed by Max's ashy smell which rode on the ensuing breeze. The crowd parted as they were led to their table, leaving Max and Jane standing alone in the entry. They had solemn expressions, Jane's eyes blank as she led Max to our booth. They slid in and Jane let out a sigh. Max crossed his hands before him, bowing his head without as much as a salutation.

I put my fork and knife down, my food remaining untouched. "What's going on?"

Jane was the only one that looked at me. I knew she had an answer, but she motioned toward Max as though to imply it wasn't her answer to give.

I bobbed my head slowly, now sensing an edge in Max's ashy scent. The smell of it was overwhelming, more so than the scent of the meat in front of me. It was bitter, and deeply hopeless. He was someplace that was very cold and alone. Seeing him this way was so different from the calm, confident Max I knew. In truth, it made me nervous. He had always been the rock, but now he was nothing but a broken man, and I didn't know why. It was just a feeling.

We finished our food, except Emily who hadn't ventured to touch hers. Jake paid the bill and we all ended up on the street in the dark. I couldn't help but yawn.

"Well, shall we go?" I pulled Emily against me, feeling discomfited by Max and Jane's somber moods.

She nodded slowly, her eyelids heavy.

"See you tomorrow at school, Jake?"

Jake snapped his fingers and pointed at me. "You betcha. Need a ride home?"

Emily was practically falling asleep against my chest. "No, I think I can manage. I tilted my neck, cracking my bones.

Jake extended his hand to Max. "Max. Jane. Good to meet you, for real. I'll see you tomorrow."

Max took his hand slowly. "Sure. You too."

My gaze skirted over Jane and Max, my eyes narrowed with

curiosity as I changed into the lion. I urged a lethargic Emily to climb onto my back. Jane smiled and gave me a brush on the head, her fingers raking through my mane.

"See you tomorrow, Wes. Take care of Emily for me."

I looked up at Jane, then turned and walked into the dark. I felt so useless when it came to helping her, but it wasn't my place anymore. The best I could do was be a friend and try to understand anything she might be going through, even if I didn't agree.

Emily's arms were wrapped tight around my neck, fingers twisted in my mane. Scuffing the ground with dirty paws, I looked skyward, just as the cry of an owl could be heard overhead.

EMILY:

I woke in the dark of my room. "Wes?"

No one answered me.

I threw the coverlet off of me, sweat coating my body. My stomach growled with hunger after skipping dinner, and as hard as I tried to remember how I got home, I couldn't.

Sitting up, I felt weak, drained—*craving.* Not only was I hot, but my room was humid, a strnge thing for Colorado. I slowly stood and walked to the window, pulling the blinds and cranking it open. I let the cool night air stream in and across my face. Sighing with tired eyes, I thought I was seeing things as a shadow moved outside, ducking behind the bend of the house. My brows pressed together, squinting in the direction but seeing nothing. A dreadful shiver broke across my skin, making me think of Greg. I leaned further out the window, trying to crane my neck around the corner, trying to convince myself that what I'd seen was nothing, perhaps just the cat.

"Emily?"

I jumped, my grip slipping from the window frame. A firm hand grabbed me just before I tumbled forward out the window, pulling me back in. I thrashed against the contact, nearly screaming before another hand clasped over my mouth. His skin was cold and sizzling, like ice thrown on a fire. He let go once I was safely rooted back inside the room. I spun to face the intruder.

"Emily, it's just me." Max loomed over me in the dark, hands in the air. His palms were blistered from touching me.

"What just happened?" I demanded.

Max's hands healed before my eyes. He dropped them. "The lingering snake venom in your blood. It does that."

"What are you doing here?" I hissed, shrugging away the chill of that feeling against my skin.

He knelt to my level to whisper. "I just heard you open the window. I wanted to make sure you were alright."

"I'm *fine*," I crossed my arms over my chest, remembering that I didn't have much more than a t-shirt on. "You're supposed to be watching Jane, not me."

Max grinned. "You're a part of Jane. So I watch you, too." He said it in a very obsessive fashion.

I snorted. "It's all you think of, seriously. Get a hobby. *Jane, Jane, Jane*," I mocked. His mind was all about it since the first day

I'd seen him.

Max shrugged and turned away from me, not giving into my attempts to fight. "Goodnight, Emily."

Just as quickly as he had appeared he was gone, a shadowy smoke dissipating in the air he once occupied.

The room had cooled now, so I shut the window, being sure to fasten the lock. I glanced once more outside by the corner of the house; there was nothing there. I gave up and climbed back in bed, twisting under the covers to get comfortable. Resting on my side, I noticed that the stuffed animals that once sat in the chair across the room had been rearranged onto the floor. They sat in a semicircle, perfectly placed, but not by me. I lifted my head from the pillow, my heart jumping. The chair they were once in was empty, but a part of me believed it hadn't been that way long. I swallowed, slowly crawling back out of bed and approaching the chair, warily keeping an eye on the stuffed animals at my feet. I pressed my hand against the fabric of the seat—it was cold, too cold…

Greg cold…

MAX:

After returning from Emily's room, I resumed standing in my place in the corner of Jane's. I watched her sleep as I always did, always *have.* Jane never knew I was here, had never felt me until now, though I'd felt her for longer than she could imagine. She was the one constant in my life. Everything else had turned out to be a lie. I wanted to be close to her in the way she desired—*I* desired—but I could feel the thread between us growing painfully tight, especially given what had happened on our visit to Winter Wood. I'd nearly killed her.

I hated myself for it, more than I hated myself for not seeing that Patrick was my father. Despite what I'd nearly done to her, though, I still wanted more. Right now the feeling to be with her was unlike anything I'd ever felt. I was addicted to her emotion. The danger of my duty to watch over her was growing fiercely challenging, and as I stood watching her, the reasons for distancing myself no longer made any sense. I just wanted to live.

What I learned today as I held her fragile life in my hands was that maybe I could control it. I had felt this life of hers like it was a ball in my grasp, something I wouldn't let go of, and couldn't. No one had ever attempted what I wanted to right now, so who knew what the real outcome would be outside of rumor? I swallowed this notion, drunk from the dim light of the room as it glowed across her face and filled me with this aching yearn. She needed me too.

It wouldn't hurt to be close to her. I really believed I could. What had happened in Winter Wood was so sudden. The emotion had washed over me without warning, but even then I had controlled it. Being near her like this right now was an emotion I could plan for. It would be easier. I *was* strong enough.

I pushed away from the corner and carefully paced across the room to the edge of her bed. I had longed to hold her as she slept, and I promised myself that would be all. It was simple enough. It was natural.

I stared at her for a moment, breathing steadily. Gently, I gathered the nerve to lie beside her, distancing myself with a few feet of mattress. My movement was light as to not disturb her sleep, afraid that if she woke, her fright would cause me to break her. I propped myself on my side, breathing in her scent and tracing small circles on her coverlet. Her chest rose and fell with each lungful of air, feeding our soul as it burned somewhere deep inside her. I was doing well with this, and I commended myself on the success of the task.

Growing braver with each uneventful moment that passed, I found myself nudging closer until my head rest against her arm. I wondered where she was, and what she was doing as her soul wandered into the land of dreaming, leaving her body behind with me. I nudged her softly, moving my body against hers and allowing my arm to drape over her.

She shifted slightly, only to reposition herself more comfortably within my embrace. I couldn't help but smile, knowing I had accomplished the one thing I'd always longed to. I brushed my finger down the length of her arm, the warmth of her skin relaxing. For the first time in a long while, I was comfortable.

I closed my eyes then, and without meaning to, I entered her dreams…

JANE:

With a strange shiver surrounding me, I saw Max walk from the edge of the field where I sat enjoying the colorful skies of my dream. The grin on my face grew as I slid a piece of grass through my fingers. There was no blood here tonight, no death at all. I'd been working on getting past the lust for it, wanting to live a real life away from my inevitable end where I could work toward making a reason of my future. This development was refreshing.

Max came and sat beside me, his body separate from mine and his emotions his own—the way it would be if he were still human. He took my hand, his fingers tracing over the ridges of my knuckles.

"I love Winter Wood." I spoke, my voice distant and soft, like a gentle breeze. Going there showed me that there really is more to life. I was going to make myself important, and Winter Wood was my place to start.

He nodded slowly. "I want you to live with me there." His gaze met mine, oceans crashing to shore. "When I said I wanted to move back, all I could think of was that I wanted you to go with me."

The sweetness of the invitation filled me with warmth. I

ran my hand through his hair, the strands long enough to wrap around my fingers a few times. He shut his eyes, the powdery blue that surrounded them much more prevalent in the light of the In-between.

"I want you to be with me forever," he added.

My hand fell to my side. "But I won't be with you forever. I can't."

He thought for a moment before speaking. "I'll find a way to follow you wherever you go. The Ever After is just another place. It's not like I can't go there, too."

I picked another piece of grass, wrapping it around my hand. "What about letting me stay in this life with you?"

Max took the blade of grass from my hand, tying a bow. "There's nothing I can do to make you stay. You are what you are. What you want only exists in faerie tales."

I lowered my gaze, watching him knot the grass. He was right. I was what I was, and with my cravings to see the other side, despite my current ability to control them, eternal life would eventually become taxing.

Max handed me the perfect grass bow and leaned against me, his hand cradling the small of my back.

"You're so good at this." I twisted the bow between my fingers, trying to figure just how he'd tied it.

He took my hand and guided me to lie down before lying beside me, his head resting on his palm and his arm hitched up at the elbow. He picked another piece of grass, brushing it down the length of my nose. "I've had a long time to learn a lot of hobbies in order to pass time." He traced the strand of grass down along the curve of my torso from my shoulder to my hip and back again.

"I love you, Jane. I want to keep you, and I will," he promised.

I cupped the grass bow in my hands, holding it against my chest.

Max smiled and leaned forward, kissing my shoulder. His lips were warm and alive in this world, a feeling so divine. I giggled as he moved and kissed my neck, then my chin.

"It's so odd," I thought out loud.

Max stopped. "What's that?"

"Feeling you like this, as though you're alive."

He fingered a strand of my hair. "Do you like it?"

I hooked my elbows under me, sitting up slightly. "I do." I paused. "Is that bad?"

He bit his lip and looked contemplative for a moment. I wasn't sure if I had hurt his feelings by saying what I had, but I was feeling truthful. Watching anxiously, his distant gaze spooled back. He looked at me and leaned close. At first he seemed reluctant, as though he'd never been this close to me before. He allowed his lips to barely rest against mine, unmoving as though testing something. Then he kissed me.

His sweet musk became a cage, the kiss like sugary honey dripping down the throat of my spirit. I lowered myself once again and reached out for him, pulling him toward me. His lips didn't leave mine as we lay back, my hands finding their way carefully down his torso and under his shirt. His muscles tensed at my touch, but slowly relaxed as I gently caressed them.

I couldn't help it. I wanted to feel his skin against mine. I wanted to melt together and feel limitless love. This was a dream, and in dreams things could be whatever they wanted, even this.

I tried again, and this time his shyness was contained.

Grasping the hem of his shirt, I began to roll it over his shoulders. He let me, only breaking the kiss long enough for the shirt to clear his head. My hands savored skin I'd never felt or seen before, and Max allowed his weight to lean against me. His lips attended my neck as I felt the length of a long scar down his side. My heart raced, wondering how he'd acquired such a gash, only now realizing the depth and danger of his life. He wedged his arm between me and the scar, again acting shy. I saw what my boundaries were, and coaxing him to allow me in once more, I respected them.

Being like this allowed me to feel his warmth like never before, the real man that was once the Max Gordon of the human world. I let myself imagine things this way, relishing his natural and protective strength holding me close. Here, we could be together forever, and I allowed my thoughts to reflect that back to him.

He groaned and stopped kissing me for a moment. "I can't do this."

His breath against my skin made me shake. I nipped his shoulder, feeling how tense his body had suddenly become. "It's okay, Max. For once, just relax a little." I rubbed my hand down his spine, imagining it ironing away his apprehensions.

He let himself feel it, permitting his hands to trace the length of my body in return. His breathing became ragged, and something inside him changed in that moment. His lips once again locked with mine. It was a furious dance, and the world around us slowly faded to shadows. The grass below my back changed shape, growing into soft, billowy threads of cotton. The warm touch of his skin became cool, like a wave of the ocean, drowning me in the ecstasy of being this close.

Before I knew what had happened, the darkness of my room had already surrounded us once again. The rush of adrenaline had caused us both to wake, though the dream itself hadn't ended. I was surprised that he'd permitted himself to be this close to me, so used to his distant persona and his vow to wait. Right now, however, the vow no longer seemed to matter to him.

His hands were under my shirt, thumbs resting just beneath the curve of my breast and fingers arched around my rib cage. He held onto me with desperation, not wanting our waking to stop us, or perhaps not realizing we'd awoken. I frantically felt for his belt, wondering how far he would allow me to take this. As anticipated, his lips left mine, his face pained, while full of desire. I slid my hands up his sides and placed them on his cheeks.

"It's okay," I whispered again, moving my hands back to remove his jeans.

His arms were on either side of my head as he lay above me, his nose brushing mine. He was shaking with such innocence that I felt I was finally seeing him for who he really was. With eyes deep like storm clouds, the glimmer of sanity that was always there was now lost at sea. Max was fighting with himself, torn between two places I couldn't understand. I hooked my hands around his waist, locking him against me. I wouldn't let him be lost there. I needed him.

I pressed myself up, arching against his hips. He bit my lip, wings beginning to flourish from his back and wrapping around us, as though his hands weren't enough. The breath was stolen from my lungs when they touched me, feeling as light as air. I reached forward, running my hand down one wing. It released a groan from deep inside him—feathers quivering.

"Jane, I can't..." He whispered again, but his voice was

unconvincing.

Hands on his back, I felt where wings met skin, and another gasp of air was stolen from my lungs. The space around me became endless, a void where I could live forever. I felt my body melting into him, his skin growing more alive with each minute that passed like this. Legs intertwined—skin against skin.

I pressed my hips once more against his, causing his whole frame to shake.

He moaned, his skin oddly hot and mine dangerously cold. Then, without warning, his hands hit the pillow behind me, making me flinch. He abruptly pushed himself away, a wave of heat rolling over me like a rush of blood to the head. I sat up straight, wavering as he stumbled out of bed and paced to the window where he grabbed his jeans off the floor. His wings were still exposed, and his whole body quaked, wracked with tremors as he fought to control himself.

"What's wrong?" There was an edge of anger in my voice. I was tired of him running away.

He'd put his jeans on by now, his hand on his forehead. Whispering under his breath, he began to pace. "I can't do this." His hand dropped, hitting his leg.

I admired his bare torso as his wings retreated, so powerful and yet so forbidden to me. Max refused me the luxury of having him. "Why?" I demanded.

He stopped and turned to me quickly. "You didn't feel that?" he gasped.

I had felt it, but it was bliss. What did he mean? "No, I—"

"You don't understand, Jane." He cut me off, voice sharp. "I literally can't do this." His face was frantic, his firm hand jabbing the air. "But, *God*… you don't know how much I want to."

"Then… then why stop yourself? I don't understand."

A forced breath of air passed his lips. He looked skyward, still pacing. "You're a drug to me—your emotions, your life. I want it so bad." He clenched his fists before him. "So bad, but I'll lose myself in you. I can't let it happen."

"Lose yourself?"

He shook his head as though at himself. "You've felt me stealing your emotion."

I nodded. "Yes, but it's not bad. I can handle it. I figured that was normal." I thought about the way I felt when he'd stolen my sadness in Winter Wood—weak and useless. But tonight, it had felt much different.

"Jane, listen to yourself. You shouldn't be saying those things. Those emotions are your own, not mine. If I go too far with them, it can kill you, which means…" His voice trailed.

"*What?*" My voice was shrill.

"Which means that I'd kill you. If I get too close like this, I could suck that life right out of you. You'd die, and I'd be the one left living your life and your feelings." He leaned his forehead against the wall.

"Why didn't you tell me this before?"

His eyes were shut, the frantic emotion he'd borrowed leaving me feeling hungry, but not for food.

"I didn't want you to worry about it, but when I found out about Patrick, I saw that hiding it wasn't right, either."

I nodded sarcastically. "Yeah, exactly."

Max draped his hands over his eyes.

I pulled the blankets more tightly around me. "So, the whole *'I want to wait because I've never done this before'*, thing was a lie?"

He stood straight, his eyes wide. “No. That’s the truth. My chastity is not a lie, but...”

My heart sank at the word but. “*But...* what?”

He shook his head. “But... I’ve never loved someone like this before, and of course it had to be you—my guarded, the one I’m forbidden to be with.”

His explanation seemed diverted from something else. “What else? That’s not all that you were going to say,” I accused.

I saw his shoulders sink, and I presumed it was because he’d been caught. He paced toward me, eyes so intense, I was actually afraid of them. “I was engaged once.” His answer seemed blunt.

“What?” My voice was louder than it needed to be. “And you didn’t find that important enough to tell me?”

Max cringed.

“What else is there?”

He bowed his head. “It was a long time ago. I called it off before the whole thing even matured. It’s not like it was my decision; it was arranged. I didn’t love her.”

“Not your decision?” The whole reality of his age came crashing down on me.

“There were other things driving me to do it, like honor, and diplomacy, certainly not love.”

I stood, dragging sheets with me, flustered by the whole thing. “And we’re not even supposed to be *together?*” All the talk about soul-mates and the way I had agreed with him suddenly made me feel foolish.

“That’s not true. We are supposed to be together, but the guardian aspect of it got in the way. The Truth told me—”

“The *Truth* is worthless,” I spat. “How do I even know you’re telling me the *truth* now?”

He was frozen, and I could tell he was trying to figure what to say to make this better.

"We're not supposed to be together, Max. That's what the universe is saying, Truth or no Truth. I mean look at us," as I drew close, he backed away. "We can't even get close." I stopped, having backed him into the wall. "You're my angel and I'm your guarded, and that's all we were ever meant to be to each other." The words didn't feel right, but I said them anyway, wanting to test them out loud.

"Jane, please." He shut his eyes. "I knew there were dangers when I saved you. I knew this was one of them, but I still believed we could love each other despite that. It's not all about—"

"Please," I snapped, raising a finger between us. "Don't start with that. Of course it matters. I won't pretend to be shy about it. You may think I sound shallow, but I assure you, I'm not. I refuse to live out my life wanting nothing but to share everything with you, every emotion, feeling and desire. I can't have that, and I can't live with the anxiety of knowing we have to be careful about being close to each other. I just want to *be.*"

I could tell he saw my point, and I could tell he knew it would come to this, though he'd clearly tried to deny it as long as possible.

I shut my eyes. "Fix this," I demanded, because I didn't know how to fix it for myself. If this was the way it was going to be, then I didn't want him near me. There were amazing things I wanted to discover and do with my life, and having this obstacle made accomplishing those things hard. This would always be a distraction, and I couldn't handle it. Just standing here before him, my eyes fixed on his bare chest and the curves of his torso I so longed to trace, was difficult enough.

I was selfish, maybe even shallow, but it was justified. I was *human!* I wanted to be near him, and not just for a simple pleasure, but because I loved him. The kind of love you know will sweep you off your feet, the kind of love you don't consider the same as any other because it feels natural—impulsive. But that was the problem. Our love could never be impulsive. If what he said was true, then I knew it wouldn't be long before I'd forget myself and get carried away in the moment. I'll end up dead, as I nearly had already. I couldn't trust myself, and that was the real problem. Impulsive was the perfect word to describe how I felt around Max. Was that such a bad thing?

When I opened my eyes, Max was gone. The room was darker than it had been before and the only thing my eyes could see was a small white origami dove lying on the corner of the bed. I walked toward it, picking it up and finding the small grass bow atop its back.

A tear rolled down my cheek as I opened the wings and gently unfolded the paper. There was nothing but a small, crooked heart drawn in the middle. Despite my behavior he still loved me. My head throbbed. I was a jerk.

"Max?" I choked, waiting a long while for a reply that would never come.

EMILY:

I sat in history class next to Jake. He had his glasses and retainer on, downgrading his looks a couple hundred notches, but it was safe. When he wore the glasses, the blue light wasn't there, and when we were in the light, it wasn't there either. As long as we hung out when one of those two situations applied, I'd be fine.

"Jake," I whispered.

The teacher was circling the room, eyeing us like a hawk as we read about the Conquistadores in supposed silence.

"I'm bored." I was too tired to deal with school. After what had happened last night, I hadn't slept much.

Jake looked sideways at me, his brown eyes hidden and dull behind the thick lenses. *Don't talk out loud, idiot. Use your mind. Besides, I'm reading. Maybe you should try it.*

I moaned, looking at the words on the page and reading the same line I'd read what seemed ten times now. *"How do you put up with this?"* I whispered again out loud, just to be impossible.

Jake glared. "I like *learning.*" His voice snaked through clenched teeth.

I smiled to myself for forcing him to play along.

Mr. Jackson clapped his hands together then. "All right class, time to break into our groups and continue working on our projects."

It was music to my ears.

Jake slowly shut his book as the class broke into a low murmur. He sighed. "Want to go to the library?"

"The *real* library?" I urged with a wink.

Jake's glance was so much smoother than his exterior would imply, a smile growing across his face. "Sure, Emily. The *real* library." He winked back.

A rush of excitement washed over me. I'd put a lot of thought into what I was doing at school, and a lot of thought into what Jake's sister was doing. I wanted to be like her. I wanted to do what I loved, though that wasn't necessarily baking. All I knew was that sitting here following premeditated steps wasn't what I loved. My clairvoyance had already taught me all I'd need to know, so school was just a giant mind-numbing experience. It was worthless, and if I could make him, Jake was going down with me.

Jake had risen from his chair, chatting with the teacher. I gathered my things and threw my bag over my shoulder.

"So, Mr. Jackson, we're going to the library," Jake finished explaining as I arrived at his side.

Mr. Jackson smiled at us in a way that made me uncomfortable—as though Jake and I were a couple and he'd found it endearing. "Sure. I'm very anxious to see what my two best students come up with." He gave us both an awkward pat on the shoulder.

Buttering him up to let us leave class and his supervision was easy, but the dreamy look in his eye was no less irritating. I conveyed that toward Jake, he shrugged.

At least it's a way to get on his good side. If he thinks we're dating, doing what we want will be easy, he explained.

I gave him laughter in return. *Just as long as it's not true.* I challenged. *I know your reputation.*

I'd never hit on a taken girl.

I pressed my lips together. *Yeah, right.*

Jake lifted one brow. *Is that an invitation?*

I put one hand on my hip. *Certainly not!*

Mr. Jackson was grinning wider now, and I realized that to him, it looked as though Jake and I were gazing into each others eyes when we were really having a mental fight. I snorted and pushed Jake toward the door.

"Bye, Mr. Jackson!" I waved over my shoulder. The class watched us leave with jealousy written across their faces. As the door shut behind us, there was a rise of murmurs, kids wanting to be granted the chance to go to the library as well, but as expected, no one else followed.

Walking down the central hall, Jake's slinky veiled light remained hidden, despite the shadowy lighting. A part of me was bummed, knowing now that his glasses were the one thing that hid it most. I'd thought about the light all night, finding that after my cold, late-night visitor, I couldn't really fall back asleep. This was when I'd formulated my notions as to what made the light appear, such as lighting, and physical obstructions like the anti-reflective glasses. As I had lain there, unnerved and tired, I remember thinking that a small part of me craved its reappearance, just for its safety. How, though, could a blue light save me?

Jake nudged my arm. "So, where to?"

I shrugged. "Last period, so we could leave grounds all together if you want."

Jake shrugged. "A part of me really likes it here. I know it sounds crazy, but it's a break from the norm."

I compulsively wrinkled my nose. "*Why?*" It came out disgruntled.

He chuckled. "I get to be someone else. I was never given the option of the life I live now, and..." His voice trailed off.

I considered where he was going with his words—he was getting personal.

"I mean, you know. I like to feel like I'm still who I was before, though I don't even know who that was."

"You're probably no different, just sweaty." I giggled.

He snorted. "I prefer *glistening*," he corrected. "And I am different. I'm *very* different."

"How?" I challenged. "I think that's in your head."

He stopped, spreading his arms. "This is not me. If I could be myself, I sure wouldn't look like a geek. I'm handsome, but no one here knows that because of all the things I have to hide."

I chuckled. "So you think you're handsome? Cocky much?"

He dropped his hands, conveying an impartial look that didn't disagree. "The worst part about being me, though, is all the rules."

Just the mention of the word made me edgy. I hated rules, too.

"I can't do anything without asking a group of elders first, and they're so uptight it's ridiculous. I'll always have someone to answer to, like a parent. Look at it that way." He slanted his head toward me and looked at me over his glasses. The silver reflection in his eyes caught the overhead lights—no blue veil. My light idea was true, too.

I pouted. "Just break a few rules then," I said absently, distracted by the mental notes I was making about the light.

Jake released one sarcastic laugh. "I can't just *break* a few, Emily. Though there are a few I'd love to. They'll kill me, and I mean it. There's no three-strikes-your-out in my world."

I began to feel bothered, imagining myself as him. "I don't envy you at all."

He weaved into me, leaning against my shoulder. "Gee, *thanks.* That really helps."

We'd arrived at the end of the hall, the parking lot outside. We stared at the freedom beyond, but I suppose to Jake it wasn't freedom at all.

Jake pressed his lips together in thought. "Here, follow me." He grabbed my arm, his hand burning hot against my bare skin.

He whipped me around and away from my freedom. Walking with determination, I couldn't help but be dragged behind him. We made our way toward the library, a place I'd thought we were going to avoid. I never liked the library, and not just because of the fact that Jane loved it. The problem was that books spoke to me here, and as you can imagine, it was distracting. We walked in, the whispers lighting up my undiluted mind. If there was anytime I would falter and want a hit of Valium, it was now—*here.*

"Jake," I cautioned. "I hate it here."

He refused to allow me to wriggle free. "That's because you can't enjoy it for what it is. For years I've wanted to show you that this isn't a place to get all worked up about."

"What do you know about what I think?" I retorted. It was a stupid question.

He glared. *Everything.*

"Why did you watch me so closely?"

Jake stopped, releasing my arm. "Because it was entertaining to watch you flounder, and truthfully, there just aren't very many mind readers left. Black Angels have taken them all and abused them for their powers. If it weren't for Max, you'd be a goner, too."

I angrily crossed my arms, refusing to look at him. "Whatever. That's sadistic."

He pinched my arm and I reeled out of my defensive pose. "Ouch! What was that for?" I was forced to look at him, and I froze. He'd removed his glasses and there it was. The veiled light had returned, the shadows of the overhead stacks inviting it out to play. My arms dropped limply to my sides, my body overcome with elation. I was being sucked into the feeling, hopelessly falling away from any anger I once felt.

Jake went about mindlessly thumbing through books. I was confused. He didn't seem to notice this light at all, and though I thought that was what he was trying to show me, I quickly learned it wasn't. Perhaps he didn't know about it?

He pulled a book out and held it before me, perfectly framed within the light as it wrapped it's blue, smoky tendrils around the cover. "See, listen to it."

Stuck hopelessly in a state of blissful calmness, poetry entered my ears. I reached out for the light, grasping the book instead as the blue wisps twisted about my fingers. Jake searched for another book, turning away from me. The hold the light had over my thoughts broke, and the poetic voices grew louder. It took all my strength not to grab him and twist his gaze back toward me. I shook my head, clenching my fists over the cover. *Stop that,* I told myself.

"Can you hear it?" his hands were above him, thumbing for

a book on the top shelf.

With so many books, the poet's words were a blur, but the melody of the syllables was beautiful and relaxing.

He brought down another book, replacing the one in my hands, along with the return of the light. "So, when you're forced to come here for class, just come to this section. It's a lot easier to digest. It's like music."

I told myself this wasn't right, using all my strength to turn away from him, still holding the book. Keeping my eyes fixed on the ground in order to avoid another glance at the light, I tried to hone in on just one voice. I hoped that by doing so, I could get my sanity back.

"Whose voices are they?" I asked.

I heard him pull another book from the shelf. "You're saying you don't know?"

I let my backpack fall from my shoulders, suddenly feeling as though it were holding me back, keeping me from some sort of freedom. "No… I don't know. I hate it here, remember?" I couldn't stop myself from glancing up. The light caught me. *What was I thinking?* I squeezed the book hard, as though it were the only thing keeping me from being sucked in.

"It's the author's voice." He pressed the book in his hand toward me, again taking the one I had been holding. I forced my eyes shut, only to open them to the cover of the new book. I flipped it around in my grasp, nervously reading the title over and over—Edgar A. Poe.

Edgar's voice dominated my thoughts, surprisingly soft and withheld. I used the sound of it to draw me away from the light, swallowing hard. "That's unreal."

Jake unhooked his glasses from his shirt and pushed them

back over his eyes. The tug toward him ceased instantaneously. I gasped.

"What?" He gave me a strange look.

For a moment I wondered if I'd allowed my guard to fall enough to permit him to hear my thoughts. I grew further nervous.

"Did you hear something interesting?" he added, narrowing his eyes.

I pulled the book to my chest, hugging it like I would my savior. I hadn't let him know, right? "Oh, *uh*... it's just amazing, is all." The sucking sensation was gone as though it had never been there. My independence had been returned.

Jake watched me for a moment. "You sure you're all right?"

"Yeah," I insisted, trying to get myself to believe it as well.

The bell rang then.

I used it as an excuse to find better overhead lighting. "Let's go." I grabbed him by the arm and dragged him out of the library, avoiding any shadows that provoked this emotion out of Jake, this emotion I don't think he even knew about.

In the hall, Jake pulled back to stop me, using a good amount of strength to do so. "Whoa, hold on." He was breathing hard as he removed his glasses once more, rubbing the sweat from his brow. No blue light came of it, just Edgar's voice as I continued to grasp desperately to the book. "What's your issue?"

With a fluttering stomach, I gazed deep into his eyes. *Where did it go?* Kids crashed out of the doors around us, leaving us in a swarm of bodies. He quickly replaced his glasses.

Everyone was in a rush to get as far away from this place as possible. I took a deep breath, Jake and I the only resistance amongst the flow. "Can we please just leave now?"

"Yeah. Okay. Come on," he gently grasped my elbow. "Let's just get out of here."

We walked to the lot in silence. I left Jake at his car with a simple goodbye, thanking him for the book, which I'd pretty much stolen. Walking on a little further, I met Wes as he stood by his car, looking toward the field across the lot. He wrapped his arm around me, not bothering to break his gaze from the field.

"Hey, girl, how was your day?" Wes leaned just enough toward me to give me a kiss on the head.

I rolled into his one-armed embrace, speaking into his shirt. "It was—*interesting.*" Edgar A. Poe whispered tragic words between us. I pulled away from Wes, seeing his gaze was still on the field. I looked in the direction he was, seeing the owl sitting on the fence about fifty yards away. "Is she always going to be around now?"

Wes looked down at me. "You jealous?"

I snorted. "No." I denied, though it did make me jealous in some strange way. "What does she want, anyway?"

Wes brushed his hand across my cheek. "Me, I guess."

I laughed. "Well, she's not going to get you." I stood on my toes until my lips met with his. I heard the owl cry, adding to my vindictive drive. I parted my lips, grasping Wes's sleeves and pulling him closer.

"Emily." He spoke against my lips, laughing. "Not here."

I grinned. "Then let's go." I insisted, popping open the car door behind Wes and playfully nudging him down into the driver seat. I tossed the book and my bag in the backseat before climbing in behind him, straddling his lap. The book had popped open, Edgar's voice filling my head, but it was romantic.

"Really?" Wes's cheeks were flushed. "Here?"

I shrugged, grinning back. "You have tinted windows," I added.

The truth was that I was nervous about what had happened with the veiled light, and it had me feeling guilty. I needed to overcompensate for my faltering feelings toward this new emotion for Jake by replacing it with a tangible one that I could control. Wes's lust was controllable, and Edgar's poems were a good distraction for my thoughts.

Wes leaned forward, hooking his hand behind my head, his lips parted as he kissed me again. I played with the collar of his shirt, his hand trailing down my neck and over my shoulders. The gentle touch continued down my arms to my waist. Wes squeezed me closer, breathing the way he did when his animal instincts began to surface. Wes bravely reached his hand under my shirt, his fingers delicately following the dip of my spine and under the strap of my bra. His hand came to a rest between my shoulder blades—our bodies rising.

I gasped in delight, and the heat in the car rose a couple degrees. The world around us fell away. I reached my hand under his shirt, unhooking the buckle of his belt. Our lips were unable to release from each other's, locked tight. The words in my head made me forget everything but this; nothing but this mattered. I lifted his shirt over his head, his skin slick with sweat against my palms. I sighed softly.

Wes's muscles were visibly tense, but his touch was so soft. He trembled ever so gently, my arms wrapped tightly around his neck. He smiled against my lips. I smiled back, but I could not hear what he was thinking. The poem in my head had overcome me as I clung to the words that had suddenly made me feel so desperate and afraid. I wanted to cry, suddenly dropping my head and pressing my forehead to his neck. I was overcome with emotion, overcome with the feeling and rush of us together.

"What?" he asked.

I just shook my head.

He ran his hands slowly down my sides to my waist. "Are you afraid?"

I laughed, thinking of the poem. It had been about a girl named Annabel Lee and a love that was forbidden. It had reminded me of how short life is, and how different our life together was always going to be. "No."

Wes nudged my forehead with his chin and my head rose. His eyes were so full of emotion, glazed with pure love. He bit his lip, half smiling. "Lost?"

I laughed nervously, nodding lightly.

He traced my lips with his finger, his other hand spread on my back where he tugged at my shirt, gently pulling it over my head. "I think I've got it from here," he confidently added. His hand traced down the center of my chest to my belly button; I giggled. His hands moved to my hips and I leaned close to him—

"Bang!"

I flew back away from Wes, my head hitting the low, tinted windshield and knocking Edgar's voice out of my thoughts. "Ouch!"

The initial sound was followed with a series of high-pitched scratching noises, like nails on a chalkboard.

"What the—" Wes had slammed against the back of his seat, looking horrified.

I looked over my shoulder. The owl was on the hood behind me, her wings outstretched and her eyes narrow. I screamed, and she chortled loudly, throwing herself at the glass.

I breathed hard as I rolled away from Wes and into my own seat. "*Wes!*" I yelled. It was frightening, watching her like this. She was hurting herself.

Wes rolled down the window, putting his hand out. "Stella, it's okay." He clicked his tongue, talking with a soothing voice.

The owl calmed a little, but her feathers were still fluffed. Her eyes flicked from me to Wes and back again. Wes wiggled his fingers, clicking again. She nipped at him. He pulled back with a frown, blood oozing from a small cut. He cursed and licked his finger.

Disgust pinched my stomach. "*Wes!* Don't do that! She probably has *worms*."

Wes laughed. "I'm part animal, Em. It doesn't matter."

I grunted. "*Gross,* Wes…" I wasn't even about to say what I was thinking.

Wes slowly put his arm back out the window. This time Stella nuzzled against it. He twisted his fingers through the downy feathers on her neck. "Even if you're not jealous, Stella sure is."

I looked from Wes to Stella. "I'm not competing with that thing." I grabbed for my shirt which had ended up in the back seat. While I was back there, I slammed the poetry book shut, grumbling.

Wes brushed his hand over Stella's head again and again, her eyes slanting closed. "We'll just have to be a little more *private* next time."

I rolled my eyes, discouraged by the whole day. Wes rolled the window back up and started the car. "It'll be okay, Emily. It was you that wanted to take it slow, remember? We haven't even officially had our *second* date. You don't want to be labeled a floozy."

An icy glare grew across my face. "I'm not a *floozy,*" I murmured. "And so what if I am? With you, it's different."

His brows elevated. "So, you really wouldn't have stopped me this time, even at the very last moment?"

I shrugged. "Maybe. Maybe not. I guess you'll never find out." The moment couldn't have been more perfect. Stupid bird.

Wes slapped his hand against his leg. "I knew my chances were good." He made a hand gesture at the owl.

Stella ran her nails over his hood one more time. We both winced.

Wes hit the dash with his hand, startling Stella. "*Stop* that."

She turned away from him impudently.

"Are you sure she's not human?"

Wes laughed. "I'm sure." He watched Stella sulk for a moment, and when she wasn't looking, he took my hand. "So much for starting over, I guess," he teased, lacing his fingers with mine.

I squeezed his hand. "We're still starting over, just… in our own way, I guess."

JANE:

I still hadn't seen or heard from Max all day, and I was beginning to worry that what I said had finally pushed Max away from me. I walked out to the lot, hoping I could catch a ride with Wes and Emily. I saw Wes's car and began to make my way across the lot. Reaching it, I caught a glimpse of something I never wanted to.

I turned away, my mouth agape. "O.M.G.," I murmured.

Quickly walking away from the car and back toward the curb, I tried to think of a way to wash my mind of what I'd seen, and find another ride. The bus had already left, and most of the students didn't like me—they only liked *Max*. Though I'm sure they'd still agree to give me a ride out of pure association, I'd feel awkward asking. A part of me knew they wondered why Max was with me and not someone that was better suited in the looks department, like Liz.

The small crane was tucked into the front pocket of my jeans, my hand grazing against it as I pulled out my cell. My shoulders sank, watching as the crane fell to the ground. I knelt and picked it up, giving it a kiss before turning my attention back to the phone. I would call my mother in a last ditch effort, though she was still working and wouldn't be able to get here for another thirty minutes. Maybe by then Wes and Emily would be finished doing… *whatever.*

I began to punch the keys.

"Well, hey!"

There was a voice from across the lot, but I didn't figure it was meant for me. There were still a few students lingering at their cars. I kept punching keys, my head bowed.

"Hey, Jane, isn't it?"

The voice was closer now. I sighed and stopped, not in the mood to be bothered but not seeing any way out of it. I slowly glanced up. At first I was confused, then surprised. The girl from the Corner Café in Winter Wood was briskly approaching, a stack of official looking papers in her slender hand. Her curls bounced behind her, her mouth fixed into a warm smile.

What was she doing here?

"Hey," she said again, reaching me. Her voice was perfect, not a hint of breathiness after her trek to reach me.

"Hi," I tilted my head, conveying surprise. "What are you doing here?" My phone was left ringing in my hand. I hung up.

Navia shrugged, making it look graceful. "I wanted to see what it was like." My eyes grazed over her, noticing her more civilian looking attire, though it did little to detract from her ethereal beauty. It looked as though she'd had her makeup professionally applied, but as I stared, I began to see it was just her natural beauty, no makeup needed—*of course.*

"*It?* You mean school?"

She nodded with wide eyes. "It's fascinating." She lifted the stack of papers to eye level. "I just applied." She was pointing to her signature at the bottom of the page. It was large and flagrant, embellished with a number of swirls and symbols. I wondered what Debbie in administration thought of it.

I laughed as she dropped the papers back to her side. "There's nothing fascinating about school," I warned. I began to wonder what it was Navia and Jake saw in this, and what they put down under 'race' on the school records. I guess when it wasn't something they *had* to do, it became something they *wanted* to do.

"Will you be my friend?" Navia hooked her arm with mine, guiding me to sit on the nearby ledge.

Her cinnamon scent wafted over me, making me think of sticky buns. "I... *uh...*" I should be happy about this, but the overwhelming feelings of sadness that were facing me after last nights fight with Max subdued my excitement. I tried to smile as best I could. "Sure."

Navia frowned. "Are you okay?"

I cursed myself for letting my emotions show. She probably thought I was weak. "Yeah. I'm fine," I urged.

Navia tilted her head, looking at me the way my mother did when she knew I was lying. "Come on, you can tell me. We're friends now, right?" She gave me a gentle nudge, crossing her ankles elegantly.

A real smile graced my lips. It felt good to have someone bug me the way she was. Typically people left it alone when sometimes I needed someone to talk to. This simple act from her made me feel important. I shrugged, tilting my head to my shoulder. "It's just a guy."

She dramatically swayed beside me, taking me along for the ride. After her long swoon she giggled. "A *boy*, huh? Well, I'm an expert in that department."

I couldn't help but laugh out loud.

She looked content to see me react this way. "I'm a pixie, remember?" she whispered. "We *love* our boys."

I kept laughing, finding her charm endearing. I could see how she could easily destroy the hearts of every boy in this school. "That's what I've heard—about pixie's, that is."

She nodded gravely. "Afraid there's nothing we can do about it. Our reputations precede us." She threw her hands in the air. "Need a ride?" She looked toward Wes's car with a brow raised and her mouth slanted. "So uncivilized. Like animals."

I laughed. "You could say that again. I do need a ride, but I don't want to impose."

Navia yanked me to my feet and pulled me across the lot so

fast that the words were still lingering on my lips.

"Well, good thing I'm here." She ushered me up to a cream colored Tahoe—*pearly* cream, of course.

She got the door for me, releasing her arm from mine. I hopped up into the passenger seat and buckled in. The interior was also cream, and smelled like a bakery in the morning. Tiny flecks of glitter floated through the air. By simply entering the car, I had literally entered another world. Staring out at the world I had just occupied, it paled in comparison.

The lingering students stared, finding us the most entertaining thing they'd likely seen all day. Clearly, they were unaware of what was going on inside Wes's car. Navia sauntered around the hood, teasing them. I felt my cheeks flush from the attention, but Navia seemed to enjoy it—or rather expect it. Boys were drooling, even boys whose girlfriends were grappling their arms—*shameless!*

"You're going to have to indulge me with every detail of this little boy problem you're having." She got in on her side and leaned toward me, acting as though we'd been life-long best friends.

"*Umm…*" I wasn't one to discuss my personal life, especially with someone I'd just met.

Navia didn't bother to pay any mind to our onlookers. She was too cool for them, but not me.

"Come on. It's a long drive to Winter Wood," she added. I knew she wasn't going to let me be demure.

I smiled and took a deep breath. "Well, then I guess it goes like this…"

WES:

A tapping noise woke me from my sleep. My eyelids were heavy as I forced them open. I turned over, my body lethargic and my mind wondering if I'd really heard the noise or not. Dim grey morning moonlight streamed through the blinds, shining stripes across my bedspread. Monday had already arrived. Emily had not stayed the night, too frazzled by what had happened on Friday to stay any night this weekend. I blamed it on the fact that she was afraid to put herself in range of another Friday car adventure. I heard the tapping for a second time, the shadowed stripes beginning to move.

I sat up, stretching my feet and sliding out of bed. I walked to the window, the tapping so soft, that it didn't post any alarm. I pulled the blinds, seeing Stella perched on the tiny ledge outside.

I cracked the lock and opened the window an inch so she could hear me. "Really, Stella, when are you going to get over this?"

She tilted her head as though she understood, though I was certain she didn't.

"Do you know what you made me miss on Friday? Do you have any idea how long I've been waiting for her to be ready for that?" I placed my palm against the window. Stella leaned alongside it, her feathers smashed against the glass and fanning out in an array of brown and white colors. “Clearly you don’t.” I smiled and clicked my tongue, thinking that if she were a cat, she’d be purring.

At least she cared enough to be here with me right now. At least she wasn’t playing hard to get. I heard a snap then. Stella jumped and leaned away. She twisted her head skyward, her eyes wide and her pupils opening to the moonlight.

I pressed my brows together, trying to look where she was but inhibited by the glass. Stella chortled, bustling her feet on the sill. The moonlight shifted, casting a shadow on Emily’s house across the alley, a swift shadow that flew across the siding and landed on the roof. From there, the shadow fluttered and moved again, growing as it descended downward. The look in Stella’s eyes became ever more anxious, but it wasn’t a fearful anxiety.

I stepped back as the shadow breached the sill, and as though it were a shadow itself, another, dark auburn owl, landed gracefully beside Stella. I hid there in the darkness of my room, not wanting this new creature to see me. I wanted to know what it was first, if anything at all.

Stella nipped at it, chortling loudly. The second owl simply leaned away from her, almost expecting her crude advance. Staring Stella down, this new owl seemed to have control over her in a way that looked like ownership. Stella cowered as the owl at last lashed out against Stella’s rude hello, nipping her neck and nearly drawing blood.

Impulsively, I left the safety of the shadows and tapped on the window. “Hey! Leave her alone.” If there was one thing I hated, it was those that preyed on the weak.

The new owl jumped, startled by my sudden appearance. It

had surprised eyes, and not eyes like Stella's, but *human* eyes. We both stood guardedly for a moment, staring, judging.

"*Who are you?*" I demanded.

The owl blinked a few times, and then looked at Stella. Stella was combing her feathers with her beak, no longer trying to battle for hierarchy, or caring. Did Stella really know this owl?

Having opened the window enough to talk with Stella before, I reached forward and slammed the window shut for good measure, making sure to lock it. Stella stopped grooming, looking angered by my action. The other owl tapped the window then, abruptly—almost frantic.

I shook my head. "No way am I letting you in," I whispered.

The owl stopped tapping, looking back at Stella. Stella chortled and nipped, but seemed to give into whatever the new owl was telling it. Stella then turned and tapped the window with as much fervor as the other owl had, as though her persuasion could sway me. I shook my head, balling my fists at my sides.

"I said *no*."

Stella only tapped louder, and I began to worry that she'd wake Gladys. I elevated my hands toward the window, palms open. Stella stopped. "*Shhhh…*" I then brought one finger to my lips.

They both challenged me with a final tap.

My shoulders sank in defeat. Reluctantly, I unlocked the clasp and slid the window open, but only a few inches. "I'm warning you. I can kill you in a second."

Both owls simply stared.

I thrust the window open all the way. Stella hopped in and onto the floor, nuzzling against my leg before continuing past me. I wanted to laugh, but my attention was far too preoccupied by the auburn owl that remained on the ledge. It waited there, its head and body frozen.

"Come in?" I ventured.

The owl understood, finally dropping from the ledge and into the room. I shut the window behind it, my gaze fixed on its back, readying myself to change into the lion if need be. Walking toward my desk, I quelled a shiver as the cold air from outside invaded the warmth of the room. Grabbing a sweatshirt off the chair, I sat down in its place.

The new owl turned, looking me up and down—continuously drinking me in. My gaze was speculative, every fiber of my body readied for whatever might come. Dull tinkering noises materialized from the corner of the room where Stella was tugging at my belongings. In my periferal gaze, she took a few and began carrying them onto the bed, clumsily traipsing them across the crumpled comforter until she found a suitable place to nest. All the while the other owl and I intently locked direct gazes. Stella then smelled the pillow beside her, the one Emily used when she stayed with me. Her feathers fluffed and she cooed angrily.

I wanted to laugh but I waited instead, hoping the auburn owl would make the first move. Another five minutes passed and I grew impatient, Stella now wrapped in her nest and resting. Finally caving, I made the first move.

"Who are you? What do you want?" I demanded.

I'd never met another shifter, but the human glimmer in this owl's golden eyes was unmistakable. Stella's eyes were flecked with wild color where these ones were smooth like mine. I sighed and slouched down, and as I did so, the owl finally broke and hopped toward the bed.

I perked up again, a renewed sense of interest toward what the owl was doing. My hand gripped the edge of the chair, biting my lip against the desire to attack. The owl sank its head under the edge of the comforter, its body changing in one fluid motion and filling the draped fabric until a head of auburn, human hair peeked out the other end.

Though I saw it coming, surprise still swept through me. I was now looking at a girl no older than Emily. Her body was completely wrapped in my blankets, her nimble hands squeezing it tightly around her. Her sudden scent was undoubtedly wild, but not at all threatening. She was plain, her eyes sharp and round, much as the owl's had been. Various shades of auburn streaked her hair, matching the feathers she once had.

Her expression was shock. "Holy *cow,*" she murmured, turning to Stella. "Missy, you were right. I just..." her voice trailed, a small hand surfacing from the blanket and covering her mouth. Her nails were dirty, her hands scarred and pale.

"Missy?" I snorted. "Her name is *Stella.*"

The girl didn't seem to care, too taken by me. "I thought you..."

I tilted my head, confused. "Thought what?"

"You're supposed to be *dead.*" She was nodding, eyes wide.

I cocked my head back, face crinkled. *"Dead?"* I elevated my hands. "Clearly I'm not dead." Palms sweating, I stood, trying to establish my hierarchy. "Who are you?" I demanded a second time.

She cleared her throat, grinning. "Who am *I*?" She seemed surprised by my question. "You don't know?" She turned her head from side to side.

"No." I stated plainly.

Her expression turned to disappointment. She sighed. "They must not have told you." Her lips pressed together. *"Figures."*

"Who?" I thought of the only people I even knew. "Gladys? Max?"

"Gladys." She nodded and sighed long and hard. "Well, I guess I could see why. She probably figured I was dead as well."

I was growing impatient, her answers giving me little information. "Okay, seriously, girl. Who are you? I don't think my girlfriend will like the fact I have a naked girl curled into my sheets."

The girl laughed with a disgusted look on her face.

I pressed the point again. "Seriously. I already feel guilty about it, so make this quick."

She continued to laugh mockingly.

"Stop!" I hissed.

She calmed herself. "You've got it all wrong, Cowboy. I'm not all too excited to be wrapped in your sheets, either." Her eyes rolled. "So don't flatter yourself." She snorted.

I was pacing now.

She leaned back. "It's not like I have any other choice." She motioned around the room, pointing out the piles of clothing both clean and dirty. "It was either the comforter, which I can only *hope* Gladys cleans regularly, or the clothes, which I think you likely never clean—you're a boy."

I felt my anger build. "Okay… so? And you *are?"* I forced through clenched teeth. She was getting sidetracked, and it was bothering me.

She rolled her eyes and let out a long, dramatic sigh. "I'm your sister, idiot." Her tone was cheeky, as though I should have known this, as though it were common knowledge.

I tried to pretend I hadn't heard what she said as I reeled backward. "Wait, *what?*"

"Your sister. Blood relative... Mom and Dad's other kid... what other way can I put it?" She pulled my comforter up to her chin, looking scared by the look of shock on my face.

"Sister?" I gaped at this auburn-haired stranger lumped up on my bed. Her dislike toward the fact she was naked in my sheets now made sense. It was a little disturbing in retrospect.

"Little sister," she corrected. "Lacy."

"Little sister?" I repeated, trying to let it sink in. "How?"

She shook her head. "Do I really have to get into the details of the birds and bees with you?"

Discomfort replaced my confusion. "What? *No...* That's not what I meant." I frowned.

Her smart-alecky attitude seemed appeased by my reaction. "Mom and dad had me a few years after you. By then they'd found a safe place to live, so they kept me," she said sheepishly. "I know they wanted to come back for you, but by the time it came time to do so, you had already adapted to this life. They were afraid it would upset you." She bit her lip in thought. "Truthfully, I suppose they figured you'd be safe here. Trust me..." She looked around the room, looking impressed despite the mess. "You've got it a lot better than I ever did."

I was plainly staring at her, the things she was saying like a dream—a *bad* dream.

She went on. "I honestly thought you were dead. I figured you'd learn about the fires and come looking for me, but you never did. Put two and two together... finito."

What Max had told me about my parents death rushed back to me, but the details were clouded by the simple fact that I hadn't really wanted to listen. "What fires, exactly?"

She rolled her eyes. "So you didn't even know about the fires?" Her brows were pressed together, voice deep. "Gladys is stubborn. I'll give her that."

"Max told me something about Washington, and my parents being murdered. Beyond that, it all went up in the air," I threw in with a shrug.

She nodded. "Yeah, somethin' like that. Our parents did die, though I didn't. We were one of the only flight families left, so escape was easy, but naturally our parents thought they could save everyone. They died while doing it." She said it as though it were no big deal. "Freakin' hippies. Out to save the world."

I digressed. "Flight family? What do you mean?"

"Yeah, you know... *birds*." Her voice was mocking in the same way mine often was. "Feathers. Beaks. Talons... dumb birds."

"I'm not a *bird*." I protested openly. "I'm more the large feline type."

Lacy shook her head and snorted. "Well, you can forget about that. You're destined to squawk, my brother."

"But..." I frowned.

Lacy grunted. "Of all the things I just told you, the thing you care the most about is the fact that you'll be a bird?" I saw that her eyes were wide, incredulous. "What the heck do they feed you around here?"

I drew in a deep breath. "Well, in my defense, I never knew our parents. They've always been dead to me. Why try to pretend I care?"

She looked stung.

"I'm sorry. But you've got to see my side of this." I tapped my chest with my hand. "I'm a little shocked as it is. I'm just trying to take this in stride. Here I am, alone and liking it that way, and this owl," I pointed at Stella, "came and decided to follow me around and then *'poof!'* here comes a sister as well?"

Lacy sighed. "Okay, well… Our parents died and I moved to Oregon, alone. I didn't think I had a brother, either, and then *'poof!'* I come looking for *her*," she looked at Stella, "and I find you."

I could see no one was going to win this. We both stared at Stella as though she were the one to blame. Stella just burrowed deeper into her nest.

I changed away from the pointless subject. "Is Stella like us?" The question had been bothering me.

Lacy glared. "Oh… *no.* No, no, *no.*" She flagrantly shook her head. "Missy is just a pet."

A condescending laugh passed my lips. "An owl with a pet owl?" I tilted one brow.

Lacy's features scrunched together. "Yeah. So?"

We both chuckled, and I was surprised by how at ease I suddenly felt. It was as though it was a natural thing—it *was* natural. Lacy's laugh matched mine, her subtle features, and of course, our hair and eyes. I could already tell she had the same defensive nature as Emily, and I couldn't help but think that they'd get along. For whatever reason, I'd already allowed Lacy into my life, no legal proof needed.

I stopped laughing. "How exactly do you know I'm your brother?"

Lacy shivered under the blanket. "I had a photo of you." She looked me up and down as I stood. "You were about ten. You're eyes give you away, though. Eyes always do for beings like us." She shivered again, more dramatically. "Geez, ever heard of heat?"

I laughed. "You're a wild animal, what do you care about heat?"

Lacy reached over and messed up Stella's feathers. "Down feathers… sort of lacking them right now. You sure are *daft*."

She had a point. I walked to the closet that was overflowing with clothes. I began to pick through, smelling each garment until I had a complete, clean outfit. "Here." I handed her the clothes.

She grasped them through a crack in the blanket.

"I can get some proper clothes from Emily tomorrow," I added.

"Emily? Who's she?"

I'd almost forgotten that Lacy knew nothing of my life. For what it was worth, it felt as though she'd always been a part of it, like I'd known she was out there, but hadn't acknowledged it. "You really didn't know I was here, alive?"

She shrugged. "No. Truthfully, I came looking for Missy and found you. Like I said: '*poof!*' my brother is alive! Not that I'm all that surprised, though."

I nodded. "I'm more surprised than you seem to be."

Lacy pulled the shirt over her head, large enough that she could do so without having to remove the comforter. "I guess I always knew I'd run into you one day. I mean, I thought you were dead, yeah." She tapped her heart. "But not in here."

I nodded, thinking that it was the same way I'd felt about our parents. Clearly that wasn't the case—they really were gone forever.

"Missy used to obsess over your photo. Some sort of crush."

She rolled her eyes. "Owls have a keen sense of just about everything. I suppose her obsession drove her to finally find you. I'd been tracking her, but where I'm not a born expert at it like she is, I got a little lost." She pulled the pants on under the comforter, finally allowing the comforter to fall away. She was spindly and tall, her features sharp. My jeans hung off her hips, her hand grabbing at least ten inches of fabric.

"So this sort of reunion is typical for you?"

Lacy giggled. "Don't get me wrong. This is wild!" Her voice grew loud, her free hand waving emphatically. "I'm ecstatic. But for our kind, this type of thing happens all the time. We're roving spirits, and if we get lost in our changelings we often forget about our human lives for years, sometimes decades. When we wise up and come back, it's holy-cow reunion time."

"What do you mean by lost?"

"Lost. Our animal spirit calls to us at all times. That's the cravings you get. You *do* get them, right?"

I nodded big.

"Right. That's healthy. It's the animal spirit inside you. You have to indulge it. If you don't, it will take more of your human spirit than you bargained for. You may end up trapped in the animal body. Being like us is like being a diabetic. You have to check your levels at all times. Listen to what your body is saying to you. Keep a constant balance."

My mouth hung open. I shut it. I tried to feel what my body wanted right now, but given the mix of emotion since she'd arrived, there was no clear answer. "Wait, so… *what?* Can you repeat that one more time? Elaborate?"

She looked at me, her smile fading. "I can see I found you at the right time. You need serious help." A light laughter escaped.

"I feel sorry for you. You know nothing of who you are."

"No. I don't," I agreed.

"Such an unfortunate thing," she murmured under her breath before stepping toward me suddenly, arms outstretched. "So, Wesley, how about a hug?"

I wrinkled my nose. "Wesley?"

Lacy didn't bother to wait for me to give her permission. She hopped toward me, wrapping her arms around my neck and giving me the biggest hug her little body could possibly allow. "This is our first hug! Can you believe it?" She sighed longingly against my chest.

I gave her an awkward pat on the back. "Sure. Okay."

She giggled and pulled back. "I'm assuming I can stay for a while, then? You don't mind." It was more of a statement than a question.

I nodded, not seeing any other choice.

"So, who's Emily?" she asked again, skipping back to my bed and hopping on beside Stella. She leaned her back against the headboard. "This is amazingly comfortable."

I resumed my position in the chair. For whatever reason, the chip I'd held on my shoulder since the day I was old enough to know about my parents began to crumble. As we talked, something inside me swelled in the region of my heart that had remained dormant for far too long—I had a *real* family.

We talked for what felt like hours, and soon, sunlight replaced the dim morning light and it was almost time to leave for school.

"Wait, so just to reiterate, Emily's *not* a shifter?" Her mouth was agape after I'd finished telling her everything about Emily, Max, Jane, and of course, Greg.

I stood, throwing a jacket on and skipping a shower all together. I grabbed my book bag off the floor, ignoring her question and knowing she just wanted to judge me again. "I need to go to school."

Lacy was still gawking, but stood. "Wait, take me with you. I want to meet your friends." She was far too ecstatic—far too much of a handful, considering the day.

"How about you wait here," I offered instead.

She stood near the door, my shirt hanging off her tiny shoulders. "*Whyyyyy...*" she whined. Clearly no one had been around much to teach her manners.

"*Whyyyy* don't you go hunting or something? You're too thin," I joked.

She frowned. "I want to go with you," she emphasized.

I laughed. "School sucks."

Her head fell. "I wouldn't know. I've never been," she murmured.

My thumb was latched under the strap of my backpack. "Then it's not worth starting now. You won't know anything. You'll just make a fool of yourself. Besides, it's not like you're missing anything fun."

She growled at me. "I know *plenty,*" she retorted. "More than you, I bet."

I saw stubbornness in her expression, the same stubbornness that burned inside me. I grinned. "Okay, then. Tomorrow I'll sign you up. Then we'll see what you're made of. But for today, just stay here. You need to settle in and get some clothes. And don't venture downstairs. Not yet. You'll terrify Gladys to death."

"And that's a bad thing?" she challenged.

My eyes narrowed. "Just stay here or fly out the window.

Wait until I come home."

She sighed in defeat. "Fine." She stamped her foot for further effect.

"I'll bring Emily along with me when I come back." I brushed past her and walked out into the hall. "*Maybe*," I whispered to myself.

She gave me one last disapproving look before I shut the door on her. I gathered myself, bounding down the stairs and out into the daylight. Emily was already leaning against the car, looking annoyed.

"What took you so long?"

My whole body was buzzing. "You won't believe what I have to tell you."

JANE:

I woke to the overwhelming sound of singing birds. Bright light invaded my vision and the smell of cinnamon and sugar filled my nostrils. I blinked a few times, trying to acclimate myself to the strange surroundings. Silky sheets were tucked perfectly around me in shades of blue, with tiny pink flowers sewn here and there.

The blankets fell off me as I sat up, my head suddenly whirling. I touched my hand to my temple and winced.

"A little too much spring champagne?" Navia swept into the room and the happenings of the night fled back to me. All weekend we had hung out, and last night she'd finally managed to convince me to give in and have a drink with her, resulting in many, many follow up drinks.

"*Ugh…* you can say that."

She had a glass goblet in her hand. "Here, drink this." She thrust it toward me. "Did you enjoy the guest room?"

I couldn't answer her, words jumbling in my head. I took the goblet, warily peering into it. It was filled with what appeared to be water, but as I touched it to my lips, I found it was minty and cold.

I thought of Max then, hurt slicing through my heart, adding to the throbbing pain in my head. I tilted the goblet back, hoping to drown the feeling. The minty liquid flooded my throat, the chill spreading throughout my body until it reached my head. Before I even dropped the goblet from my lips, my head felt better, as though I'd slept sound and pure all night.

Navia snatched the goblet from my hand. "I made some French toast as well. Come, join me in the kitchen." She pulled me from bed, a nightgown of silk falling around me.

"What's this?" I looked down at my foreign body.

Navia giggled. "I couldn't let you sleep in your frumpy clothes!" She handed me a matching robe that had been hanging on a hook.

I took it, hoping it covered more skin—it didn't.

"You need a new wardrobe," she added with wide eyes.

"So I've been told." I caught a glimpse of myself in a mirror across the room. My hair was a giant knot on my head and mascara was smeared around my eyes, making me look like a raccoon that had broken into her house. "*Uh*… is there a restroom?"

"Of course, silly!" She pointed to a door beside the armoire. "You should know!" She gently elbowed me. "*You were a little sick last night,*" she added in a whisper.

I felt mortified. "Oh my gosh. I'm so sorry."

Navia fanned away my remark with her hand. "No worries!"

I held myself in comparison to her. She looked as though she'd already gone to the salon for four hours, but in reality she'd just been cooking breakfast. I melted from the envy of it.

"You're so lucky."

Navia looked confused. "Me? Lucky? *Why?*"

I snorted. "You're naturally gorgeous, and look at me." I motioned to my reflection.

Navia put a hand on my shoulder. "I may be lucky in looks, but trust me, luck is subjective."

I wondered what she meant, but I could tell that was the end of her comment.

Slipping into the bathroom, Navia went back to the kitchen. I splashed water on my face and swished a little in my mouth. I ran my fingers through my hair as best I could, but I knew no matter how hard I tried, I'd never compete with Navia's effortless curls.

I exited the bathroom and joined Navia in the kitchen where I took a stool at a white marble bar. The whole place was carved in marble, and from what I can remember, was set into the mountainside far above Winter Wood. A carving by the door read 'Winter Retreat', indicating the fact that there was likely a summer, fall and spring retreat as well—I could only wish for such a thing.

"I've been thinking a lot about your predicament, my pet." Navia delicately dipped a perfect piece of French bread into a batter that looked rich with cinnamon, eggs, and cream. "I may have a solution."

I lifted my brow. "Really?" This, I wanted to hear. The champagne had allowed words to fall freely from my mouth and Navia had been subjected to listening to me go on and on about Max. The more I remembered about what I'd told her, the more ashamed I began to feel.

"This Max fella. He sounds like a handful." She was nodding along with her words. "Angels are tricky." She sighed.

"They are?" I wondered if they had a reputation as prominent as Element Pixies.

"Sure are." She patted the toast with a spatula. "I loved one once. That bastard broke my heart," she said matter-of-factly.

I couldn't help but laugh. The word 'bastard' was unnatural when formed by her lips. "You did? What happened?"

Her whole body shifted as she flipped the French toast with as much expertise as a French chef. "He changed his mind, I suppose. Right out of the blue."

"Just like that? No warning?"

She sharply shook her head. "None at all."

I shrugged apologetically. "Well, Max didn't change his mind. He just didn't divulge the whole truth to me. Like I said, he was engaged once."

She looked up at me, pausing her actions. "To whom, I wonder."

I shrugged. "He didn't say—and I didn't want to know."

She stared at me for a long moment before flipping the toast onto a plate and placing it in front of me. "I'd give you syrup, but I assure you it's plenty sweet as it is."

"Thanks." It looked amazing, and after a night of drinking champagne, I needed it. "So you're sure you don't know Max?"

Navia threw another toast in the pan and it sizzled loudly. "No, can't say that I do."

I shrugged. "Well, he hasn't really been to Winter Wood for a handful of decades."

"*Ah*... see." She was intently concentrating on the toast. "I moved here not that long ago. I definitely wouldn't know him."

Despite her explanation, I was still surprised. Navia seemed to know everyone I'd mentioned, human or not, long dead or alive.

"But, back to what you can do. Sounds like it's not a matter of you two not *liking* each other, but that you can't..." she giggled, "be *together*."

I shook my head, enjoying her innocence toward the subject.

Navia scraped at the corners of the toast. "I may know a way we can level the playing field, though. It might sound harsh, but I assure you it's easy." She flipped the toast, leaving me in suspense.

"What's that?"

She hummed a small tune, plopping the toast on a second plate before joining me at the bar. She nimbly prepared herself a bite with a measured slice of butter and ate it. She chewed politely, at last swallowing so she could answer. "You need to become an angel," she said plainly.

I nearly dropped my fork. "Become an *angel?*"

Navia took another small bite and swallowed. "Sure. It's not that hard. You just have to die saving someone and give them your life in their place." She made it sound like directions for cross stitching—as though even my grandmother would know it. "Dying is nothing new to you, but the catch is that you need a reason not to leave and go to the other side, and I believe we both know what that reason is." She gave me a little nudge and a wink. "When you have the chance to walk across that bridge to the Ever After, simply don't."

"What are my chances of succeeding? What are the dangers?" I wasn't asking because I was considering it, but because I knew there had to be plenty of dangers, thus justifying the fact that I wasn't going to do it.

She shrugged. "Nothing, really."

I snorted. "*Nothing, really?* Then why are angels so rare?"

Navia laughed. "Most people are selfish! How many people that you know of will willingly take the fall for someone else? People don't just willingly hand over their lives."

I laughed. "This is true."

She smiled proudly.

"But what about my Seoul bit and my near death experience when I was little? Won't it be dangerous for me to be tempted with death again, especially when it's what my body craves?"

Navia's back straightened. "No! Not at all! If anything, you'll probably be able to resist it better than anyone, because you know how it feels."

I could no longer deny the fact that I was actually beginning to consider this. I looked at my watch then, seeing it was nearly time for school. "We better get going. We're going to be late."

She giggled slightly. "So?"

I let one laugh escape my lips. "It's your first day!"

She slid from the stool, stepping on her toes as she took my plate and spun away from me. "Well, who cares, right? Besides, you need a makeover first, and we pixies are known for that as well."

Dread washed over me. School sounded like a better idea.

EMILY:

"No *way!*" My voice filled the car.

Wes nodded enthusiastically. "I swear, Em. I have a sister."

I sat back against the seat, feeling so many emotions for Wes. I was excited for him, mostly because I knew his dismal attitude toward family was destined to change.

"And, what? She's just up in your room, chilling out?"

He was still nodding. "Yeah, can you believe that?" He started the car. "I guess Stella is hers, too."

"Really!" My voice peaked once more. "You mean that little brat of an owl that's been all but humping your leg is actually a family pet?"

Wes grunted. "Yeah, sure. Though I'm not sure that's how I'd explain it."

I stomped my feet, overwhelmed by the news. "*Wow.*"

Wes put his hand on my leg. "Calm down, freak." He changed the subject. "But I'll need to borrow some clothes until she can get some for herself. She's a stick, so it should work just fine size-wise."

I frowned. "Are you calling me fat, or are you saying that I'm too thin?"

Wes tensed. "Neither?"

I laughed. "I'm just *teasing,* Wes."

He grinned uneasily and we backed out of the drive. The ride to school was quiet, both our minds occupied with thoughts of Wes's sister. He did a bad job hiding it, but whereas it was rather exhilarating news, it made sense. From his mind I learned what she looked like, what they'd talked about, and whether or not he'd spoken fondly of me, which he had. She seemed a little wild, and I knew that would bug me, but for Wes, I'd deal with it.

Lost in these thoughts, I saw a shadow fall across the hood of the car, then another. I leaned forward and looked up through the windshield, just as we slowed to turn into the school parking lot. Two owls were flying above the car.

Wes didn't bother to look, grumbling instead. "I told her to wait."

I pointed to the auburn-gold one. "Is that her?"

"The sassy looking one?"

I laughed. "Pretty sure they're both sassy."

He finally brought himself to steal a glance. "Yeah, the auburn one, unfortunately," he muttered. "She was supposed to stay in my room."

"I can see the stubbornness is a family trait," I added.

"Tell me about it." Wes shook his head, trying to ignore their presence. "Where's Jane this morning?"

I shrugged and leaned back. "I don't know. Mother said she was with a friend, I suppose."

"A friend? Where's Max?"

I looked at him with a baffled expression. He'd never ask about Max. "No idea. I haven't seen him except for last Thursday night when he came into my room. Usually he's always around, but maybe he's just busy."

"Max came into your room at night? What was he doing there? Why didn't you tell me?" Wes demanded.

I put my hand on his arm. "Chill out. Max just thought he heard something and came in to check on me." And he probably did hear something. Last night, the same incident reoccurred, though this time Max didn't show up to check. I woke to a warm, humid room and another cold, empty chair, audience of stuffed animals and all.

It was Greg all right; I was convinced. Luckily, with the venom still in me, I knew there was nothing he could do but stare in the dark like the freak that he was. I didn't want to tell Wes, especially now that he had a sister to be excited about. Bad news would dampen his mood, and it wasn't like anything was going to happen. Based on the way Max had sizzled when he touched me, Greg inevitably would, too.

"That better be all he was looking for," he further warned.

I nodded big. "It was. Don't worry."

"Do you think he's got that other pixie chick on the side?"

I let one laugh pass my lips. "You mean the Avery girl he almost married? He better not." I punched my fist into my hand. "I'll kill him if he does."

Wes shook his head, the familiar protective thoughts for Jane sneaking through his otherwise silenced mind. "Me, too." He thought for a moment as he parked the car. "I think Jane deserves to know about it. I bet he hasn't even told her."

I agreed. "And if he hasn't told her, then my admiration for perfect Max is beginning to change."

"So, we should tell her, don't you think?" Wes shut off the car and grabbed his bag from the back seat.

"I think we should." I unbuckled, my hand resting on the door handle. "At lunch, okay?"

AVERY:

I shifted my weight on the vanity bench, grinning inwardly as I stared at her reflection. I reveled in the feeling of my new pet beside me—Max's pet. She was so naïve, so... *impressionable.* I powdered her cheeks with makeup, wanting to dress her up like the little doll that she was to me. Besides, it was worth enjoying her while I could.

Jane coughed. "Whoa, Navia. That stuff really gets up your nose, doesn't it?" She choked.

I gave her a little pat. "Try not to breathe too deep, darling." *Try not to breathe at all,* I thought. If only she were frozen in time like a real doll, then I could keep her always like a trophy.

I ran my hand down the length of her dark hair. She was so soft and delicate, and I could almost see what Max saw in her. It was like having a little bird, so diminutive, with her life in your hands. If I wanted to, I could crush her with one finger, but that would defeat my goals of making Max suffer.

I'd decided that she needed to be caged in a place Max

could see her but could never touch. To do that, all I needed to do was make the temptation of eternal life and limitless love too tempting for her to pass up—so tempting that she stupidly attempts to become an angel. Already I could tell she was leaning toward my idea, but what I hadn't told her was the practical certainty that it would result in her death. She'd end up trapped on the other side, away from Max, tragically just out of reach. What they face now in their intimate life is nothing compared to the torture they will face when I'm done.

"There. You're beautiful." I set the silver compact back on the vanity. I had to admit, she was gorgeous once you put a little makeup on her. If I hadn't known her, I'd venture to believe she was an Element Pixie in her the fall season, even. At least until she opened her mouth to speak.

Jane twisted her neck and faced the mirror. "Wow. I love it."

I ran my hand down the back of her head one more time, obsessed with petting her hair. "Lovely, my pet. The boys will fall all over you today. Just you wait."

Jane giggled. "I'm excited to see the look on my friend Liz's face. She'll be red with jealousy!"

I sighed, taking it as a compliment. "As all women should be, my pet." And I meant that in so many ways, even for me.

MAX:

The ceiling was fifty feet overhead, making me appear as small as I felt in this room. My hands were clasped before me, waiting. Jane's scent still lingered within the fibers of my jacket, my throat tight because of it. No matter how hard I tried, I couldn't stop thinking dangerous thoughts about the other night: The way her skin felt so close to mine, the feeling of her life as it made my heart beat in a way it hadn't in too long. I wanted to taste her, the pain of being away from her dehydrating my very spirit.

I drew in a deep, shaky breath, hearing the distant sound of footsteps approach. I shut my eyes one last time, hoping to hold myself together long enough to ask for forgiveness. I assured myself that this was the right thing to do, saying it over and over in my head, beating with each step that echoed. The sound was sure and strong, just as it had been years and years ago.

"Maximus!"

My eyes sprang open, seeing the Crown just a few feet before me. He was smiling, and as he drew close, his arms welcomed me in. I was surprised by the action, but stepped into his embrace, giving him one pat on the back before stepping away. My eyes became fixed on his.

"Maximus, I am not ashamed to say I'm relieved to see you. I've worried about you immensely over the years."

I nodded politely. "I find myself surprised to hear it, Srixon." I wanted to feel nervous, but forced myself not to.

He laughed. "Please. What happened I could never blame you for. I fear you feel that way, but I realize that what happened was my fault. I should have never put you to the task of caring for Avery, let alone expect you to love her when I knew you didn't. I regret to admit that I was desperate, and felt it would fix what was destined for her. I am not shocked to find that it has only fueled the fire."

Guilt overcame me, despite his kind words. "She's turned, hasn't she?"

The Crown nodded gravely. "I have received word that Avery has been spotted in many of the Black Cities, though I do not believe she has yet committed to their side through any of their members."

"I took her light," I admitted with shame. "That's why she turned."

Srixon placed one hand on my shoulder. "Believe it or not, dear son, but her light was taken long before it disappeared under her love for you. Avery was claimed, years before you came into our life. Her light had a destiny, and it was to fade."

"She had already been claimed by the Shadow Pixies? Why didn't you tell me?" I felt further betrayed by Winter Wood. Anger flashed in my eyes, replacing my remorse.

Srixon's expression was dark. "I'm sorry, Maximus. Of all the lies, I did not want Avery's fate to be another one." His head bowed. "When she was small, an elder Shadow Pixie visited me in my chamber one night. She warned me of the Shade's intent to destroy me, and placed a curse on my head. She said great despair would fall upon me, and my bloodlines would end. At the time,

I did not know what she meant, thinking I would be stripped of the ability to produce an heir. Clearly, when Avery came along, I saw that those notions were untrue. For many years, I forgot about the Shadow Pixie's warning, until Avery came of age. She began turning toward dark magick, taking an unhealthy interest in such things as torture, fire, shadow dust, and other heathen things. I soon realized what the warning meant, that the Shade was to claim my children and leave me void of an heir that way. At first I denied it and did everything I could to force Avery away from the darkness, but clearly, that did not work. She's their queen now."

"Avery will inherit the Shadow throne?"

Srixon nodded slowly. "My own daughter will become my greatest enemy." His face became deeply grim and pale. One day he would have to face her, and I could see that already he knew he'd lose. "The Shade was smart this time. I fear we're facing some dark days."

I couldn't think of anything to say, too blown away by the whole thing. Could I have stopped her by staying here, or would it still not have made a difference? Worse yet, would the Shade have come after me if I stood in his way?

Srixon drew in a deep breath and re-gathered his composure. He changed the subject. "I learned of your father, Maximus. I'm sorry," he admitted. "I assure you that if I had known Patrick was your father before his death, I wouldn't have allowed the lie to continue."

"How did you learn of it?" I demanded.

Srixon took a moment before speaking. "I received a letter from Patrick that arrived just after his passing. He told me about his regrets by way of you, and wanted me to be the one to tell you who he really was when he was gone. By then, I had no idea where you were. I'm sorry that you never knew. I know he'd tried many times to tell you, but I'm afraid he just couldn't."

Hearing Srixon inform me that Patrick was too much of a coward to tell me he was my real father hurt. "How did you know I knew about Patrick being my father in the first place?"

Srixon lifted one brow. "I'm not a fool. I knew you had come back. Someone from the faerie community, a waitress at the café, said they'd seen you. Aside from her claim, I also had people watching over the apothecary, hoping you'd show up one day. I knew that you'd eventually figure out who Patrick was when given access to Patrick's things. It was only a matter of time." He paused. "We've been waiting for you to return for a long time. I'm not ashamed to admit that we need you."

I felt my muscles relax with mutual understanding. "I need the Priory as well."

Srixon nodded with a noticeable relief. "If we could have brought you back sooner, we would have, but you didn't make it easy to be found. I knew you had taken a human to guard, and I figured that had become your sole priority..." his voice trailed.

I felt Jane as he mentioned it—I felt her laughing. "I did. She did."

Srixon pressed his lips together, a look I knew all too well.

"You disapprove?" I asked.

Srixon's eyes met mine. "It's not that, Maximus. It's *who*."

"Who?"

Srixon leaned close. "I suppose in retrospect you couldn't have chosen a better muse, but it still concerns me. The faerie I mentioned before recognized her right away, given that the faerie is a Light Seer." He lifted one brow. "She's John's child, isn't she?"

I nodded. "I did not know he had a daughter, let alone two, not until..."

Srixon sighed. "I don't blame him for hiding it. He was a Priory member with a particularly dangerous marriage to a human. He was trying to protect them."

"What about Jane is any different than any other guarded?" I ventured. Why had Srixon made such a point?

Srixon rubbed his chin. "She's yours, at least. That alone gives me hope."

He hadn't answered my question. "But why Jane? Why the emphasis, and why did the seer recognize her?"

Srixon bit his lip. "There's a Truth about her."

Just the mention of the term angered me. My Truth had caused me nothing but pain, false hope and confusion for Jane, and now another Truth?

"She's been seen in it, but not as you'd think."

"How?" I demanded, feeling my protective nature begin to surface. Jane was supposed to be mine and mine alone. She was my Truth, so having her in the Truth of Winter Wood brewed jealousy.

"I honestly can't say because telling you would put the outcome at risk. Already we've removed the faerie from the streets of Winter Wood for her own safety. This future has to remain a secret."

"Please, tell me something," I pleaded.

Srixon closed his eyes. "All I can tell you is that Avery is involved." His eyes opened. "Saying that is mistake enough. There are so many things that will have to happen for the Truth to come to pass, and right now, it leans in our favor, but barely. If anyone affects the outcome at this point, it could be catastrophic. It was always about fate, all this time, and now it's all finally coming to pass."

I clenched my fists. I wanted nothing more than to be able to read his expression, but it was too vague to offer further answers. My personal problems with Jane were now shadowed by the gloominess of this new development. "So Avery will return."

Srixon drew very close. "Maximus, you need to watch that girl of yours. I cannot press the point enough. Avery is my daughter, but I will be the first to tell you that she is not who she once was, and never will be again."

I swallowed, knowing Jane didn't even want me around. Because of my stupidity, I now had to suffer in the shade, watching her the way I always had, without her.

"Find your guarded, Maximus, and do as you've sworn. That is our best hope for keeping this Truth in our favor."

WES:

At lunch I found Emily outside. I sat beside her. "Have you seen Jane yet?"

She frowned. "No, not at all. I don't know what's going on, but she almost never misses class."

"You said she stayed with a friend all weekend? Who?"

Emily shrugged. "The only person I know of that even remotely resembles a friend to Jane is Liz." Emily rolled her eyes until they were glaring right at the culprit in question. "And see, given it's a miracle, she's here."

I looked across the yard as Liz walked briskly through it, her coat wrapped tight around her and her minions acting as the second layer between her and the cold. I nodded and laughed. "I can see that."

Emily sighed long and hard, leaning her head against her arm as it rest on the table.

"What's up with you?" I wrestled my sandwich out of its small plastic bag. It was the third peanut butter and jelly sandwich I'd had today.

"I'm just tired, is all. I haven't been sleeping very well."

I chewed through the soft bread, the jelly leaking through the air holes and onto my hand. "You should stay with me tonight."

Emily smiled slightly. "I'd love to." She blushed. "But you have your sister there now. Not to mention the fact that my mother would never allow it."

I shrugged. "You've done it before. Your mother didn't seem to mind it then."

Emily began to look frustrated. "Yeah, but she will eventually. That's the way she is. She gives you a little room and then she…" Emily's voice trailed, her eyes fixed over my shoulder.

"What?" I turned as I said it, no longer needing an answer.

"Jane?" Emily whispered. "Is that really her?"

I was thinking the same thing. Jane, or rather this being that held Jane somewhere deep under a layer of makeup and preppy clothes, walked across the lawn toward us. There was a blonde you'd think came right out of a Victoria's Secret catalogue linking arms with Jane, who was smiling widely. I found myself at a loss for words. I may not love Jane the way I used to, yet I couldn't help but notice how good she looked, even if all that makeup wasn't really my thing.

"Who the *Hell* is that with her?" Emily snorted.

I glanced back at Emily in shock. "I don't know. Doesn't look like anyone from around here, though, if you know what I mean." I nearly choked on a hunk of gooey white bread.

Emily gave me a reproachful glare. "Do you really think she could be from Winter Wood?"

I nodded slowly, mouth agape. "Either that or she's from some model cult in California."

I could practically feel Emily's glare burning holes into the back of my head. "Real nice, Wes."

I shook my head. "I'm serious. It's unnatural to be that..." I tried to choose my words carefully. "*Well formed.*"

The tart smell of jealousy seeped from Emily's pores and wafted across the table.

I glanced back at her once more. "Trust me. I'm not at all interested. Looks like that come with an inherit bitchiness, not to mention a mess of makeup stains."

Emily's jealous scent faded as she laughed and agreed. "That is so true."

"Hey, guys." Jane stopped as she reached us, striking a pose.

Emily and I just gaped in return, not willing to encourage this behavior, nor understanding it.

"This is Navia." Jane's grin grew. "She's from Winter Wood," she added in a sing-song voice.

I gave Emily a *told-you-so* look. Emily rolled her eyes at my need to flaunt the fact that I was right.

The girl stepped forward, releasing Jane's arm. "Hello. It's nice to meet you." She reached out for my hand. I gave it to her with a shake as she bowed lightly.

Emily's heart rate surged in my head. Navia must have noticed as her eyes fluttered to look behind me. She dropped my hand and backed away, tilting her head and giving Emily an innocent smile.

"You must be Emily, Jane's sister. I've heard a lot about you." She paused, likely waiting to see how Emily would react.

Emily said nothing.

"You're very brave!" Navia went on. "Being abducted by a Black Angel is an experience many don't live to talk about."

EMILY:

Navia stepped forward and extended her hand to me over the table. At first I stared at it, my gut wrenching in the worst possible way. I had tried to crack into her thoughts since the moment she'd gotten close enough, but it was like Fort Knox on Independence Day.

Navia held her hand in the air, patiently waiting. "I admire your strength," she added, layering on the charm.

My stomach settled and I finally took her hand and shook it. "Thanks for the... *er...* compliment?" It wasn't exactly a compliment but rather a 'lucky you', but still. Being abducted by a Black Angel was an experience I was still dealing with, especially considering what had been coming to my room the last couple of nights.

Navia smiled, a smile that appeared genuine, but there was something more to it. I couldn't figure out what it was, and my stomach wrenched again. Holding her hand allowed me to dig deep under the walls of her mind, but there was still no way in. Her mind was well trained. She shared nothing.

"Do you guys want to join us?" Wes asked nervously, shell shocked by her beauty. I couldn't really be mad at him, though. Being around such unnatural splendor would make any man's resistance crumble—it even made me nervous.

"Of course!" Jane sang, plopping down beside me as Navia took the bench beside Wes, opposite Jane.

Navia watched Jane closely, in a manner that reminded me of a girl and her pet. I laughed to myself, figuring the only way Jane would ever allow anyone to make her over as Navia had meant she practically had to be their pet. Liz had tried many times, but she had little finesse when it came to convincing Jane of anything. What scared me was how easily it seemed Navia had succeeded at the task.

Navia glanced at me on the diagonal. "What was the Black Angel like?"

I frowned. This was hardly a subject I wanted to discuss with Wes and Jane, let alone her. "A jerk." I answered simply, hoping she'd take the hint.

Navia jutted out her bottom lip in thought, but didn't press further. Wes sat up straight, demanding attention as he eyed me. He cleared his throat.

"So, *uh*… Jane. Where's Max?"

Jane snorted. "Since when do you care where Max is?"

Jane's reaction was hard to read. There was bitterness, but also concern in the way she said his name.

Wes shrugged. "Just wondering. He just seems a little *here-today-gone-tomorrow.*"

Jane's eyebrows pressed together. "What do you mean by that?" She'd sensed Wes's sarcasm.

"Nothing." Wes was torturing her. He was making it obvious he knew something.

Jane sighed dramatically. Navia watched him intently—curious. "Okay, Wes. Spill."

A smile snaked across Wes's lips. I was surprised by how much he was enjoying this, and was seeing old emotions flair in him. His eagerness to destroy Jane's love life because of all she'd put him through would forever, as I'd thought, be a factor. "I heard something interesting about Max when we were in Winter Wood, that's all. Just makes me a little nervous about his absence, and I wonder how it is you can trust him."

My gaze shot from Wes to Jane, wanting to see her reaction. Jane's eyes narrowed. "Heard from whom?"

I looked back to Wes.

"From Jake Santé. It was something about Max's past, in terms of relationships. Saw it as a red flag." Wes took a huge bite of his sandwich, acting cocky.

Jane's lips pursed ever so slightly, her eyes narrowed. Navia's attention to the subject only grew more intense, her eyes darting between Wes and Jane, as mine were.

"And exactly what did you *hear?*" Jane pressed impatiently, though her voice was controlled.

The tension was thick. So thick, that I was certain I could reach out and grasp the mass of it and crumple it up in my hand.

"I heard Max was engaged once, to some pixie chick." Wes glanced at Navia. "No offense."

Navia shook her head slowly. "None taken."

"Guess Max was a real heart breaker," Wes added.

Jane didn't flinch, suggesting this was something she already knew about, possibly explaining why she was *sans* Max.

Navia took a sharp breath and leaned toward Wes. "Did Jake tell you who?" Her head tilted with interest, an interest I assumed was due to her belonging to the pixie community and in being Jane's new bestie, but there was also something else.

I tilted my own head, the whispers in her mind trying to break through. They sounded anxious, but were quickly squabbled. Again finding myself at a dead end, my considerations turned back to Jane. I could practically hear her swallowing down dread beside me. Wes's reply would now be the only thing that could shed light on the situation.

Wes relented. "The Crown's daughter, apparently. Avery was her name."

Jane stopped breathing all together. By the looks of it, it seemed that Max hadn't provided Jane with a name.

Wes twisted his head to face Navia. "Do you know who that is?"

Navia shook her head slowly, her lips a narrow line. "No, never heard of her." Everything about her suddenly ceased to move, as though she'd been frozen.

Wes shrugged. "So, anyway. I thought you should know, Jane. That's all."

Jane was just as frozen as Navia. I was scared by the whole thing, never before seeing Jane so affected by one simple word or name. After a moment passed, however, I was relieved to hear her draw in a long breath of air.

"I knew about it," she murmured, dropping her head. "I just… didn't know her name."

I bit my lip, seeing the sting in Jane's eyes and regretting the idea of bringing this whole thing up. This morning it had seemed like a good idea because I thought she didn't know, but apparently our news was a bit late. Broaching the subject was nothing but pouring salt on a freshly opened wound.

"Is that why Max hasn't been around?" I put my hand on Jane's back, trying to comfort her.

Navia remained distant.

Jane nodded, looking like she was about to cry.

I looked at Wes, feeling increasingly bad for Jane. What was happening? Max and Jane had been so in love, but now it was falling apart. I guess anything could. "I'm sorry." I rubbed my hand in circles on her back.

Jane shrugged me away. "I'm fine." She sat tall, sucking down her sadness, her face like stone.

Navia was peering off into the distance. Was she really telling the truth, or did she know who Avery was?

Jane stood. "Come on, Navia. Let's go."

Navia's attention came back to us. She grinned and stood, taking Jane's arm. My gaze remained on Navia, her eyes flashing darkly just as they broke from mine. I drew in a discreet, tiny breath when I saw it, sensing the danger in it. Though I wanted to grab Navia and ask her why, they had already turned and walked away just as quickly as they had come.

"That didn't exactly go how I'd imagined," Wes admitted once they were out of earshot.

I shook my head distractedly, still trying to figure if the darkness was my own apprehension toward new people, or if it had really been there. "No, not at all."

Wes stopped eating for a moment. "Are you sure you're alright, Em?"

I swallowed, hiding the concern for now. "Yeah, babe. I'm fine." I smiled as best I could, but something deep in my stomach lurched again.

AVERY:

"Well, that wasn't very nice." I squeezed Jane's arm with the force of my nervousness. She shied away from me slightly. Jane's friends already knew about Max and me, a factor I hadn't considered. Luckily, they didn't know what I looked like, but considering my rather prestigious place in society, it wouldn't take long before they found out. I needed to execute my plans, and soon.

Jane snorted. "So much for friends, right? I'm so sick of their mockery, teasing... *judging*."

I smiled through my unease. "Well, you have me now." At

least for a little while, I thought.

Jane nodded in agreement as we passed through the school doors and into the hall. She gently shrugged out of my grasp. "I better get to bio lab."

My pet was sad, something I secretly enjoyed, but was required to convey otherwise. Still though, I had grown fond of having a pet, and I had to give Max a little credit—it was fun. I nodded sympathetically and gave Jane a hug. She smiled bleakly before shuffling pathetically down the hall.

As she turned the corner, I felt him beside me.

"You called?"

The hall was empty except for us. "I did." My shoulders drooped with the pending pressure. "We need to accelerate the plan."

Greg snorted. "I don't even know what the plan *is*. Are you ready to share?"

I turned to him, giving him a sassy smile as I traced one nail down the length of his nose, then kissed it. "We're going to kill her."

Greg chuckled as though my words were impossible. "Not to be a Debbie Downer, but I think Max will notice."

I laughed to myself. "Oh, Greg. He won't."

Greg shook his head. "If Jane turns up murdered, he's going to dedicate an eternity to finding whoever did it. He'll find you. If there's one thing Max can do, its hunt his prey."

I wrapped my arms around Greg's neck, leaning against him. I clicked my tongue. "That's why I'm not just going to kill her, my darling. I'm going to convince her to kill *herself*. If Max believes she did it, then the story ends." The words alone excited me. "And best of all, he'll blame himself."

I could tell I was rousing Greg's desires as his hand grasped my hip. "You're going to make her kill herself? How will you manage that?" He leaned close.

My gaze rose to meet his, allowing the darkness in my eyes to show. "Just watch, dear Greg. You'll see." I pulled out of his grasp, smoothing my dress over and down my body. "Have you been doing as I ask?"

Greg's look conveyed his distaste for being left in the dark, and left empty handed. "I have."

"And?" I elevated my brows, thus lifting my chin.

"He's gone to your father, just today."

"He did, did he?" Max had more gumption than I'd thought. "Well, then I will assume he will be looking out for Jane a little more closely." There was a ping of betrayal in my heart. My father would have surely told him about my darkness. "If he sees me with her, the whole thing will be ruined." I sighed. "Please, keep me informed of his whereabouts at all times, won't you, darling?"

"He's here right now," Greg challenged with a smile, getting back at me for my coy behavior.

My smile sunk to a frown and my stomach fluttered with the statement, a reaction I hadn't expected. I was over Max, wasn't I? I bit my lip and sloughed off the feeling as fast as it had come, finding an excuse for it. Max held my light, my soul. I craved it and that was all. This was the only reason that made sense to me. Max was a mere memory of my past life.

"Doing alright there, Avery?" Greg's voice brought me back to reality, the smug grin on his face all I needed to ignite my anger.

I changed the subject and challenged him in return. "Been

visiting your pathetic little girlfriend, have you?"

Greg looked confused. "What? Who do you mean?" He snorted. "I don't keep girlfriends.

I laughed lightly. "I know you've been continuing to visit that Emily girl. Her mind may be protected, but not from me. She was wildly thinking about it just a moment ago: you sneaking into her room in the dark, watching her… It's all really quite *romantic.* You must have left a lasting impression on her." I shook my head mockingly. "Can't you just let it go, Greg? That's what's truly pathetic." I turned away from him, quickly ending this meeting. "I should go."

I disappeared before he got a chance to reply, leaving him instead with a shocked expression, something I never got tired of seeing.

JANE:

I felt increasingly ill as I placed one foot in front of the other. I didn't expect that knowing her name would do this to me.

Avery.

It washed across my thoughts like waves on a beach—constant, unchanging, and worst of all, unstoppable. *What did she look like? Was she like me? Was I like her?* I felt increasingly self conscious just thinking of Navia and how beautiful she was.

Avery had to be at least as attractive. They all were. I was, in comparison, quite literally plain Jane.

But the questions didn't stop there.

How long were they together? What did they do for fun? Did Max break up with her, or did Avery break up with Max? A part of me felt Max had left her, but I hadn't bothered to ask details, too devastated by the simple existence of a former woman in Max's life, and not just any woman, but a *fiancé.*

A chill fell over me then, a sweet, soft chill. I stopped in my tracks and turned on my heel.

"*Max?*" I whispered, frantic and drunk with the feeling.

Holding my breath, nothing happened. No one was there. I bit my lip, placing my hand on my chest as the breath I was holding began to sting. I released it and shut my eyes, wanting to cry, but nothing came. Opening my eyes, I turned back and continued on down the hall. When I reached the bio lab, I was relived to see it was empty. Normal students were still enjoying lunch, only geeks like me liked to arrive early—and, well, geeks like Jake, normally.

I stared through the small window into the dark room, knowing I should go in, but not sure if I was prepared to be that alone. A moment ago it had seemed like a good idea, but I knew I really just wanted to get away from Navia for a moment. She was suffocating me.

I didn't like being weepy, and worst of all, I didn't like being predictable. Running away from my problems to sulk by myself in a dark room was definitely 'predictable Jane'. I dreamed of running someplace new for a moment, like the ice cream shoppe or the park. These were places that could actually comfort me for a change, but then I remembered I had no car. Finding this the only choice, I placed my hand on the handle of the door and pressed down against all my body's screams not to.

My footfalls echoed as I made my way to my regular spot and sat down, stool squeaking. I sighed, looking up at the board where equations were scribbled. Everything about this room felt like an old friend. There was a smell of alcohol from the beakers that sat filled along the far wall. The scent seeped toward me, burning my nostrils and making me forget about the scent Max had given me—the scent of me.

Another sweet chill fell over me, and I didn't know if it was from the thrill of forgetting, or something else. I shut my eyes, indulging my mind.

"Max?" I asked again. *"Please?"*

The chill grew stronger. I opened my eyes, but again, no one was there.

"Why are you doing this?" I asked, but deep inside, I already knew the answer. Just then, something white caught my eye on the stool beside me. I twisted my head, my heart leaping into my throat. There was a paper crane sitting there, facing forward as though it had been there all along. I couldn't help but smile.

I reached for it slowly, relishing the moment as I unfolded its wings.

I have to fix this. That's what you want.
That's all that matters.

I ran my hand over the letters, the ink still fresh. It was my fault he wouldn't let me see him. I had been right. My request for him to fix this had not been taken lightly. I should have known enough about his nature to understand that he wouldn't come back until all of my requests were fulfilled. I lifted my head, feeling more alone than before—he was punishing me.

The door to the lab opened suddenly. I jumped, crinkling the paper in my hand to hide it. Navia waltzed in. I could not escape her.

"Seriously. Why are you here?" She snorted—albeit gracefully. "I think I've had enough of this school stuff for today, how about you?" Her eyes grazed the room, looking sharp.

I had to agree. "Yeah."

She sat on the stool beside me, looking at the paper in my hand. "What's that?"

I squeezed the wad of paper tighter, the ring on my finger burning into it. "Just a note."

Navia crossed her legs and folded her hands on her knees, looking like a politician on stage. "From?" The corner of her mouth curled.

My mouth mimicked hers. "Max."

She leaned back, her mouth forming an 'o'.

"What?" I accused.

Navia giggled. "Love letter?"

I laughed once. "Hardly." My fingers felt the sharp crinkles of the note as began rolling it over my fingers.

"Well…" She placed her hand on mine. "I have just the thing to get your mind off it. I was just invited to a Halloween party Friday night, and I think we should go. Finding the right costume is enough to keep you distracted for days, trust me."

I tried to be happy about it, at least for her sake, but there was no hiding my continued sadness.

Navia sighed. "I want to help you feel better." She paused. "Have you had a chance to think about what I said?"

"About?" I was in no mood to remain sharp about everything she'd mentioned in the last forty-eight hours, especially given the added factor of champagne.

"About the whole becoming an angel thing?" she reminded me pertly, as though it was obvious.

"Oh… *uh…*"

Navia didn't let me finish. "Just think. It would solve all your problems. You'll no longer be Max's guarded, so you know what that means, and you'll live as long as he does."

I let the thought take hold. "How will I find someone to save? It's not like people just drop dead everyday in Glenwood Springs, let alone from an event requiring saving."

She brought her finger to her chin. "Well, then save *me.*"

"You?" I leaned forward, holding back a laugh. "How does that work? Are you in need of saving?"

Navia shrugged. "I don't know. I could be."

"No, you're practically immortal. I know because you have no death." I shivered. What I was doing was considering my own death, and it felt awkward talking about it as though it were a plan to go to the mall or something.

"I could still die if I wanted to. How about I jump from a cliff, and you break my fall?"

I burst out laughing. "Navia! That's weird."

She giggled. "I know, right? And so *typical.* I just love cliffs, though." She tapped her finger on the table, her words so out of place in the world I once knew. "How do people die these days?"

I stopped laughing. "I dunno. I suppose in car accidents, fires, falling down the stairs."

"Drowning!" Navia jumped up. "Drowning! I'll drive a car

into the river and you can save me."

I swallowed. I always thought that drowning would be the worst way to die. "That doesn't guarantee I'll die, though."

She shrugged. "Well, just be sure you do! It shouldn't be that painful. Just jump in before you take a breath."

I shook my head. "But isn't it a little too… *staged?*"

Navia frowned. "Yeah. You're right. We need to find a real someone to save."

"This is beginning to sound like an impossible idea."

Navia bit her lip. "I thought this would be easier."

"Yeah, well. If it were easier, we'd have a lot of angels, right?" I laughed. "And a lot of dead people," I added.

Navia was staring into the distance. "I'll come up with something," she murmured. "Don't worry."

WES:

Sitting in the driveway, I shut the car off. "Okay, Emily, this is it."

Emily laughed. "You make it sound so… *daunting.*"

Having Emily meet a sister I'd only known for a handful of days *was* daunting. Luckily for me I had put it off, but it came at an expense. Every night with Lacy had felt like a barrage of grenades, her pestering to meet Emily so constant, I had to give in. Emily had also pestered me, but at least understood that I wanted the chance to understand my sister for the sake of safety. Lacy was wild, and if she decided she hated Emily as much as she suggested, I was afraid Lacy would hurt her.

I smiled nervously, putting my hand on hers. "Let's just say she's a little strong willed."

Emily rolled her eyes. "And I'm not?"

I bowed my head. "That's what I'm afraid of," I murmured. Listening to Lacy go on and on about how wrong it was to date someone that wasn't a shifter was bad enough. The simple act of introducing Emily to Lacy at all was pure madness.

Emily got out of the car before I was ready. My body felt like a lead weight. Emily crossed her arms, staring at me through the windshield. Her mouth formed the words '*come on*', though I couldn't hear her. The nerves in my stomach made the muscles in my arms begin to ache, seeping across my skin in a wave of carnal need—carnal *fear.* It was a pack, or *flock* thing, I suppose. Emily and I had become a sort of pack, but Lacy and I were a pack by blood. I didn't want to be put in the position to choose between the two. But I was getting ahead of myself—they hadn't even met.

I swallowed down another animal instinct that was rising inside me—the need to run. Opening the door, I stepped out. Emily met me at the hood, locking her arm with mine as though to say, *'you're not getting out of this'*.

"It's going to be fine, Wes. Everyone loves me." Her naked lashes fluttered innocently.

Emily's skin against mine felt soothing. She was right, everyone did love her. Her powers of persuasion were impeccable, and where it's probably her ability to read minds that assisted that talent, it worked, and that's all that mattered.

We walked together up the path and onto the porch, Emily's paper bag of extra clothes swinging at her side. Just as I went to grasp the door knob, it flew right out of my hand. The door swung open, far faster than I knew Gladys could possibly move—but it wasn't Gladys. We were face to face with an excited Lacy, her hair fluttering in the wind that had been created by the force of opening the door.

"Hi!" She yelped, her body swimming in a pair of my basketball shorts and long T-shirt.

Emily looked surprised at first, but quickly collected herself. "Hello."

"You must be Emily." Lacy stepped forward until their noses practically met. Lacy's eyes were narrow, seemingly inspecting Emily's very soul. *"Hmmmm."* She stepped away.

Emily tilted her head. *"Hmmmm,* what?" she demanded.

I felt my heart rate surge to life.

Lacy slouched onto one hip. *"Hmmmm,* you're pretty. That's all."

Emily nodded slowly, a look that meant she wasn't buying Lacy's vague explanation. "Right, well… so are you."

I was trying to understand what was going on. I wasn't so naïve to take it for face value. There was some sort of *'fluffing of feathers'* that was happening somewhere I couldn't see.

After another moment of staring down Emily, Lacy turned to me. "I like her, I guess." She shrugged. "Even if she isn't one of us." Lacy flashed Emily a look. This was going to be an impossible afternoon.

Emily snorted. "Gee, thanks."

I tried to change the subject. "I thought I told you to stay in my room?"

Lacy's demeanor changed. She pouted. "I was going to, but it's been *days* that I've been locked up in there. Do you know how boring that is?" She closed her eyes with a delighted look on her face. "I smelled something good from downstairs." Her hands were squeezed into fists in front of her. "Human. *Food.* Do you know how long it's been since I've had human food?" Her eyes opened wide.

I lifted my brows. "No. I guess I didn't consider it." I was being sarcastic.

Lacy frowned at me. "Anyway, I figured Gladys wouldn't freak out too much, and she didn't. Just a little scream, but she got over it once I explained myself. At first she actually thought I was you." Lacy glared at Emily once more. "Her vision apparently isn't very sharp. I don't see the resemblance."

Emily rolled her eyes.

"You both have red hair," I offered. But in truth, there was a lot of resemblance. "I could see the mix up."

A disgusted snort passed Lacy's lips. She didn't need me making up reasons.

Emily crossed her arms. "I thought you *liked* me," she challenged.

Lacy pressed her lips together, her pose mimicking Emily's. "Like is not love, missy. If you were a shifter, then maybe you'd get an upgrade, but you're just a mind-reader, a cheap trick."

A sharp breath passed Emily's lips. She turned away from Lacy, looking as though she was about to storm off toward home.

I conveyed to Lacy a look of anger and disappointment.

Lacy silently tried to protest, but soon gave in. She reached out and grasped Emily's arm, stopping her. "Sorry, I didn't mean that. I just..."

Emily furiously twisted back to face her.

Lacy searched for the right words. "I just get used to things being a *certain* way—traditional, or at least what I know as traditional." She released her grip on Emily's arm. "I guess things are different here."

I gave Lacy one last glare. Her excuse was good, but not good enough.

Lacy grumbled at me, and then sighed. "Please, don't go." She said it with as little enthusiasm as I could see possible.

Emily's eyes flashed with a competitive spark. "Fine." Her stance screamed defensiveness, and I could see she was formulating some sort of plan—Emily always bit her lip when she was. "But I'm not letting you borrow my clothes." She pulled the paper bag behind her back.

I shut my eyes and drew in a long, deep breath, trying to remain sane.

Lacy gasped dramatically. "What! Why?"

Emily gasped right back. "Because you're a brat!"

Lacy set her jaw in determination, attempting but failing to look benign.

Emily ignored it. "Be nice, and maybe I'll lend you one thing that I brought."

I could practically hear Lacy's teeth grind together. This wasn't going well, but at least Emily hadn't bolted. I heard Gladys then, her voice low, but demanding.

"Would you all just *calm* down!" She came to the door, opening it wide until she could fit in the frame beside Lacy. "I may be old and slow, but my hearing ain't."

Emily looked surprised by Gladys's sudden authority.

"You all sound like a bunch of badgers in a fight. Go on now, play nice." She squeezed Lacy and Emily together, collecting them in a group hug. *"That's nice, yes?"* Her voice was muffled as she spoke into Lacy's chest. Leaning away, Gladys's frail frame had to be supported by the handle of the door. Her beady gaze found mine. She was beaming. "Glad to have your sister home? Glad to be what you are?"

I grinned despite the fact that I was angry that they'd never told me about my genes, or that Lacy was even alive to begin with. But, as Lacy claimed, perhaps they just didn't know about Lacy's status, or that I had made the transition. "I am, ma'am."

Gladys's smile sank, her once kind eyes narrowed. "Then act like it." She turned and stormed back into the house with as much 'storm' as an old lady could muster.

I stood there, stunned by her sudden sauciness.

Lacy and Emily both giggled discreetly, eyeing each other.

"Whatever," I huffed.

AVERY:

"Greg?" I whispered as I reached the wood. I'd left Jane at home, her attitude having turned all sulky and doubtful since Monday—I hated it. Having a pet was becoming more work, all of a sudden. I was glad she would be gone soon. *"Greg?"* I called again, a little annoyed that he hadn't immediately appeared. I

heard a branch rub gently, a sound so minute, but not of nature.

"What?"

I twisted to meet Greg's gaze as he peered out from behind a tree. He had been sitting behind it. He flicked a leaf on the ground until it crumbled.

I rounded toward him.

"I need you to get Emily. We need a sacrifice," I barked.

Greg didn't bother to move. "No." His voice sounded irritated. He was used to being the ringleader, not the henchman.

I put my hand on my hip. "*Excuse* me?"

He looked up. "No. I don't want to... I *can't*."

I shook my head, looking to the sky. "What do you mean you *can't?* Do you love her or something? Don't want to see her dead?"

His eyes narrowed, and in that small gesture, I saw that he really did love her, though he wasn't about to admit it. "No. that's not it. It's because of what happened a few weeks ago with some snake incident. She's poisonous to me now. I can't touch her," he said simply.

I grumbled. *Why hadn't I known that?* I refused to let it stop me. "Find a way. I need you to threaten her life so that Jane can take her place. You know, be the hero and die doing it."

Greg suddenly looked more intrigued. "You mean, attempt to kill Emily, but then I'll get to kill Jane instead?"

I nodded.

A sly smile snaked across his face. "Why didn't you say that before? In that case, I'll find a way to take Emily."

I nibbled my bottom lip. *Not that taking Emily was really going to bother him much,* I thought. "What makes killing Jane so enticing to you? What's your beef with my pet?"

"Your pet?" He lifted one brow mockingly.

I growled at him.

His mockery retreated. "Same reason it's enticing for you—I want to hurt Max." He pulled his feet under him, lifting himself off the ground. "I've wanted to kill Jane since I failed to years ago. I hate the fact that she makes him so *happy*." His face was twisted with loathing, brushing the leaves off his pants. "And she's annoying."

I laughed. "Wait, you've tried to kill Jane before? Why didn't you tell me that?"

He shrugged. "You didn't ask. Besides, I figured it was common knowledge that I don't like her. I don't just hate from a distance. I typically like to do something about it."

I stared blankly. "I'd considered a lot of things as to your hatred toward her, but not that. I mean, I never knew you'd made the attempt to kill her. I knew you wanted to kill her, but I didn't know you'd actually tried. I'm impressed."

He approached me, looking smug about the fact. Based on his pause, I could tell he was relishing it. "I had lots of reasons to hate that girl, long before Max, even. Her family was mixed-breed. The mother was human, her father was magickal, and not just that, but a member of the Priory. I killed her father, John. I hoped to kill the whole family, but when Max stepped in and stopped me—"

"That was when he made her his guarded, isn't it?" I interrupted. "When you killed her father, and then tried to kill her. I mean I knew he had saved her, but I didn't realize it was a result of something you did. This just keeps getting better and better! What a small world!"

"I know." He was idly fiddling with his fingers. "That's

why I agreed to help you. It was servicing my own cause—my unfinished business of killing her, or at least that's what I hoped your end game was."

"Well, that is my end game. Happy?"

"Very."

I allowed my excitement to sink in. "So, then you have no problems and we're on the same page."

"We are."

I smiled wide. "I want you to take Emily on Friday, after the Halloween party. I'll get Jane sloppy on spring champagne. She's gullible that way. Friday will be our night, the perfect night. I just love the way death sounds on Halloween. I've always wanted to try it. What better way to celebrate the day of the dead than with murder, or should I consider it sacrifice?"

"Both," Greg answered confidently, an annoying twang to his voice.

"Go now." I shooed him, growing tired of his face.

He didn't look very impressed by it. "As you wish." His eyes rolled as he turned away from me.

WES:

"Here," I handed Lacy the costume Emily had handed me. They'd warmed up to each other, but not enough to yet transfer gifts hand to hand. I was still the mediator.

"What's this?"

"A witch costume," Emily answered for me, her head still buried in the wooden chest of costumes we'd found in the attic.

"Witch?" Lacy's nose crinkled. "So cliché. Don't you have anything better?"

Emily sat up, something pink and purple in her hand. "Of course I do, but I'm wearing it. Besides, a witch suits you perfectly."

Lacy grumbled and marched to the other side of the room, holding the witch costume up in front of her. "I don't even want to go to this stupid thing."

"Then don't," I interjected, growing tired of her constant pessimism.

Stella was perched on another trunk in the corner, her eyes closed, unconcerned by the drama that was unraveling before her—apparently she was used to it happening, and that's what scared me.

"Here, Wes, catch." Emily tossed a wad of green fabric at me. I caught it just before it hit me in the face. "And what is this?"

"Peter Pan."

Lacy turned back to us, giggling. "I guess maybe I don't have the worst costume, then."

I unraveled the fabric, pulling at a bit of plum colored nylon that turned out to be the leggings. "Seriously?"

Emily turned and smiled a smile that was full of recollection. "It was my father's once. I was a lost child that year, and he was my Peter Pan."

I shut my eyes, seeing there was no way around this. Lacy was still giggling lightly, though her back was turned, her hands untangling a black wig.

"What time does this thing start?" I was stretching the purple leggings, hoping they wouldn't castrate me by the end of the night.

"Eight." Emily had a small grin on her face, the faerie wings in her hands unfolding as she straightened the wires. "Isn't it funny? Here I am, about to wear faerie wings and they're nothing like what real faeries are like. I should have feathers in my hair and tattoos across my skin."

"People would think you were a biker-*bird*," I added.

Emily's energy only grew more excited. "I know! But that's what the fairies in Winter Wood are like."

Emily couldn't get enough of Winter Wood. We'd gone there every day after school with Jane and Navia for a snack at the café. I wasn't too keen on it, but watching Jane's new friend made it worth the trip. It's not that I had a crush on her or anything, it's just that, well, she was breathtakingly gorgeous. It was like staring at a real life swimsuit model, only better. Luckily, I kept these thoughts in the vault of my mental mansion, behind a lead door that was three feet thick. I couldn't risk having Emily hear them, and I couldn't stop thinking them if I tried. Pixies had that effect, I guess.

"Emily!" Emily's mother called from the bottom of the attic ladder. "You're friend is here!"

Emily's face popped out of the chest once more. "Jake's here," she announced a second time, as though we hadn't heard.

"Clearly," I murmured.

Emily ignored me and went back to rummaging in the chest, pulling out a black, furry lump of fabric. My brows were pressed together with interest.

Footsteps ascended the ladder, and Jake's head popped

through the hole in the floor. Since he'd revealed himself to us, I'd grown used to seeing the shiny eyed, clean cut version of Jake, but today it was all nerd, and he'd laid it on thick. A pair of suspenders held his pants above his waist, his glasses like thick picture frames around his dull, green eyes. "Hey, guys." His braces made his voice wet and annoying.

"Hi, Jake." Emily didn't seem to care whether he was the nerd or the suave vampire. To me it just meant she didn't find him attractive like every other soul in Winter Wood seemed to—that was all that mattered. Because he was a non-threat, I could be friendly to him.

"Here," Emily tossed him the wad of fur.

"What's this?"

"A gorilla."

An uncontrolled snort escaped my lips like a laugh. Peter Pan suddenly seemed like designer duds in comparison. Sucked to be him.

Jake glared at me for that comment. "I'll sweat to death in this," he protested.

Emily shrugged. "But I figured this way you wouldn't have to wear the getup," she motioned to the glasses on his face. "You can hide behind the mask instead."

Jake grumbled, but conceded, trying on the mask that covered his head in a layer of black fur. Lacy eyed him sideways, and then leaned away. I'd told her about what Jake was, and she wasn't too excited by it. She'd told me about shifters who had been attacked by vampires in Washington, thinking they were animals but quickly discovering otherwise. By then, it was too late to save the shifter.

Jake removed the mask and eyed Lacy in return. "Don't

worry, darlin`. I don't like poultry, either."

Lacy frowned, her cheeks turning a bright red that was accentuated by her fiery hair. "Good," she grumbled. *"Imp,"* she added under her breath.

"Have you ever met a real imp?" Jake shot back. "You'd reconsider your accusation if you did."

"Ass," Lacy didn't care what it meant.

Jake shrugged. "That's gettin` better, a mule."

"What about Jane and Navia?" I asked innocently.

Emily looked up, a frown replacing her smile. "What about them?"

"Are they coming?" I refused to look at her, afraid she'd find a way into my vault.

Emily slammed the chest of costumes shut. "Yeah."

Her anger wasn't directed at me, but rather the names themselves. I grew curious. Drawing closer as Jake and Lacy continued their banter, I whispered, "What's wrong?"

Emily was furiously detangling something in her hands, the wings she'd flattened now attached to her back by two loops of elastic around her arms. "Something about Navia bugs me. I don't like what she's doing to Jane."

"You mean all the makeup?"

Emily's eyes met mine. "Yeah, the makeup, the… I dunno."

I brushed my hand across her face, drawing her attention away from the tangle in her hands. I leaned in and gave her a peck on the lips. "Don't worry so much. You're starting to sound like Jane."

"Ewwww…" Lacy squealed from across the room. "I told you guys to stop doing that kissy stuff in front of me."

I looked toward her, seeing that Jake also appeared awkwardly disturbed by our display of affection.

"In front of *us*," Jake added.

"Sorry." A half smile lifted my cheek.

Emily blushed with embarrassment, once again fumbling with the fabric and turning away. Jake and Lacy had their costumes just about on.

"Help me?" Lacy turned her back to Jake, exposing the unzipped zipper of her *muumuu*-like black frock. I was amazed to see them working together.

"And Max?" Emily whispered.

I turned back to her. She had given up on the fabric.

I shrugged. "I still haven't seen him."

"I wish I knew what happened." She pulled her hair back in a pony tail, fastening it with a sparkly clip.

Max and Jane's supposed split was something we'd all been obsessing over all week. Jane's explanation at lunch on Monday had given us zero leads, and we couldn't understand why something so seemingly perfect could end so fast.

I shrugged. "Maybe Max will be there tonight. Then we can ask him. I'm much more comfortable asking him, you know, man to man and all."

"So now you're willing to talk to him." Emily sighed. "Regardless, I doubt he'll be there." She looked at her watch and sighed again. "We should get going."

A chill ran down my spine, remembering my first and only party experience a few weeks ago, when Greg had shown his first signs of provable insanity with Emily's friend, Alexis. She hadn't been the same since, and her parents ended up removing her from school all together, not that that act alone hadn't done the school some good. Emily picked up on my apprehension.

"He's gone, Wes. This party will be much more normal, I swear. Come on. Let's go." She stood and met Jake and Lacy, ushering them down the ladder.

I went down last, shutting the attic latch behind us. Fully dressed a few minutes later, we all met in the hall for pictures.

"You guys look great!" Emily's mother exclaimed, snapping photos from low, then high, having us sit on the stairs. "What's your name again, sweetie?"

"Jake." Jake's voice was muffled by the mask.

"Give me a big *grrrrr*."

Jake obliged.

Emily rolled her eyes. "Okay, Mom. We really need to go." She took the camera from her mother's hands, placing it on a nearby table.

"Awe… Bye, guys. Have fun!" She wiped her nose with a tissue, looking as though she was going to cry, though it was more likely just the remnants of the flu she'd had.

We all piled in my car, and on the way to the party, Jake was already complaining.

"I feel like my butt is swimming in sweat," he disclosed from the backseat.

I heard Lacy gag slightly. Stella was perched between them and even she was leaning away from Jake at this point—no deodorant would have been strong enough to stifle the scent. We all laughed except Emily. She had remained distant since the conversation in the attic.

"Here!" Lacy squealed, making me jump. "This is *so* the place!"

I looked where she was, seeing a house up ahead, swarming with teenagers in any array of costumes.

"This is so awesome," Lacy added. "My first human party!"

"Sure, *now* you're excited," I teased.

Lacy shrugged. "A girl is allowed to change her mind."

I parked on the street and shut off the car. *"It's not that great,"* I mumbled.

JANE:

"Really, being Disney princesses feels a little young to me, don't you think?"

Navia fanned me away with her hand. "*Pish posh,* darling. I've been around much longer than you and I know for a fact that Disney Princesses are the best princesses in the world, except for us, of course!"

We were crammed into Navia's other car, her white BMW sedan. Why we didn't just take the Tahoe was beyond me. We stopped at a light, our blue and yellow dresses like layers of meringue. I felt funny, but I knew that every year the senior class went overboard with their Halloween party—hopefully this meant I would be fitting in with an outfit like this, unlike my dress in this car.

The light turned green and we turned onto the streets of suburbia. I had no idea where we were, but Navia seemed to know her way as though there was also a GPS embedded in that perfect, little head of hers. Soon, the loud pump of music began to shake the car and I knew we were close. Turning another corner, our destination was obvious. We drove past rows of cars I was used to seeing in the school parking lot, now lined down the street. Each car we passed was a reminder of just how far I would have to hobble in three inch heels. Navia had to fight to find a spot. After what felt like miles, we at last parked. Navia backed against the curb without utilizing her mirrors, ever aware of her surroundings as though every move was a well choreographed dance at the ballet.

She shut off the car. I popped open the door, feeling like I'd just opened a can under pressure. The hoops of my ridiculous Belle costume nearly sprung me right out and onto the sidewalk. Navia's Cinderella dress naturally flowed in comparison as she gracefully spun out on her side of the car. Her curls bounced, so perfect and platinum it was as though Cinderella Barbie had suddenly become life-sized. If I could walk her through Disney World at this moment, packs of screaming girls would surround her, demanding an autograph.

I tried to steady myself as best I could, hobbling to meet Navia near the bumper. She took my arm, nearly lifting me off the ground as she did so and making walking so much easier.

"Better?" She wasn't even struggling to hold my weight.

I nodded. "Much."

We pranced toward the house at an alarming rate. The smile on Navia's face looked permanently carved there, just like a Barbie's would be. I saw Wes's car parked thirty cars closer to the house, and wondered how early he'd arrived to snag such a spot. Reaching the door, the pounding music penetrated my soul. Navia simply walked in, demanding attention as she swept into the front hall. It was as though she were arriving at her own personal ball. I felt grand on her arm as everyone seemed to stare.

"Jane!" I heard Emily's voice above the music, the crowd pushing and shoving until her red hair burst through, wings on her back.

Navia released my arm, floating into the crowd and chatting with Liz, who looked noticeably angry about Navia's matching Cinderella attire and the fact that Navia looked infinitely better in it.

"What are you doing here?" I frowned at Emily, so used to her old partying ways that I instinctually feared a night of endless stress. Then I remembered that she was with Wes—a senior, and a responsible one at that.

"I'm with Wes and Jake," she grumbled, clearly irritated by my accusations. "When are you going to get over it and accept the new me, Jane, seriously?"

I ignored her. "Where's Wes?"

Just then Peter Pan broke through the crowd and approached us. I laughed.

"Right there," Emily giggled.

I looked at Wes's purple tights. "Nice."

Wes grumbled. "Are you here alone?"

Emily took his arm, leaning against him with a smile and answering for him. "No. She's here with *Navia.*"

I saw Wes's eyes twinkle slightly, a hidden joy glowing somewhere deep inside. He was a man, and like every man I'd seen in the vicinity of Navia, they all fell hopelessly in love her.

Emily bit her lip, and I knew what question would come next. "And Max?"

I drew in a deep breath, my hands gripping at the mass of

yellow sateen that was draped from my waist. All I could do was shake my head.

Wes puffed out his chest a little, looking as though he was trying to summon strength. "What happened, Jane? *Spill.* It'll make you feel better."

I felt the chains wrap around me—I was out of excuses.

Emily touched my arm. "Come on. I hate to see you like this, and truthfully, we miss Max, too. It's not that Navia isn't great, it's just…" Her voice trailed, and I sensed a familiar feeling of disappointment from her.

I swallowed, gathering my emotions and packing them up like a parcel for the mail, ready to give it to them straight. "I told him to leave."

Emily gasped, quickly cupping her hand over her mouth. Did she have to be so *dramatic?*

"Why?" she crooned.

I played with a ruffle near my waist. "It turns out that as his guarded, he and I can't…" I stopped myself, knowing how shallow and naïve this was going to sound to an outsider.

"Can't do what?" Emily pressed.

Wes gasped, getting something Emily wasn't. *"It?"*

I blushed and nodded. At least Wes got it. He knew that look on my face all too well—the look of disliking the term.

"What's *it?"* Emily asked dumbly, still not getting it.

"Sex." Wes said bluntly, looking Emily in the eye.

I blinked a few times, taken aback by his direct remark. He'd never been so outward with the term before. "Well, in so many words, *yes,*" I said sarcastically.

Wes snorted. "This isn't really a subject I want to discuss, especially with you, so…" He shook his head, releasing Emily's arm and walking away. Wes was pouting about it.

Emily just rolled her eyes. "Seriously? Why?" She leaned in, cupping my elbow and pulling me closer. At least she could respect some of my privacy and reasoning, and it made me want to respect her in return—a rare feeling.

"I guess it's something in the way we're connected. Max borrows my emotions in order to protect me, but I suppose he can take that too far. If we were to..." I once again stumbled over the term.

"Have *sex?*" Emily blurted, just as Wes had.

I scorned her. "Yes. *That.*" I rolled my eyes. "If we were to do that, his draw on my emotions could get carried away. Max would suck the life right out of me."

Emily leaned back, looking mildly stunned. "Wow... *really?* That's kinda heavy."

Her remark was less than impressive. I ignored her. "I mean, you can see why I'd send him away, right? I loved him—*love* him—and being around him, and wanting so much from him, how do I know I won't get carried away one day? I certainly can't leave it up to Max to be the only responsible one. That's just *ir*responsible."

Emily grasped both my elbows this time, holding me square in front of her. "I can understand, Jane." She shook me gently. "Besides, what we're learning about Max's past isn't exactly..."

"Reputable?" I finished her sentence for her. It was the perfect word.

Emily shrugged. "I mean, I was going to say *savory* because I thought it sounded cool, but sure. I guess that works. I mean, everyone has a past, his just happens to be a little more... *intense*... and well... *extensive.*" I could see she was trying to play an even field, but there was also an understanding in her words, as though the issue was her own. "I know how it feels to overcome past... *um*... romances. I mean, you know, you and Wes and all." She stumbled over her words. It wasn't a subject we'd addressed in a whole lot of detail.

"Emily, you know I don't have feelings for Wes, and knowing and loving Max as I have now, I know that I never did. It was a comfort thing with him, that's all."

Emily had dropped her hands to her waist, fiddling with a lump of my yellow dress as it invaded her space. "I know that. I do. What I'm saying, I guess, is that I understand. I want you to be able to talk to me about these things, and not just..." Her words trailed.

"And not just what?"

Emily let go of my dress. "And not just find a new friend, like that Navia girl to confide in. She doesn't know you like I do. Frankly, the chick gives me the creeps."

I couldn't help but laugh and nod. "She is a bit different."

Emily nodded along with me. "And I know what you're going through with the whole... *intimacy* issue." She was suddenly acting modest about it.

I laughed. "Like you and Wes have any issues," I teased.

Emily snorted, her eyes wide. "We do when I'm too chicken to even do it!" She blushed a deep crimson.

"What?" I tilted my head and snorted. "With your history, how are you scared?"

Emily bit her lip, shifting her weight on one foot. "I don't have a history, Jane. You just assume that I do."

I let the idea sink in, finding it impossible. "No way."

Emily laughed nervously. "I'm not joking! It was just

comfortable having you think I was a moral-less person. Allowing you to believe I was someone else kept you at a distance. It kept you from finding out about my mindreading." She tapped her head.

Flooded with relief and happiness, I pulled her into me, unable to control my need to hug her. I was full of pride and guilt at the same time, pride for her chastity and guilt because I'd assumed the worst from her for so long. She pushed me away gently.

"Maybe you should listen more," she dared. "Like I do," she added with a grin.

I giggled. "I promise to try and ask more…" I was nodding and smiling, but Emily's face had suddenly drained of all color, her eyes fixed over my shoulder and behind me, searching frantically. My happiness quickly faded. "What?" I felt a flutter of nerves in my stomach at that look, knowing it couldn't be good.

Emily narrowed her eyes, ignoring my question. I turned and looked in the direction she was, behind me and through the rooms of the house toward the kitchen. There were more guests now than there had been when I arrived a few moments ago, the hall overflowing, but not with anything out of the ordinary.

"*What?*" I repeated, looking back at her and giving her a little nudge.

Emily's eyes pried away from where she'd been looking. She shook her head as though shaking away an image. "Nothing. I just thought…" she stopped herself, pressing her lips together as Wes returned, balancing four cans of beer.

"Want one?" he asked, looking proud to be serving us.

I scowled at Wes for cutting short Emily's answer. "Emily, I thought we just promised to tell each other everything? You can't just do that and expect to avoid an explanation."

Emily frowned and reached over me, snatching a beer from Wes's hand. She snapped it open and began drinking. Seeing that Wes was now struggling to balance the remaining beers in his hands, I quickly assisted him, grabbing two cans that were about to fall to the floor. Wes regained his balance. Emily's abrupt change in attitude was confounding.

"What's gotten into you?" he barked at Emily.

Emily had her eyes shut, her head tilted back as she drained the can. She crushed it in her tiny hand, looking brutish doing so. "Just anxious is all. Thanks for the beer."

My brows were drawn together. I once again looked over my shoulder, but there was still nothing to warrant her strange and unexplained behavior. What in the world had just happened?

EMILY:

I gave the empty can back to Wes. He took it with a confused look that rivaled Jane's. I nervously glanced back across the house where I had seen it—seen *him*. Greg. It had to be a figment of my imagination, but what if it wasn't? My lack of sleep the last week had been hard on my already flawed concentration. I wouldn't be surprised to find I was seeing things now, too. Then again, if Greg really was in my room, then he could really be here and I wasn't seeing things at all. My spine steeled, body shaking.

Where was Max?

If Greg were really here, there was no way Max would not know about it. Lover's quarrel or not, Max was still sworn to protect Jane for the rest of her life including those she cared about, like me… at least that's what he claimed the night he invaded my room. Now, more than ever, I actually missed having Max around—he would be able to tell me the truth—was Greg really here or not?

I know it seemed a stupid thing to obsess over, but no one saw what Greg did to me—what he made me *do*. I was trapped in my body, his every wish my duty to fulfill. Granted he didn't take advantage of me, at least not to *that* degree, but he did make me kill a man. My hands sliced the heart right out of his poor soul, the blood forever staining my skin. I could never forget the way the man looked at me, my face the last he saw.

What Jane and Wes knew about my abduction was vague and loose. I hadn't been able to open up about it yet. Given that, being terrified by the simple possibility of Greg's proximity at this party made my reaction at this moment understandable. I certainly wasn't about to foot my burdens of that experience on them here and now. This meant leaving Jane with unanswered questions, though I had promised not to.

Wes seemed to shrug it off rather quick, idly sipping his beer. "I brought one for Navia, too. Where is she?" I was glad Wes was changing the subject away from my weird and sudden behavior.

Jane stood still, holding the two extra beers and staring at them with a frown on her face. "I don't know." She looked around for a place to leave them, finding a side table in the corner behind her. I watched her maneuver the mass of yellow sateen fabric, setting the beers on two coasters—always the polite one.

"Well, did she go to mingle?" Wes pushed.

Wes's pressing interest in Navia's whereabouts sent an irritated twitch down my spine. On top of everything else I had to deal with, now I had to deal with the fact that Wes clearly had a thing for Navia, even if it was a superficial attraction to her super model looks. He thought I didn't know, but he wasn't as great at hiding it yet as he thought he was.

Jake approached then, and my whole body tingled with his nearness, hungering for the relaxation the veiled light could provide. Given the ape suit, however, there wasn't so much as a glimmer.

"Hey, man." Wes put a hand on his shoulder. "Got a beer over there for ya, on that little table thingy next to Jane."

Jake groaned dramatically. "Oh, you're a *god!*" He practically lunged for it, popping the top and chugging it down, finishing with a flagrant *'ah'*. "Now that's good."

I rolled my eyes away from them, leveling my gaze across the room where the same, dark figure I'd seen before now leaned against an arched passageway—closer now. I felt my heart stop, my eyes lingering on the figure: undoubtedly a man, undoubtedly Greg. His face was shadowed by the overhang of the arch, his pose somehow coy and confident at the same time. I allowed myself to open my gaze to him, hoping that by doing so, he would disappear. He didn't.

Black leather jacket and dark jeans—all the smoldering, dark romance he possessed was put on display. A sick part of me enjoyed it.

I shut my eyes hard this time, trying to quell the emotions that were mixing inside me—hatred, love, murder, and lust.

Opening my eyes with the emotions haltered, I saw he was gone. Though he had once again disappeared, one thing was for certain. This was real this time. This was not just a figment of my imagination anymore.

What did he want?

Jake reached for the last beer. Leaning back into his place in our circle he snapped it open, but before he could bring it to his lips, I snatched it out of his grasp. I slammed the fizzy amber liquid down my throat once more. I would not let this scare me. I was poison to Greg, and I needed to remember that.

Tilting my head back, I choked on the beer, surging forward in a fit of coughing. Jake caught me in his arms, patting my back.

"What in the *world?*" he remarked, aiming the question toward Wes. "What's wrong with her?"

I stood up straight, wiping my chin.

"What's your problem?" Jake asked me directly, looking from Wes and back to me. He squeezed my arm.

I yanked myself out of his grasp. *"Nothing,"* I hissed. The beer was already beginning to get to me.

"We already tried that question," Jane filled him in. "It doesn't work." Her dry sarcasm was annoying.

The three of them were staring at me like a sick person.

"What?" I barked.

They just shook their heads. Navia approached with a look of concern on her face. She sidled alongside Jane. "What's wrong with your sister?"

Was it that obvious? I felt my teeth grind together, wanting to rip her perfect little head off. She did not belong in our group. She did not deserve to fit in with us. And most of all, she did not deserve to know my problems.

"Maybe we should go." Wes wrapped his arm around my waist, gripping tight. I gave up and allowed myself to sink into him, though my body didn't want to. My weeks of clean living made me more receptive to the poison of alcohol, and right now, I was feeling not only overly emotional, but easily persuaded.

I saw Jane nod in agreement. "I'm not sure she's ready for this type of scene just yet."

I hated her for saying that, as though I couldn't control my actions. Then again, I couldn't control my thoughts, either. Greg had invaded them the moment he'd arrived, and he was laughing at me.

~

I woke with a start, gasping for air. I sat up fast, looking to the chair in the corner of the room. My faerie wings from the party were crumpled in the seat. It was as though they'd been sat on, the chair still rocking. I'd tried to stay awake and wait for Greg to come, but that hadn't lasted long as the beer forced my eyes closed. Now, though, I was definitely awake, and he was *definitely* here.

"Greg?" I stammered. "I know it's you."

The words were hard to say. Lips trembling, I cursed myself for admitting it out loud. I knew that once those words left my lips, there was no turning back.

The floor creaked, opposite from the still rocking chair. I drew in a sharp intake of breath and shot my gaze in the direction of the sound. I could barely see a thing, my eyes straining against the darkness.

"Greg?" I foolishly asked again.

The air was thick and warm, so warm that any movement encouraged perspiration. I heard another subtle rustling, like a mouse, or perhaps a figment of my imagination. I pressed myself back against the headboard, pulling the covers up to my chin. Something in the room shifted then, and the shadows began to move. My eyes had to be deceiving me, but as the warm humidity melted to a cold chill, deception turned to reality.

The shadows crept across the floor toward the foot of my bed, snaking up and over the covers. I tried to stay within the little light the moon provided, but the shadow did not seem to care about the safety of my light. It stretched endlessly toward me in billowing waves. Ringlets of cold air tickled the skin on my face, like a door left open in the middle of winter. I'd been holding my breath, my lungs now stinging. The shadow halted and I exhaled, a cloud of steam releasing from my mouth and falling upon it.

"Who are you?" I tried again, my voice shaking.

The smoky shadow blew away like sand in a wind storm, revealing what was hidden beneath. "Just me." Greg had been discarded in the receding wave of sand, his mouth twisted into a wicked grin. "Did you like the entrance? I've been working on it for a while."

I stopped breathing as I jolted back, my head smacking against the headboard.

He laughed. "I wanted to impress you, and give you a start. I succeeded."

Collecting myself as fast as I could, I sat up, hands in front of me and ready to defend. "What do you want?"

His brows were sewn together. "I could ask you the same thing." His footfalls echoed across the wood floor as he took a few steps back and stood straight, hands resting at his sides. I could see he was avoiding getting too close, telling me that what Max had said about my poisoned blood was definitely correct.

"Why do you keep watching me?" I lunged forward a little, testing the theory. Greg jerked back, avoiding the burn.

He was nimble and unfazed, but careful nonetheless. "I'm not watching you."

I grew more confident. "Yes. You are."

Greg shook his head. "Why does everyone keep saying that?"

"Everyone who?"

Greg moved and sat at the end of the bed. "You..." his eyes met mine. "And Avery..."

His icy chill crept over the comforter, falling upon me. "*Avery?* You know her?" I gasped.

Greg bounced on the mattress, leaning back on his elbows. He looked at me, his eyes amused. "Avery was almost kin to me. Of course I know her." His sarcasm wasn't welcome. "But now she's my new partner in crime." A delighted half smile spread across his olive skin. "You may know her best as sweet *Navia*."

My mouth fell open as the name sank in. I saw her face in my mind, puzzling together the various clues to her distant attitude at lunch the other day. "Navia is... *Avery?* But..." Why hadn't I guessed that? It suddenly made sense.

"I can't believe you didn't pick up on that. I thought that you were smarter." Greg sighed long and hard. "She's gorgeous, though, isn't she?" He traced his finger over the pattern on my bedspread. "Though I still like you better. You've got a certain spark I crave." He clicked his tongue and shook his head. "Too bad we didn't work out, but… luckily for you… it seems we'll get a second chance."

My hands felt cold and clammy. "There are no second chances with us, Greg. So leave me alone."

He sat up, looking hurt, though I knew it was all for show. "*Aw,* don't say that! We had great times, remember?"

Images suddenly invaded my head, images of murder, lust, and greed. The images were attached to a carnal need to be close to him, a need to feel our bodies intertwine, breath becoming one. My stomach lurched, trying to push this demon out. He was brainwashing me.

"*Leave me alone,*" I seethed through clenched teeth. I was stronger than him, and pushing hard, the images disappeared.

He laughed. "I'm impressed! You've grown strong."

"Stop coming here. Stop watching me sleep!" I yelled, feeling the release of his wicked energy inside me.

He stopped laughing. "I haven't been watching you *sleep,*" he said again, annoyed. "That's far too cliché for me."

I wrinkled my face, confused. "You haven't?"

Greg snorted. "No. If I wanted you that bad, I'd just come and take you."

My back steeled. "Then who was it? Avery?" If he hadn't been the one in my room, then who was left?

"*Avery?* You think she has time to watch you when she's busy ruining Jane? You're not *that* important." He laughed once. "Yeah, right." He thought for a moment, looking infuriatingly confident. "But, listen…" his weight shifted closer to me. "I really do have to take you now."

I felt my heart rate quicken. "But you can't touch me."

He inched his way over the sheets. "Yes. I can… if I have to."

"Why?" I spat.

Greg traced his finger down my arm. The touch sizzled, making him wince. "You're supposed to be bait. If you haven't already guessed, Avery wants to see your sister dead. The best way to lure her in is with you, as we've seen before." There was a look of envy on his face. "I guess Avery knows how to take jealousy to the next level."

My throat was tight, and I found myself at a loss for words. I looked around the room, looking for a way to escape. Knowing Greg's agility, however, there was no point in trying.

"I'm sorry I have to do this again, my dear." He tilted his head and leaned into the curve of my neck, just under my ear. His breath singed the hairs that were standing there. "I promise that this time, though, I won't let anyone take you away from me. This time, we'll be together forever," he whispered, the very mention of it felt like cold lead entering my ears. He brushed his nose against my skin, wincing again as he leaned back, angered by the reaction between us. Grasping the edges of my sheets, he pressed me against the backboard. "There's something enticing in this, isn't there? A forbidden pleasure, perhaps?" His teeth flashed and he winked, the green halo of his eyes glowing. "I must say, our connection sure has a new flash to it that it didn't before."

I wanted to scream, but my voice had frozen. I tried to wriggle free, but Greg only pressed harder. He was laughing softly, mockingly, the way he did when he'd forced my hand to murder.

Mustering all the strength and concentration I could, I spoke forcefully. "*Please,*" I pleaded. "Please just let me go."

Greg wrapped the sheet around me, hands careful but fast. He tucked me into a cocoon, and just as he was about to lift me from bed, he lurched suddenly. Looking at him, I saw his eyes were wide and surprised, his arms around me releasing. I was flung from his grasp and I fell back onto the mattress. Rolling onto my side, I was quick to detangle myself from the sheets.

Breathing hard, the room was too dark to see what was happening to him, but I could hear Greg struggling. I rubbed my eyes, trying to regroup. When my eyes at last began to accept the shadows, I pieced together what darkness I could, surprised when I saw Jake's soft veiled light floating amongst it. I drew in a sharp breath of air, the safety the light offered like a shot to the heart. The struggling continued, and sitting there, with my breath held tight, I traced the broad outline of Jake's arched back. His hands flailed at Greg's face, swift and silent, his ability to see in the dark far surpassing Greg's.

"Jake!" I gasped. *What was he doing here? How—*

Jake looked at me, his eyes flashing with the toxicity of that soft, veiled light. I froze.

Jake had a look of guilt on his face, catching ever so slightly in the moonlight from the window. The room grew warm once more, and that's when I realized what had really been the case. Jake had been my late night visitor. Jake had been the watcher as I slept—not Greg.

"*Jake,*" I whispered.

He stole a glance. *I'm sorry,* his mind read.

Greg tossed him off, seeing the opportunity. Jake fell to the side like a sack of grain, discarded with little effort. I swallowed hard, my hopes of rescue shattered because of me. Greg slowly rose from the ground, brushing himself off with an amused grin on his face.

"You've gotten yourself a rabid bat to protect you, I see." Greg straightened his long black coat, smoothing his hand down one sleeve.

Jake moaned from the corner, trying to sit up. Greg approached him, eyes on me. He clenched his jaw as he kicked Jake in the stomach, getting a rise out of the horrified look on my face. Jake coughed hard, spitting blood onto the floor before slumping into it, unmoving.

"Jake!" I whispered harshly. I wanted to cry, but my breath caught in my throat as Greg's arms wrapped around me, squeezing tight. I could hear him struggling against my poisonous skin, but it didn't stop him. He balled me in his arms, my gaze trying to remain on Jake, hoping he was alright as I let Greg take me. My arms were weak, my heart tired. I knew that struggling was useless.

"Jake..."

MAX:

Sitting in the dark office of the apothecary, I tried to think of what to do. Jane didn't want me around, but I had to be there to protect her closer than ever, preferably visibly beside her. How can I make amends with her? How can I make her see that there are more pressing problems we face, other than the simple problem of our connection? On the whole of things, Jane needed to know that danger was out there waiting for her. I could not keep her in the dark this time.

On the desk sat a bronze rose. I was again reminded of the day when I first learned of Jane, and the rose I'd bought for Avery. It had been an empty gesture of dying love, but the look on her face was pure innocence despite that. Avery had been a harmless creature, and I was having a hard time imagining her as the Shadow Pixie in Srixon's explanation. In all the time I had known Avery, I never once saw a glimmer of that evil. Would I recognize this new, darker version of Avery if she were standing right in front of me?

Finding her was my primary task, but from what Srixon had told me, Avery hadn't been seen in years. For all I knew she lived halfway around the world. I bit my lip. What would she do when she saw me, and what kind of danger did she pose? Did she know about this supposed foreseen future with Jane? And in what way would Jane be important to any of it? In what way would Avery?

Jane was just a girl, just a human thrown into this world as a Seoul. I sighed, knowing that wasn't entirely true. To me she wasn't just a girl. To me she was everything. Jane held a spark of something I'd never seen before, and that wasn't just our soul inside her, but something larger than that. Was my purpose here not solely to find her, but to truly be the one to protect this important being whose future was bigger than any of us could even imagine? Would she finally bring peace to the war between human and magick?

I wished I knew more, and I wished I could see this Truth

involving them, but it was kept hidden for a reason, and that's what scared me the most. From what I gathered out of Srixon's vague explanation, it wasn't hard to see just how big of a deal this was. I had never seen him act so grave, so serious. Bottom line was I needed to watch Jane.

I needed to watch Jane.

I stood abruptly, knowing what was required only to be knocked off balance by a sharp blow to the face. I fell to the floor, startled as I looked frantically around the room, but no one was there.

Gregory.

The pounding pain in my cheekbone stopped as abruptly as it had come. I took a moment to understand what had happened and what it meant. No other pain followed. When nothing more ensued, I stood from the floor and brushed myself off. In a snap I disappeared, headed to Jane's room.

Appearing at the foot of her bed, I was perplexed to see she wasn't there. I circled the bed and felt her sheets—they were cold. Disappearing again, I appeared in Emily's room, hoping she'd know where Jane was. Her bed was also empty, but not cold. Her sheets were in disarray, thrown about the room—then there was a moan. My eyes darted in the direction of the sound, surprised when I saw Jake lying in a small pool of his own blood. Falling to his side, I carefully supported his weight and hauled him to his feet. With the back of my hand, I wiped his face with the sleeve of my jacket.

"Jake, what happened?" I whispered firmly.

Jake struggled to open his eyes, murmuring inaudible sounds from his bloodied lips.

"What?" I leaned closer and shook him gently, trying to

convey the importance.

"Greg," he managed to say, louder this time, the words draining him as he fell against me. I looked at the puddle of blood on the ground, fearing the amount he'd lost. He needed blood, and now. I pulled a knife from my pocket and cut into my own skin at the crease of my elbow, where it would flow freely. Holding Jake against the wall, I guided the slow flow of blood to his lips. He took it unwillingly.

I sighed long and hard. Jake grimaced, but the light was returning to his cheeks as his body heat once again rose well above a human temperature. After a minute, the cut on my arm began to heal over and Jake was able to stand on his own two feet, his lips pursed as though he'd just bit into a lime.

"Bleck!" he remarked. "What does Emily see in that?"

I chuckled with relief. Hearing him act like the Jake I knew was a good sign.

He wiped a hand across his continually perspiring brow, streaking it with blood. "Emily's gone."

I looked at the stain on the carpet. "Greg took her?" I didn't see how, but I could smell the lingering burn of his flesh.

Jake nodded. "Yeah."

"Did you hear anything else?"

Jake rubbed his stomach. "He was going on about how he needed her, and then something about Avery. I can't be sure just what that means. I was pretty livid at that point. It's hard to know just what he said."

I gave him a reproachful glare. "You shouldn't have been here..." I put my hand on his shoulder. "...but I'm glad you were."

Jake shrugged. "I can't help it." I could see the look in his eyes, the look of a man barred from what he loved—a look like my own.

"She has Wes, Jake," I reminded him, as I have before.

Jake became flustered. "I know. I know that." He began pacing. "Can we just..." he stopped, helplessly holding his hands in the air before slapping them against his legs. "Never mind." He gave up. "There are more important things to do right now than discuss this, don't you think?"

I had to agree. "How did Greg take her?"

Jake snorted. "Like anyone does—hands around waist, *'come on darlin', you're mine'*, you know?"

I shook my head. "I get that, but he's supposed to be somewhat... *allergic* to her."

Jake shrugged dramatically. "I don't know! I just walked into this. How am I supposed to understand that?"

I shook my head. "And you remember nothing about where they were going?"

Jake thought for a moment, being cooperative. "No. I don't think he bothered to mention that." Jake's jaw clenched. "He's a real *jerk*."

"I know that."

Jake's eyes narrowed. "So are you."

My head tilted as I glared. "That's not helping this situation."

Jake grumbled.

I took a moment before adding to the circumstances. "Jane's gone, too," I admitted, ashamed that I'd lose track of what was most important to me as an angel, and a man. My head dropped.

Jake approached me, brows raised. "Taken?" he asked.

I shrugged, conveying it wasn't quite like that, at least not initially. Jane had simply left me.

Jake snorted. "She left, didn't she? I'm not surprised. With your track record…" He stopped talking as he saw the look on my face. Shrugging his shoulders he bravely added, "Just sayin'."

I denied my desire to blow up at him, fixing my hands at my sides. "I need to find Avery."

Jake's brows lifted with surprise.

"Will you help me?" I added, further swallowing my pride.

Just then, two owls flew through the window. I knew one was Wes, but I didn't recognize the other. Wes looked up at Jake, and then to me.

"Emily's been taken," I said bluntly.

Wes looked to Jake. His mind raced with confusion, his thoughts still directed toward me as anger rose in the waves of his mind.

"Yes. Jake was here when it happened." I tried my best to remain neutral.

Wes's eyes narrowed at Jake as the questions continued to pour out of his mind.

I shrugged. "I don't know why, Wes. Why don't you ask him yourself? He's right there."

Wes's feather's fluffed in defiance. Diverting my attention away from them, I briefly looked to the new owl behind Wes for an explanation as to who she was. The owl divulged her relationship to Wes openly.

"You're his sister?" I asked in a whisper while Jake and Wes were occupied.

Her head tilted.

"I never knew." I added.

The wild owl flew through the window then, landing beside Wes's sister. Everything began to make sense.

Jake shifted his weight and shook his head, bringing my attention back to him. "I'm not here to take your girlfriend, Wes, so chill out."

I gave Jake a warning look to behave, hoping Wes wouldn't see it. Jake only glowered.

"I can't take your girlfriend," Jake added, sounding shamelessly disappointed by that fact. "Remember? There are rules."

Wes chortled sharply.

"If there weren't rules?" Jake laughed. "Then things would be different."

Wes lunged at Jake but his sister stepped in, grabbing his tail with her beak.

I cringed and swiftly closed the distance between me and Jake, pinching his arm and giving him my last warning. "Stop." Now is not the time to tell Wes about this. I cleared my throat, addressing everyone. "Has anyone seen Jane recently?" I felt ashamed to ask. I should know.

Jake was the first to answer. "She's been hanging out with this new pixie friend of hers, Navia. She doesn't seem to care much for us anymore, or you, apparently."

My teeth ground together. That was a low blow. "What pixie? I haven't seen a pixie."

"Last I saw them was at the Halloween party earlier tonight," Jake added.

"What was this pixie like?" I asked again.

Wes scratched at the floor to get my attention, explaining her to me in great detail—too much detail.

I swallowed hard. My gut was telling me that something about this new friend of Jane's wasn't right. I felt my hand begin to shake—it was too much of a coincidence; besides, pixies didn't make friends with Seouls, only Shadow Pixies did because they liked the death surrounding them. My next statement proved difficult to say aloud.

"I'm afraid that pixie she's with is a very old friend of mine. I'm afraid she's with Avery." Those simple words put an end to the tension in the room.

Wes's already large owl eyes were now larger. He hopped over to Emily's bed where he slid under the covers, his head popping out the other end—human.

"*What?*" he gasped.

I shrugged. "I came upon some information that may suggest that this old friend of mine, Avery, may be out to get Jane. From what you tell me of Navia, I believe it's the same person," I explained. "I'm not sure just why, or what she wants with Jane, but I can assure you it's not good."

Wes's gawking expression didn't change. "I know who *Avery* is, Max. You don't have to refer to her as your *old friend*. She was your fiancé," he added bitterly.

I glanced at Jake, my patience with him just about worn out. "You told them, didn't you?"

Jake nodded brazenly.

He was really testing my trust today. I shook my head. "How much has she been around?" I asked Wes, not wanting to hear Jake speak.

"Like every living second since you left, it seems." Wes laughed, but nervously. "She gave me the creeps she was so gorgeous. I can't believe you were engaged to her once."

Jake snorted, taking another jab at Wes. "I thought you loved Emily," he challenged.

"Jake. Stop," I demanded, my voice booming and on edge.

Wes grinned, amused by my anger toward Jake before turning his attention back on the main subject. "Her name was Navia, though, not Avery. Are you positive you've got it right, because pixies all seem to look the same to me," Wes added.

I nodded. "It has to be her." Avery used to tell me all the time how she wished she had a more distinctive name, like Navia.

"So, it's really her?" Wes recognized the truth on my face.

"I think that's what the man is saying," Jake snapped.

I nodded again, more slowly, still ignoring Jake. "I think so. She's extremely dangerous, too. I don't think you can even understand how much."

Jake frowned, looking at his hands. "She's a Shadow Pixie, isn't she?"

I allowed myself to answer him this time, nodding gravely.

Jake shook his head. "I knew there was something funny about her."

Wes swore under his breath. "Well, this can't be good." He grunted. "Even if I don't know what a Shadow Pixie is, it just sounds bad. Not to mention the fact that Jane and Avery both are, or *were*, romantically involved with you. That's never a good thing. It's like two roosters in a cage."

Wes knew enough about disgruntled ex-girlfriends to see that the two of them being friends was a premeditative and dangerous thing.

"What the heck does Avery want to do with Jane? If she wanted to kill her she would have done it, considering the fact they've been locked at the hip the last week. Avery didn't really appear violent toward Jane, either," Jake interjected naively.

Wes and I both looked at him.

Wes laughed. "Just because she hasn't done anything to her doesn't mean she won't. Chicks are crazy. Avery's probably just playing with her first. It doesn't take a genius to put the pieces together as to why. Avery probably wants revenge for what Max did to her. She's just playing it cool until the right opportunity comes along to… do whatever." Wes looked at me nervously.

Jake ignored the look of concern Wes and I were sharing. "At least I'm not the one naked under a sheet right now."

Wes's sister chortled angrily at Jake, Jake disregarded her anger.

Wes shook his head. "Lame rebuttal, man—*lame.*"

I could see where this was going. I'd been here with Wes before. "Come on, guys. Seriously… *stop.*" Aside from removing their tongues, I didn't see how this was ever going to end. It was better to just move on.

Their glares both turned to me.

"Alright then, smarty pants. What do you propose we do?" Wes's anger was transferred, his sister still perched like his shadow, fluffed and ready to defend Wes's honor should I threaten it.

I sighed long and hard. "We just fix it."

WES:

I spiraled to the ground with Stella outside Emily's room, watching Jake climb from the window as though he'd done it before. How had he gotten there faster than me, and all the way from Winter Wood? Yeah, *right.* He had been closer than that.

I'd woken the minute I felt her heart surge to life. I knew that Emily wasn't just having a nightmare. The fear from her was eminent, and her every heartbeat was like a drumming alarm. Granted it took me a moment to gather myself and Lacy, but I had arrived as soon as I could. There was no way anyone could have been faster, aside from Max, maybe—*apparently*—but that was Max.

My talons ripped at the dirt below my feet as I considered the possible reasons for Jake's timely appearance. They were all bad.

Max stood beside me, looking down at me. I looked up at him. I didn't like the look on his face. It was pity. Why was it pity? What did he know? Like I said, having Max get there before me came as no surprise—it was Max. But the sweaty vampire? A slow, *clumsy* guy? Was he really agile enough to arrive before me? For the most part he was just human. He couldn't fly, couldn't even run very fast.

He must have already been there?

Was he involved?

Was he… I chortled loudly. Stella nudged me, trying to calm me.

Max scowled. "Concentrate on finding Emily, Wes, not that. You're driving me nuts."

His remark only made me angrier. Of course I was concentrating on finding Emily. She was all I cared about. Lacy flashed me some images of a hug, comfort—it was our way of communicating. Stella flashed me similar images, but with a bit more zest to it. I tried to reprimand her, thinking it was hardly the time. Stella looked hurt, but she was just a bird.

Annoyed, I quickly flew up to the window of my room. Lacy followed me. I dove in, landing on my bed and gathering some clothes in my mouth. Lacy did the same and we quickly changed, creeping down the stairs as quietly as possible and out the front door. I was going to need to be able to communicate more openly, so for right now, the animal in me was going to have to wait.

"What about the house?" I offered, catching up to Jake and Max as they stood on the lawn, discussing possible places Greg could have taken her. "Like before."

Max looked at me, a glimmer in his eye. "He's not there."

His reply was loaded.

"How do you know?" I pressed.

"Because… I destroyed it." Max turned away from me, walking toward the street where his Land Rover Defender was parked at the curb, already running.

"You destroyed the house? When?" I followed after him.

Max looked over his shoulder, but the spark in his eye was furious. Something inside him had changed. There was darkness.

His typical comfortable confidence was fading to disgruntled exhaustion, like a man grown tired of life's pointless games. There was a chip on his shoulder that wasn't there before, and it was a big one.

"I did it recently," was all he said, lacing it with such bitterness, that I knew it was a subject I no longer wanted to venture into.

Jake brushed past me, hopping into the back seat of Max's car.

"Surprised you didn't take the front," I challenged.

Jake turned to Lacy as she arrived at my side, her red hair flowing. He gave her a wink. "Ladies get the front."

To my disdain, Lacy giggled.

I hissed at her, but she ignored me. Circling the car, I took the other back seat beside Jake. I didn't want to be near him anymore, but at least I could keep an eye on him here.

"What about Avery? Where are her hangouts?" Jake leaned forward between the two front seats. Max turned onto the road, the car whipping fast as we all held on.

"The problem is that Avery always had a lot of hang outs."

"It's got to be someplace private, wouldn't you suppose? She wouldn't want to risk anyone recognizing her while she was with Jane."

"You would think."

Just then Max's eyes grew wide and he slammed on the breaks. We all flew forward as the car skidded sideways. Then there was a thud.

I looked up fast, feeling it, feeling *her.* "Emily!"

I fought with my seatbelt, but Jake was faster. He got out of the car just before me. Pushing harder, the buckle finally released and I scrambled out behind him. My gaze crested over the hood, seeing Emily was sitting up on the pavement, rubbing her head. Jake was already at her side, rubbing her back.

"Are you all right?" he asked.

"Yeah, I'm fine. It was my fault." She was looking at him in a daze, her eyes buried deep within his.

My whole body tensed. I stormed toward her and shoved Jake to the side. *"Get away from her."*

Emily moaned as I hoisted her off the ground, cradling her in my arms.

"Emily, what happened?"

Max had appeared before me, skin whiter than I'd ever seen it before. "Are you all right? I didn't… I didn't even see you."

Emily nodded, smiling at Max. "I'm fine. Most people don't see me, so don't worry."

"Did Greg let you go?" Max pressed.

She shook her head. "No. I just… I got away."

Max leaned closer, hand hovering just above the skin on her arm. I looked where he was, seeing streaks of freshly raised blisters across her skin. I suddenly held her more gently, having not noticed them before.

"He couldn't keep me," she whispered. "I burn him."

I grunted. "It looks more like he burned *you*."

"Where did he take you?" Max withdrew his hands, unable to help her as her poisonous body was as much of a detriment to him as it had been to Greg.

"Not far. Into the woods." She pointed ahead of us before turning back, expression hopeless and scared. "They're going to kill Jane," she warned.

"Was Avery there?"

Emily nodded. "Max… I had no idea that was her. I should

have seen it."

Max gave her a look of confidence. "It's my fault. Not yours."

Just then, two giant shadows rose behind Max. I took a step back, not understanding what I saw until Max lifted off the ground, carried by heavy tarps of feathers. "Jake, follow me. Wes and Lacy, take Emily home and keep her safe."

I watched as he rose up, his giant grey wings unlike anything I'd seen before.

Jake jogged up to me. "Take care of Emily, will you?"

I growled.

Lacy grasped Jake's shoulder and spun him away from me. "Leave them alone. I think you've done enough."

"I'm just trying to help." Jake shook his head and backed away. "Sorry." He plunged into the front seat of the Rover and slammed the door. The tires spun with a final look, but the look was only for Emily.

"What a *creep*," Lacy murmured, watching Max's car disappear around the end of the block.

"Come on. Let's go." Emily's fingers grasped at my shirt, her head nuzzled under my arm as my other held Lacy's. I tried to pull her along with us as I turned, but her feet remained planted.

"No, brother. I think I should help." She slid out of my grasp and clicked at Stella, guiding her up onto her shoulder.

My expression grew fierce. "No. You shouldn't. You have to come with me." I wanted to grab Lacy and drag her inside, but my hands were already full.

"Let me do this. I need to."

"*Why?*" I spat.

She shrugged. "Because I didn't help before, and now our

parents are dead."

Mouth agape, Lacy didn't allow me the chance to reply. She changed into the owl, clothes falling to the ground as Stella picked up the air that had been dropped beneath her. Together, they both followed in Max's direction, and I was left split between the only two things that mattered to me—family and Emily.

AVERY:

"Perfect." I looked skyward, hearing—*feeling*—him approaching.

"What's perfect?" Jane asked, stumbling beside me.

I handed her the bottle of champagne, our Disney dresses dirtied from our little hike in the woods. Jane thought we were being adventurous, free spirited teens, taking on our right to be young and reckless, but really I was luring her to her death. With her out of the way, Max would suffer, and then I would come along and sweep him off his feet. I would make him happy. I would finally get my light back.

"Just the night, my pet. It's *perfect.*"

We stopped.

Jane plopped herself on a fallen log. "It's *dark.*" She frowned dramatically.

I laughed. "Yes. I know that." I snapped my fingers, igniting a spark of fire in my hands. A handy trick I had acquired from Max.

Jane gasped. "I can do that, too!" She narrowed her eyes and concentrated hard on her hand, faltering as sparks flew. *"Ouch,"* she murmured, burning herself.

I discreetly rolled my eyes.

The spark in her hand finally ignited, illuminating her frustrated face as it turned to elation. "Ha! See!"

I nodded. "Very good! I didn't know a Seoul could do that."

She sighed and slumped forward, staring at the light. "Max taught me."

"Oh, did he?" Of course he had. I tried to act interested.

I heard a rustle then, but not a rustle anyone but me could have heard. Looking up, I saw the faint shadow of Greg behind a tree, just out of the light from our fires. I smiled. Jane took another swig of champagne, stretching her feet out before her. Her flame was messy and blue, sparks singeing holes in her yellow dress.

I opened my mind to Greg. *Where's Emily?*

She got away.

What?

He shrugged.

"My sister doesn't like you, I don't think." Jane admitted, her words buttery with champagne.

"Not many girls do like me," I mindlessly answered.

How did she get away, Greg? I pressed, subduing my desire to stand and smack him.

She's got that stupid snake venom in her. It makes things a little tricky.

You better fix this. I wanted to do this tonight.

"I don't see how girls could hate you, though. You're so nice!" Jane exclaimed, turning to me with a lopsided grin and squinty eyes.

"I threaten them, I guess."

I already have fixed it, Greg added, his upper lip catching the light with a sly grin. *Seems we'll even have the audience you desire. Max is coming.*

I already knew Max was coming. That was a feeling I couldn't ignore. *And just how did you fix it?*

Before I could get an answer, there was a distant scream. Jane jumped, dropping the champagne bottle on the ground with a thud. "Oh my gosh. What was that?"

I wanted to ask the same thing, but turning back to Greg, I saw he was gone.

Jane stood, a thick billowing smell of adrenaline seeping from her skin. "Should we go look?" Her eyes met mine, nervous.

I shrugged, disliking the fact that I'd lost control of this game. I no longer knew what was happening. "Maybe it's someone to save," I stood slowly, trying to play along.

"*Um…*" Jane was faltering.

"Come on, you know you want to do this." I paused, looking in the direction the scream had come from. "Let's just go check it out. It might not be anything at all. Could just be a group of kids like you and I, out in the woods goofing around." I gave her a nudge on the arm, plucking the bottle out of the mud and placing it in her hands.

She took one last big gulp, properly placed under my spell. Her mind was malleable and confused, and I would mold it.

JANE:

Something about that scream was not innocent, and something about it felt familiar, like the way chocolate tastes. I lowered the bottle of champagne from my lips, letting the last bit of sweet, perfumed liquid trickle down my throat. My heart began to pound.

"Okay," I agreed. "I'll do it." It felt like a detached part of me had been the one to say it, not me. My insides were screaming for me to listen, to stay put, but for whatever reason this new part made me ignore all that. I shook my head, trying to straighten myself out.

Navia took my hand, yanking me forward before I got the chance.

I stumbled over logs and brush behind her. "Can we slow down?"

She shook her head, her ringlets shaking off a cloud of glittery cinnamon. "No. We might miss the opportunity! We have to hurry."

My heart felt like lead, but my body kept moving. What if this really was it? What if this was my chance to get out of the spell Max and I shared and rise as an equal. This could change everything for me. I would live as long as Max did. I could be as strong as Max was.

We could be *together.*

My arms tingled with the thought, practically feeling the way his skin had felt against mine, the intoxicating cloud of love that locked us together. Then the cloud grew dark, and that other part of me sent out one last warning.

What if this would ruin that?

What if Max's love for me was just because I was his to guard? I hadn't thought of this in great detail. I dug my heels into the dirt, but Avery was stronger than me. Instead of stopping, I toppled over onto the muddy forest floor.

I heard her gasp as she let go of my hand. "Jane!" She knelt, hooking her arms under mine. "What in the *world* are you doing?"

I forced myself to my knees, mud slopping from my arms. "Just wait, okay?"

"Wait for what? This is what you *want,* Jane. Trust me." She let go of me.

There was another scream then, louder this time as we'd gotten closer. It was a woman's scream, and something about it ripped into my soul.

Avery's once pleasant demeanor fell sour. "Get up, Jane. I'm not giving you a choice. You need this."

MAX:

I flew as fast as I could, but something in my gut told me it wasn't fast enough. The spot where Emily had managed to free herself from Greg had long since been abandoned, his trail leading farther up the mountain. It twisted and wound, confusing me, stalling me.

What was he doing?

Then there was the scream, and I knew what he'd done.

JANE:

I was confused by Navia's sudden change. "*What?*" I gaped, knees sinking into earth.

"I'm not giving you a choice," she repeated, this time with a smile. "I know this is what you need, even if you don't see it."

I'd sworn that the first time she'd said it she hadn't said it with the same wash of friendliness. No part of her first statement had felt like she was looking after my best interests, but rather commanding me. I looked to the ground, wondering what I was doing here, wondering who I was.

"Come on." Navia offered me her hand.

I didn't want to take it. I didn't want to touch her, but that something inside me that was controlling me against my will felt too warm to ignore. Taken by the tone in her voice, I saw my arm reach up like a puppet until my hand was placed in hers. She hoisted me off the ground with little effort.

"That's right. You can do it." She smoothed my tangled hair from my face. "Now let's hurry."

Navia pulled me after her once more, dodging trees and bushes, until finally, the forest opened up. The smell of wet moss was in the air, and just then, a cool mist hit my face. The rushing noise I was hearing became the recognizable sound of water, and I knew we'd made our way to the river.

Navia halted, and I ran into her.

A voice welcomed us. "There you are."

I didn't have to see the person to know who it was. My back steeled, and I cowardly hid behind Navia.

"Who are you?" Navia commanded.

I shook.

"Let that woman go," she added.

There was the distinct sound of someone struggling. Knowing Greg, I also knew he was about to kill them. That's what he did.

Greg laughed. "Not your concern, *pixie*. Besides, I wasn't talking to you."

My breathing stopped all together, my hand clasping onto the blue silk of Navia's bustle.

"Come out, Jane," Greg teased.

I slowly peered over Navia's shoulder, eyes cresting the arc of her neck.

"There you are!" he announced, hands in the air.

My throat closed up. He had a rope in his hand, and as my eyes followed it to the cliff behind him, my heart sank when I saw who it was attached to. The woman I had heard screaming, the woman whose voice struck my soul, and the woman that was my mother. She was his prey. I was hit with a wall of déjà vu, taken back to the vision I'd had in the kitchen the other week—Mother falling from a cliff.

Greg walked to the ledge where he had her lying on the ground. He picked her up, holding her with one arm as her feet dangled over the edge. The rushing sound of water reminded me of the assuredly sharp rocks below, nature cursing at itself as water carved through the earth.

That déjà vu had felt so real, and now I knew why. What I'd seen in her future death was coming true, but how? It had always been a silly thing, but this was exact, right down to the minor details of what my mother was wearing. How had I seen this? How could it have come true?

"Jane!" My mother screamed. "Jane, get out of here!"

A chill ran down my spine, finding my visions suddenly more than a game, but reality. I stepped around Navia. "Mom!"

I felt a hand on my arm, stopping me. "Jane, wait. That's *dangerous*," Navia warned.

I looked back at her, confused. Since when had she changed her mind?

She shrugged.

I shook my head. "You were right. I have to do this. That's my *mother*."

Navia gasped, her delicate hand covering her lips and releasing from my arm. "It *is?*"

I narrowed my gaze, sensing a fake energy from Navia, but I didn't have the time to question it.

I turned back to Greg. He was watching Navia with a look in his eye, a look I couldn't decipher. "Greg." I got his attention.

He coolly looked away from Navia, sighing dramatically. "Well, darling, are you going to save your mother?"

"What do you want?" I demanded.

He began to laugh. "I want you *dead.* I want my brother back, and as long as you're here, that won't happen." He jostled my mother in his arms.

Mother released another scream, one that resonated deep within the pit of my stomach.

He spun my mother into him, clasping a hand over her mouth. "You're a virus that won't go away, Jane. For sixty years you've plagued me. *Sixty.*" He spun my mother away from him, swinging her toward the cliff.

I screamed a scream that was so loud it should have been in a dream, only to clasp my hand over my mouth as Greg halted, saving my mother from going over the edge. *"Mom,"* I whispered painfully to myself, reaching my arm out toward her and taking another step closer.

"Don't," she stammered, her eyes watering with tears. "Your father wouldn't... He wouldn't *w*—want this. Let him kill me."

I froze, dropping my hand. Everyone was silent. Everyone was staring at me.

My mother slowly began to sob, hands muddied and covering her eyes. Mother had known about us, about father, about *everything.* I could see that now. For whatever reason, I saw a lot. Flashes of time sprinkled across my mind: The way my father looked at my mother, the way she always seemed careful, hindered. Most of all, it was in the way she looked at Max, as though my mother knew who he was. Her innocence was just a disguise.

With Mother whimpering, Greg once again teased me as he lifted her, toes dragging across the ground until there was no ground at all. My gaze was fixed on her feet, dangling above a final expanse that would be her end. I saw her future death, repeating over and over in my head, the same way it had in the kitchen that day. I had already seen her die a million times. Since I was seven, her deaths had played out to me in many forms, with many endings, but this was the one that had mattered. I could not bear to see her die again, even if it meant my own death to achieve that.

"You won't die," Navia whispered behind me. "Remember, Jane. You can be the angel this time. You can become strong enough to defeat Greg. Just *think*."

I gritted my teeth; she was right. Though I could never kill Greg, having the ability to stand against him meant a lot. There was this possibility, and that's all I needed.

Greg's smirk grew then, his hand around my mother's waist slackening. "I'm tired of waiting for an answer from you. One way or another, someone's got to die."

My mother began to squirm, hands grasping at anything they could.

A spark ignited inside me, a spark I hadn't expected. I lurched forward, seeing the world pass by me in slow motion. Greg's arms released from my mother's waist all together, his laugh following in a slow succession, like the beat of my heart.

My feet barely touched the ground as I ran, kicking up dirt of an Earth I was about to leave, but only for a moment. Seeing my mother begin to fall, I knew I wasn't nearly fast enough to make it. Speeding up, I also knew I was running too fast to ever stop myself before reaching the cliff. There was no turning back now. I had already made my choice.

Greg stepped out of my way, my mother's arms unable to grab hold of his leather jacket. Falling, *falling,* the cliff's edge began to swallow her. Taking one last deep breath, I leapt, closing my eyes as I saw the last death I would ever see: my own. I smiled as I felt my hand touch my mother's skin. I clutched tightly, my whole human life leading up to this singular end. With the force of my forward movement, I pulled her back like a basketball player keeping the ball in play. I felt her breath as it passed my ear, imagining her heart beating for years to come. She was thrust behind me where I knew she would be able to grasp onto the edge of the cliff. I leapt, eyes still shut, but seeing all I needed to within the pictures of my mind. I felt suddenly free, and the world stopped turning. Air caressed my skin like a hundred fingers, silent, silent…

…silent.

Silence gave way to ambient noise. I opened my eyes, feeling as though no time had passed. I hadn't felt a thing.

Looking around, I was no place new. This was the In-between I'd visited every night for ten years. This was like home. I smiled, letting out a yelp of accomplishment and jumping in the air. I knew how to get home from here, and I would.

Facing a field, I turned and was met with a long meandering river that cut through the middle of everything. This was new, but I knew what it was all the same. This was the edge of the In-between where the world met the Ever After. I smiled again, the free feeling I'd felt jumping off the cliff remaining with me. I felt refreshed, in love, and alive in a way I hadn't felt since my father's death.

"Jane!"

A bridge appeared over the river, or had it been there before? It was arched, long, *inviting.* My eyes traced the enticing curve of it, and on the other side stood my father.

"Daddy!" I screamed, voice cracking with years of pent-up emotion. Unable to resist, I ran toward the bridge, halting just where the grass met the planking.

"Jane, darling. I never thought I'd see you again."

I felt as though I were floating. "I've missed you so much." I shook my head. "Why did you have to go?"

He simply smiled at me, tilting his head. "Come, I want to give you a hug." He opened his arms before him, the way he used to. There was a strong tug to go to him, but a part of me wanted to resist, a big part of me.

"I don't think I can," I whispered, unconvincingly.

"Please, Jane. I've missed you so much." His face became pained. "I've been so alone here."

My heart strings tugged. I took a step forward.

Daddy smiled. "I won't make you stay. Just a hug." He took a step toward me, but stopped.

"What's wrong?" I asked.

He frowned, his mouth curling in such a familiar way. "I can't go any farther."

I felt a horrifying need to help him flow through me. I took another step, and then another. Before I knew it, my father was only a few feet away. My senses washed in and out of consciousness like the water below the bridge. "Why didn't you tell us about any of this?" Wind from the Ever After blew across my face, smelling not like death, but something far better.

"I couldn't. It would have put you in danger. Besides, it was not you that had the gift of magick, but your sister." He tried to reach for me, but some invisible force held his arm at bay.

"I deserved to know." The words felt wrong—selfish.

Father did not reply.

"I'm sorry." I bowed my head.

He nodded in acceptance of my apology. "It's all right, my darling. You're here now."

I looked up at him, his brownish red hair looking just like Emily's, his eyes like mine.

"I've missed you so much." He sighed, backing away. "And I shouldn't tempt you like this." He turned his back to me. "You should go."

I felt angered by his cold shoulder. How could he turn his back on me again? "No, Dad."

His head lifted and he looked over his shoulder. Tears stained his face.

I couldn't bear to see him this way. He had been all I'd ever cared about. He was my best friend. I wanted to be with him. I no longer wanted to go back to a life where he would not be there.

He turned once more, offering me one last chance at a hug.

I took a deep breath, taking the final few steps until I was welcomed into his outstretched arms. He held me tight, his embrace warm, real, *safe*—

"My *pet*," his voice changed, hand circling my back. "My dear pet." I lurched away, tumbling backward onto my heels. Horror struck me, deceit and lies. Navia was standing in my father's place. Her eyes were black, like ink in a vial with no bottom. Her face was twisted into an unmistakably evil grin, and all sense of courtesy had vanished.

I turned to run, but the bridge was gone. I stood on the water's edge, pulled back and away from it by an unseen force. I bowed back to Navia, scared. "Navia? What is this?"

She sighed long and hard. "Avery," she began. "My name is *Avery*."

"Avery?" I narrowed my eyes.

She sighed long and hard. "I know. I hate it, but it's my name." She shook her head, eyes locking once again with mine and spearing my heart. "I almost didn't do this, my pet. You're so much fun after all, but like most good things, they have to end. I had to remember what my goals were."

"I don't understand." My mind was a blur, looking for the bridge. Was I still in the In-between, or the Ever After?

"You were in my way, plain and simple. You don't think I could just let you waltz into my life and tear it apart without my eventual revenge, did you? No, no, no. *No.* You have to pay, just as I did." She walked up to me, pushing me with her finger, strong enough to knock me off balance. "You do not deserve what was to be mine. You deserve what I got instead: a broken heart."

I steadied myself and swung at her, but my hand was like smoke, passing right through her.

She laughed. "Nice try, darling, but I'm not the dead one here. *You are*."

"You touched *me,*" I challenged childishly.

She shook her head. "Pixie magick. Nothing but a trick. I can come in and out of the Ever After at my leisure because I'm the Shade. Where do you think I've been hiding for so long?" She snapped her fingers and my father suddenly appeared. "I guess you can have him now, though. Consider it a consolation." She shoved him toward me and our two ghostlike clouds passed through each other. I stumbled to the ground.

"Jane," my father gasped, my real father.

I sat up to look at him. "Daddy, is that really you?"

He crawled toward me and tried to grasp me but couldn't.

"Ah!" Avery screamed dramatically. "So touching, and yet so *tragic!* Finally you get your daddy back but you can't even touch him!"

I scrambled to my feet, or what could be considered feet. Standing still, the cloud around me concentrated once more, making me appear whole. "You tricked me!" I screamed.

Avery chuckled. "You're finally realizing that?"

I clenched my jaw, running at her once more, but again, my ghostly cloud crashed right through her, splitting into a billion particles of dust. I struggled to put myself back together as she stood over me, arms crossed.

"I better get going, my pet. I have a life with a fiancé to rekindle." Her grin already haunted me. "Happy Ever After." She backed away, beginning to disappear with her hand in the air, fingers dancing. *"Ta ta!"*

And just like that, she was gone.

MAX:

"Greg!" My feet slammed into earth, heart aching. I stormed up to him, noses inches apart. "*Where is she?*"

A silvery cloud appeared beside him, emanating with the smell of cinnamon.

"There you are." Avery appeared, her familiar voice twisting my stomach.

She was so different, and yet so familiar. There was shade all around her, her once beautiful eyes bleeding shadows. I backed away, suddenly overcome with nausea. Falling to my knees, I buckled over. Greg did the same.

"You feel that, don't you?" Avery laughed, her footfalls so silent that I hadn't heard her close the small distance between us, her mouth right next to my ear. "Don't you, *darling?*"

"You didn't tell me this was going to *hurt!*" Greg complained from where he rolled in the dirt beside me.

Avery's weight shifted, gravel crunching below her feet. "Oh shut up, baby." She spat over her shoulder before sighing and turning back to me. Hooking one long nail under my chin, she lifted it. My eyes met her dark and empty ones. "Hurts, doesn't it? When someone rips your heart out?"

I heard Jane's mother's frightened breathing, barely able to look up to see the blur of her body near the cliff.

"What *d*—did you *do?*" I demanded shakily.

"You don't know? You don't feel that life inside you, making you alive again?"

I could feel it. My body was warm and tingly. Every emotion I once felt from Jane was now mine alone.

"I took the only thing that mattered to you, darling. But look what I gave you in return!" She grasped my shoulders, pulling me to my feet with little effort. "I wanted to show you how much I love you. What better way than to give you your life back?"

My legs felt like jelly. "I don't want my life back."

She frowned. "Like being an angel too much, do you?"

I heard an owl's cry then, and I cringed. I didn't want them to come. I didn't want more death.

Avery grumbled and dropped me. My knees buckled, sending me crashing to the ground. She looked skyward, noticing the owl as well. "Now what?" She marched back to Greg, kicking him in the side. "Get up, you idiot. Take care of this."

He moaned, but managed to stand. The pain of my split from Jane was over, but the emotional pain still left me shaken. The owls descended, landing beside me.

Are you okay? Lacy asked, eyes darting between me and Avery.

Her pet just stared at Avery, feathers fluffed and eyes nervous.

I nodded, but my mind spoke otherwise.

I felt Lacy's anger and saw her thoughts turn irate.

Don't, Lacy. It's not worth it.

She ignored me, slowly turning square with Avery. Her feathers inflated, and her wings were held extended at her sides.

Lacy, don't. I tried one last time.

Foolishly, Lacy ignored me, lunging toward Avery. Avery welcomed her attack, simply swatting her away with one hand. Lacy's body fell to the ground, alive but stunned.

Avery laughed. "Seriously pathetic. You need better friends."

The other owl did the same, angered by her master's defeat. Avery swatted her to the ground just as she had Lacy, only this time she finished by stomping on the owl's head. I heard a crack.

"Foolish animal," she spat. "She deserved to die."

I shut my eyes, saddened and feeling worthless. I knew that owl was dead for no reason, and for no fault but my own.

"*Well,*" Avery sounded flustered. "I can see you need some time to come around." She kicked the owl carcass away from Lacy and to the side where it rolled against a rock. "But when you're ready to be with me, as you *will* be, you know how to get a hold of me."

Greg arrived at Avery's side, holding his stomach. I looked at him, my eyes crying out, why?

For a moment I saw remorse in his green gaze, but he looked away. I thought about our life before. I thought about Patrick, and what Greg had known. Something about him still wanted for a better life, I knew it.

"*Please,* Greg," I managed weakly.

He turned away, Avery doing the same as she hooked her arm with his, sashaying her hips into the darkness of the woods. I took a moment to gather myself, the silence of the forest like the calm after a storm. Finding my hands beneath me, I pushed myself off the ground. Lacy's body had since changed into human form. She lay unconscious and covered in dirt, her side badly bruised a deep purple. I removed my coat, every movement I made toward her like a million needles to the skin.

Jane's life made me weak, and I could not allow it to happen. With Greg as my enemy, I had to stay strong. I had to remain an angel. The life in me was not mine, and never could be. I had to give it back to the universe to be born to another.

I put the coat around Lacy's bare shoulders.

She roused, taking a moment as she stared at me. "I'm so sorry, I…"

I put my hand to her lips, shaking my head.

Her eyes fluttered, tears forming. She reached for my hand and removed it, grasping tight as she felt my warmth. "You're alive, aren't you?" She let go, knowing what that meant. "I never knew her, but I know how this must feel for you."

I clasped my hands around her shoulders and helped Lacy to her feet. "I won't keep this life inside me. I can't."

Lacy zipped the jacket which was like a dress on her. She shook her head, brows stitched together. "Do you even have a choice?"

I nodded. "It was my life to protect. I can do with it as I please."

"You can't give the life away."

I pressed my lips together. "It's already left her as mine left me. My life has been given to another somewhere in this world. I know you're afraid this means I'm giving away her soul, but that doesn't happen. A soul can only belong to one. This…" I thumped my chest, "is just a life, and it's not mine. It must go."

"I don't understand," she frowned.

I nodded. "You will."

"Well, how do you get rid of it?"

"Like this," I shut my eyes and let go. It was hard, my body craving it, wanting to hold it inside my bones. I felt my temperature drop, and before I knew it, the feeling of it was gone all together. An immense drought of emotion blew over me, and I felt more alone than ever. I shuddered as my legs faltered. Lacy was quick to support me. The longer I held on to the life, the harder it would have been to let go. It was the right thing to do.

"So, just like that you're an angel again?" She looked me over, not really seeing the immediate difference.

I nodded. "I never lost the angel in me. That can never be taken away no matter how hard I try. What I would have gotten was mortality and the ability to live a short, human life of emotion and weakness. Sounds uneventful, but in my eyes it's a luxury."

"Oh." I watched her let the idea sink in, looking down at her body. Her mind traced over the idea of what it felt like to be me. She understood, eyes leveling with mine once more. My gaze darted away from her to the nearby rock where her owl lay lifeless, changing the subject.

Lacy followed my gaze and gasped quietly. "Missy." She rushed to her side, carefully running her hand over her crumpled feathers and broken neck.

I turned away from them, looking to the edge of the cliff where Jane's mother stood, back to me, head looking down and over the edge. I felt my chest tighten, though no emotion existed for me to take. I walked one foot in front of the other, arriving at her side with my eyes looking out ahead of me.

Sarah reached for my hand and I felt her pain resonate through it. Finally, I gathered the strength to look down, seeing the one thing I never wished to see on the bank below. Jane's body lay on the rocks, curled gently into herself. For a moment I wanted to believe she was simply sleeping, but this being on the rocks was just a shell, just a projection of the soul that once owned it. Her spirit had been ripped apart, her soul locked in the Ever After where it longed to be.

"Will she come back?" Sarah asked.

I squeezed her hand. "She has to," I whispered, fingering the chain around my neck with my other hand. It hadn't released. This wasn't over. "I promised her I'd fix this."

THE MASTER laid the owl's dead body on a rock, her feathered head broken by the devil herself. *"My Missy,"* the Master whispered.

The owl heard her but could not reply. All she ever wanted was to be human. All she ever wanted was the chance to finally meet him and win his love. Since the day she saw his picture, her animal instincts had changed. She was stuck in a body that was not her own, and now she was dead inside it. Hope was lost.

The Master left her on the rock with a kiss, her guardian and friend for so many years. From above the owl watched as wind tickled at feathers she once possessed, feelings she once felt, and hope she once believed in. Her soul lingered for a while over the body she once called home, now filled with nothing.

Just then, as she floated above a world she was destined to leave, a blue light drifted toward her through the air with no direction. It was a strangely enticing blue light that drew her in, all the while still above the lonely body she once owned. She watched it curiously, danced around it until the light no longer danced back. Staring longingly at it, the owl was no longer able to avoid its beauty. The two collided.

Alone in the woods, a new life was born to a human girl, left lying on a rock where a friend once left her. Opening her eyes, the world seemed foreign, and quickly, the past she once knew faded away. Slowly sitting up in a body so suddenly natural to her, she noticed that around her lay a bed of brown and white feathers. Her soft, human skin was in strange contrast to these feathers she felt she knew, but something inside her forgot how.

"Who am I?" she asked out loud. The words sounded foreign on her tongue, but words she knew and understood nonetheless. The world whispered back, but it was too quiet to hear.

"*Who am I?*" she asked again, gently plucking a feather from the rock and inspecting it, pulling her knees to her chest against a chill.

The world whispered back on another gust of wind, but still she did not understand. Twisting the feather in her hand, a strange sensation overwhelmed her. "*Stella,*" she whispered, but she didn't know why. In a second her body had changed, owl wings flanking her side. She did not understand how or why she had so quickly changed, but again it did not surprise her. A part of her felt this was what she'd wanted all along. Testing her theory, she once imagined the soft skin of before, and before she knew it, she again found herself sitting on the rock with human hands that were full of lose feathers.

A Natural Shifter had been born to a life already used...

About The Author

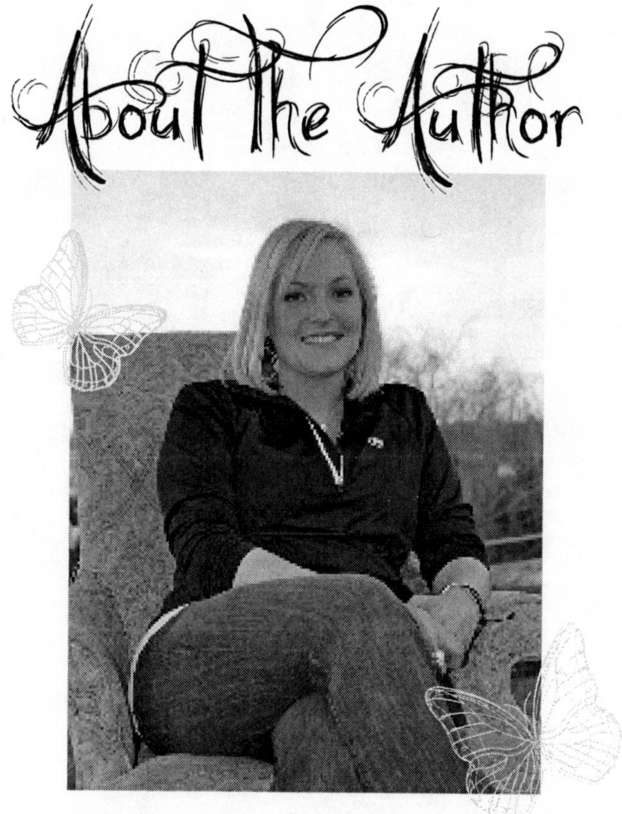

Abra Ebner lives in Washington State with her husband and two cats. She loves to golf, read, cook, write, and dream. She graduated from Washington State University with a degree in Graphic Arts, as well as studying abroad at the Queensland College of Art.

Aside from writing, she says there is nothing that gives her as much joy, other than love and memories. Every day we live our own story. Never forget that.

Visit her blog at:

www.AbraEbner.Blogspot.com

Visit her websites at:

www.KnightAngels.com
www.FeatherBookSeries.com
www.ParallelTheBook.com

PREVIEW

:::

PARALLEL

The Secret Life of Jordan McKay

:::

Letter
Found in the Personal
Effects of Patient #32185
Vincent Memorial Hospital, Boston

July 12, 2009

My name is Jordan Mckay, and if you've found this, then you have seen the consequences of what led me to my death. There may be things about me that you will find strange, but if you could understand the life I've lived, then you will know more about the nature of my makeup. I am different from everyone; special, unique. I am what I have come to understand is called a Shifter.

Within the boundaries of our life from birth to death, we can travel from one age to the next, leaving a foggy line between our present, past, and future. Here we are able to see how events can change the world, or at the very least, change just one life. If we can manifest a thought hard enough, then we can go there. This is the key to our talent.

I am not completely certain how many of us there are, or why we were created, or even where we came from. I can only guess that it's a glitch in human kind and a chance at playing God. In this world, we learn to fend for ourselves and fight for our basic need for selfish gain. For me, my gain was the love of a woman. A selfless act in my eyes only, but now as I grow to learn what it's done to her, I can see that it was all a mistake that I can no longer take back.

Either way, I have seen that there is a pattern for disaster in this world, and a fear so dark it could swallow the night. I have learned now that you cannot hope to erase all the wrong, only replace it with another. After all, you cannot change your luck; you can only try to change the events that caused the misfortune in the first place.

Manipulation of time is a powerful tool but something I fear is deadly if not completely understood. I hope to reach out to those like me, to save them as I have failed to do for myself, and to tell them that no matter what you do, you cannot hope to make things better. My personal belongings will tell the story...

Jordan McKay

Statement from Dr. Ashcroft,
Vincent Memorial Hospital, Boston
August 3, 2009
11:56 p.m.

Agent Donnery:
When did you meet him?

Dr. Ashcroft:
I met him at twenty-five.

Agent Donnery:
But it say's here that you knew each other since you were six? How is that?

Dr. Ashcroft:
I met him a couple times throughout time, but if you understood what Jordan can do, then you would understand what I mean when I say that we met for the first time when I was twenty-five, and he was twenty-seven. At least according to his driver's license.

Agent Donnery:
What do you mean, according to his license?

Dr. Ashcroft:

Think of Jordan's life as a timeline, only his timeline has been chopped up and rearranged in an order that does not fit science. He could leap around from one place to the next, each place revealing something that has changed, each a parallel life of the one you were just in. When I met him at twenty-five he may have been in the body of his twenty-seven year old self, but his mind had just been six. It's a terrifying thing to have happen to you when you think of it.

Agent Donnery:

I see. So what happened? How and why do you believe, or I suppose know, all this is true? (laughter) It just seems far-fetched is all. I'd like to hear your side of it.

Dr. Ashcroft:

It's hard to believe, I know, but considering the fact that you're from a branch of the C.I.A. that is set up in order to research just such happenings, I believe that there is more out there than I can even try to understand, and that you actually do, or can, believe me.

Agent Donnery:

I can see your angle. It is true that the somewhat fictional nature of what happened here is not too uncommon. Our world has been polluted with so many chemicals and synthetic agents that you would not believe the things I've seen, the things you never thought possible, but of course, you'll never know of them either.

Dr. Ashcroft:

(laughter) Except this.

Agent Donnery:

True, but I also expect your explicit secrecy on the subject.

Dr. Ashcroft:

I'm a doctor, Agent. I'm good with confidentiality.

Agent Donnery:

Then we understand, so please, tell me about Jordan McKay.

Dr. Ashcroft:

(pause) It's difficult for me to accept, even still, but my life was stolen from me. If I had known all along about what was happening, I suppose I would have tried to stop it, though it would have been hard. I have been lied to, led down a path that I no longer see as my own but I am now forced to live. When I was a little girl I used to think I was lucky, that all the great things in my life were God's choice for me, but now I see that God had nothing to do with it.

Agent Donnery:

So you believe that you were at the mercy of Jordan instead?

Dr. Ashcroft:

Yes, he made the decisions, took over God's roll, so to speak, but I only saw it as my reality. I did not know I was like a modern day puppet. (pause) There is nothing left of my real destiny but the stories of a man describing a life I thought was no more than a faint memory, imprinted on my mind like a dream.

When I think back, I can remember it all but it hurts too much to imagine. As I sit here I still can't believe that I fell for it, that I took the easier path that ended with a life that was false.

In the end, I suppose all I can do is live with the cards I have been dealt. I'm in love with my fate, the fate that took me on this parallel path into a place I was never meant to be. I only hope that grace can still find me here, and that I will be forgiven. After all, if God was no part of it, then I guess love is the devil's creation.

Agent Donnery:

I see, so you loved him too?

Dr. Ashcroft:

Yes, I suppose that no matter what, I would have always found myself drawn to him. It was fate after all.

Agent Donnery:

Will you tell us how it happened?

Dr. Ashcroft:

I can try.

Agent Donnery:

(pause) Here, these are the journals you requested, that we found in the office, splayed across the floor.

Dr. Ashcroft:

(pause) Thanks, I (pause) I'm sorry it's just that that the last time I held these, everything changed and my whole world came crashing down.

Agent Donnery:

I understand. (pause) We've gone through it and tried to make sense of it all, but unfortunately it jumps around and it seems things may be missing, or are out of order. Many of the dates are very old.

Dr Ashcroft:

(laughter) Agent Donnery, I'm certain it isn't out of order, that's what you need to understand. See here, each page is numbered in order from beginning to end. You cannot go by date because his world never worked that way. (pause) Here, let me begin telling you what I know, what he knows...

Formulated from the journals
of Patient #32185
May 21, 2009
9:34 p.m.

I was ripped from the park bench where I sat eating the melting popsicle and dreaming about my life, now thrown through a dark tunnel, landing with a sudden crack on the seat of a bus. I grabbed my head in agony, the blood pounding through my swollen veins, making me lightheaded.

A woman in a pink nurse's uniform ran toward me. "Sir, are you okay?"

Her concerned green eyes blinked rapidly, and her figure blurred as I tried to focus on her face.

"Sir?"

She referred to me as sir, but I was only six, or so I had thought. The pain in my head subsided and I sat up, looking at my hands. At first I was confused by the size of them and the aged appearance of my skin, but upon closer inspection, I found they were still my hands, as the scar I had gotten when I was four lingered on my palm but was faded as though healed over time.

"Sir?" she asked again, her voice reverberating loudly in my aching head. I quickly put my hands into the pockets of my jeans to hide them, also shocked by the size of my legs as they protruded from the seat.

What was going on? I looked at her as I finally nodded,

swallowing to ease spit down my dry throat as I looked around the bus, unable to handle her stare for too long.

Was I dreaming? I had to be dreaming. I pinched my leg through the pocket of my pants but it didn't work. I then thought about the fact that if I were dreaming, I wouldn't be wondering if I was because in dreams you typically aren't as conscious as I felt now. As far as I could tell, I was wide awake.

As my eyes darted around the bus, I noticed that the nurse and I were the only ones on board. I could see the driver eyeing me from the front seat through his large rearview mirror, judging me in a way that reminded me of the mean teachers at pre-school. Looking away, nerves overcame me and I grabbed my head as it throbbed like a swelling bruise. The driver cleared his throat and shifted in his seat, and I knew I was making him uncomfortable.

"He's alright!" the lady yelled to him, also noticing his discomfort.

The driver looked relieved as she said this, and he nodded, focusing his gaze on the road ahead.

I rubbed my eyes with my giant hands, feeling as though my brain had somehow expanded in the split second since I had leapt from the park bench to here and I feared it might leak through my ears. It seemed that all I had once known had tripled in size as though someone had plugged a microchip into the back of my head, filling it with years of information and knowledge.

"Sir? What is your name?"

I looked back into the woman's green eyes, finding

them piercing and beautiful as a feeling I had never felt before rushed over me like a hot wave of water. I shrugged, finding myself at a loss for words, my memory too scrambled to speak. I had no recollection of how I got here, no clue as to where I had been.

"May I?"

The woman motioned to search my pockets and I nodded, feeling like a scared little boy. She felt in the lapel of my coat for something, finding whatever it was and pulling it back toward her. I was wearing a green coat that I recognized as my father's, except I now filled it out like I never had before, my body like that of a grown man. My brow began to sweat below the black baseball hat on my head, so I pulled it off, resting it in my lap as I pressed my sweaty curls back, my hair an unacceptable length and a far cry from the maintained crew cut my father had forced me to wear.

A wallet now lay in her grasp and she flicked it open, fishing inside with her dainty fingers, her fuchsia nail polish chipped around the edges. I watched her as she scanned through the compartments, my gaze turning to her face where I noticed a scar. It spread from the right side of her nose back to her ear, leaving a large discolored patch of skin that had tried to mend itself over time, as though a burn from her childhood. Her hair was a deep auburn that was pulled back in a messy ponytail and fastened with a pink rubber band. A few thick strands fell on the right side of her eyes, shielding what it could of the scar, though the attempt was useless.

"Is this you?" She pushed the wallet toward me and I tried to focus on the tiny image as I looked down at the card behind the clear plastic cover. There was a dusty driver's license squeezed into the slot and I touched it with my dirty finger, finding the dates and photo all wrong as I furrowed my brow, my stomach now nauseated. I swallowed hard, reading the name and recognizing it as my own; Jordan McKay, blue eyes, brown hair.

I opened my mouth and narrowed my eyes.

"Er…yes."

I swallowed, frightened by the deep tone of my own voice as I brought my giant hand to my throat, shocked by the Adam's apple that now protruded from the front like a broken bone.

"But…" I brought my hand back to the image and tapped my finger against the plastic, looking at her.

Her green eyes scanned my face.

"It looks like you," she assured.

I nodded, taking her word for it.

She sat down beside me and looked about the bus with frantic eyes. She seemed to be trying to formulate some sort of plan for me, her lips parted as a gentle breath escaped into the air. She looked down at the wallet one last time, her mouth forming words as her eyes traced the blurred letters of the driver's license and address. She perked up then, causing me to shy away out of sudden fear.

"Driver, next stop please!" She looked out the dusty windows that reflected the neon lights inside, searching for some sign of where we were on the route. I couldn't stop watching her and I wondered what was wrong with me, and why I still felt the same strange wave of warmth crash over me, again and again. Another sudden sharp pain racked my body but this time in my stomach, and I winced, grabbing my side.

"Oh!" The woman touched my arm and my mind forgot about the burning in my side and instead focused on her warm hand. "Are you alright?"

I nodded and gave her a shaky smile, forcing down the pain. She focused back on the bus, looking out the windows. I watched her blink as I continued to shut out the pain and swallow the sick taste in my mouth.

My grandmother had often taken me on bus rides, so I was used to the ride and motion, though my large body was hard to keep still. I looked back down at my hands and legs, wondering what had happened to the time between ages six and now. I must be dreaming but it felt real, as though that time had been stolen from me, like what I imagined would happen if I had been in a coma. I wiped a bead of sweat from my brow, my hand scratching across the stubble that grew on my face. I felt my chin, amazed by the feeling of it as it scrubbed my fingers, reveling in the fact I was man enough to grow a full beard.

The bus screeched to a halt and she hooked her arm under mine, lifting me from the seat as I stood on weak legs, the altitude a far cry from that of a three-foot tall preschooler. It was then that I caught a glimpse of my body in the fogged reflection of the bus window, my eyes shocked by the large figure staring back at me. I froze for a moment, taking in the reflection of myself in the green coat, my hair just below my ears, and my face rough and tanned. This could not be real, this could not be happening to me. I was lost.

She led me down the stairs as my body shook. We stepped into the cool night, my hot skin welcoming the cool air as it soothed the warm feeling that still plagued me. She looked from side to side, looking at house numbers as she craned her neck to see over each stoop.

She exhaled sharply, and I could tell she was annoyed but I didn't want her to leave either. She brushed the hair from her face, mumbling something under her breath as she pulled me to the left. I stumbled over my big feet as we went past one stoop after the next, stopping at each to assess the house numbers.

Finally, her pace quickened and I struggled to keep up as a few fat drops of rain fell from the sky.

"Oh thank God," she whispered, stopping before the last stoop on the street and looking up at the numbers.

The few drops of rain turned to a sudden downpour, and she pulled me by the arm up the steps to the door. This time she didn't bother to ask as she rummaged through my coat pockets and found a key. She fumbled with it in her hand, the shiny silver catching what little light there was on the street. I heard the metallic clink of it as it met the lock, turning with a soft thud and releasing the jamb.

She pressed the door inward and pulled me with a firm grip as she searched for a switch. Light erupted across the apartment as she succeeded, and my eyes fell on a scene that felt comforting somehow, as though my brain and body recognized it but my soul did not.

"Ok," she breathed, releasing a relieved breath. "You're

home." She looked around the room and removed her sodden coat and scarf. "Do you mind if I borrow your phone?" Her hair was dripping from the few stray strands on her cheek.

I looked at her and then around the room, wondering where a phone even was, unable to recognize anything but the feeling in my gut that this place was mine. I nodded and shrugged, finding there was little else to do.

She let go of my arm and I steadied myself on my feet as she walked in a brisk pace toward what looked like the kitchen, trusting her instincts as to where a phone could hide. I blinked and looked around the room, taking it in and finding that as I looked closer there were a few things I did recognize like pictures and a few trinkets; all now tattered with age.

Looking up I saw that there was a mirror across the room above a fireplace, and I made my way toward it, moving my hand from one object to the next, hoping each was sturdy enough to support me. Though my large hands had scared me, I found they were much easier to use and could grasp things in their entirety. I supported my weight with my arms, the muscles flexing as they never had before, like He-man's did in my comic books back home, wherever home was.

As I got to the hearth, I placed my hand on the sill, like a newborn baby learning to walk. I could hear the woman in the other room on the phone, whispering in hushed tones that were both frantic and a little scared. I turned my attention to the reflection before me, recognizing nothing but the child I had known underneath, my eyes telling the truth as they still held the twinkle I had known.

My face had grown considerably and the once soft

youthful skin was replaced by stubble and pronounced features. I nodded to myself, finding that overall I was pleased with the way I had turned out, relieved that I was in fact quite handsome despite what my father had said. I watched as I blinked, almost fearing the man in the mirror, still unable to completely accept that he and I were the same entity.

I turned my head and inspected the side view. My nose had the same small hook it always had and my ears were just as big, though the size of my face had now caught up to them. My deep grey-blue eyes were full of the youth I had seen everyday though now pressed into the mask of a man I struggled to know. I did not look much older than twenty-seven, but it was hard to tell as I had never been twenty-seven before.

I saw the woman exit from the kitchen through the reflection of the mirror, coming toward me with reddened eyes and a saddened brow. She kept her gaze away from mine as though ashamed by what had just transpired over the phone, afraid that if she looked at me, she may fall apart.

She tried to gather herself as she cleared her throat. "I told my husband I was working late and missed the bus so I'd just work through the night."

My gut ached with guilt as my eyes followed her lips as she spoke, a soft crimson that reminded me of my mother's when she was upset. I could see in her tired eyes that her husband had been a horrid man. I knew this because I had seen the same look from my mother. Her husband was probably drunk and mean as my father had been and it made my heart throb with pain. I doubt he noticed how beautiful she was, the kiss of a freckle on her cheek, the sharp green of her eyes.

I turned to face her, finding the overwhelming need to give her a hug, to comfort her when it seemed no one would. I put my arms out toward her, and to my surprise she fell into them and began to sob without hesitation, as though I were her best friend. I felt awkward holding her, my body looming over her small frame and my arms wrapping around her almost twice.

After a moment she pulled back and wiped the tears from her face, her scar reddened by the blood that had rushed to her cheeks. "I'm sorry, I must seem crazy; inviting myself in and hugging a complete stranger." She blinked and looked me in the eyes.

"Oh…" I paused, still surprised by my own voice. "It's alright." I cleared my throat. "To tell you the truth I don't what happened to me, either, I feel as out of sorts as you."

She blinked some more and narrowed her eyes. "You must have some sort of amnesia or perhaps you had a seizure?"

Her attention turned away from the phone call and back to me. She grabbed my cheeks and looked into my eyes, inspecting them before grabbing my hand and leading me to the couch in front of the fireplace. She sat me down, taking the cushion beside me, her movements graceful.

"Forgive me, but something about you seems different." She put her hand out and grabbed my cheek to turn my head to face her.

I shied away from her touch, but she was stubborn.

"You have the eyes of a child, but the body of a man." Her eyes were full of a depth I doubted few could understand the way I did now. It felt so sudden, so strange to feel this way about someone I hardly knew. I found it hard to justify the connection, but there was one. It was as though I had grown up with her as her best friend, been there for every stage of her life.

"I…" I paused, finding the words I was about to say absurd.

She looked at me with an eager stare.

"I don't expect you to believe me, but I was six just a short while ago, and now I'm here and I'm…"

"Twenty-seven?" she finished my sentence.

I nodded. "Sure, I suppose."

"It was on the license," she nodded and pursed her lips, taking a moment to think before looking back to me, content with her answer.

I glanced around the room and took a deep breath. I could tell she didn't believe me, more likely she just believed I was crazy, but it didn't matter. I needed to say it because to me it was real. "I think I may not be in the right time, if that makes sense. Do you think that's possible?"

She laughed. "I'm not sure but I wish that were true." I saw her roll her eyes and turn the scarred side of her face away from me. "I wish I could change things and go back in time." she allowed herself to imagine it.

I laughed in return. "What would you change? You seem wonderful." I was surprised that she was willing to entertain the idea and it distracted me from the fear in my stomach.

She smiled and I could see tears welling in her eyes. This stranger before me felt like much more than that, as though she were an old friend, someone whom had risked many things to save me tonight, to make me feel as though I was not lost.

She let out one chuckle. "I would change everything."

My heart stung as she said it, feeling the hurt and pain in her words. It did not seem fair that such a beautiful creature could become so forgotten by God, left to fend for herself in a world where no one would lend a hand.

"I would take back all I've done." She ran her hand along the hem of her nurse's scrubs. "I would change this." She touched her face and ran her hand across the scar. "It changed everything for me, took my beauty, my confidence." She pressed back tears. "I used to want to be a doctor, but when you look like a monster, everything is hard."

I watched her with focused eyes, my heart breaking at her every word.

"And my husband…" She shook her head.

"You deserve better." I knew what to say because I had longed to tell my mother the same thing for years but I never got the chance before she died. I always thought that when she got cancer it was God's answers to her prayers. My mother wanted to die; I saw it in her face everyday and now I saw it in the woman's as well, the look of an empty soul that had been left alone in this world.

She nodded and sobbed into her hands. "I'm twenty-five with so much future left to live but I fear I don't want to, I fear my own mind. I have tried so hard that now I have given up.

What other choice do I have but to accept my awful fate?"

I placed my hand on her back. "If I could I would save you," I mumbled, and in my mind, I made it a point to save her. No matter what life I was now living, this was my single focus from here on out.

She laughed with tear stained eyes. "I would love you for that."

She looked at me then, and for the first time since reading Cinderella, I felt what love at first sight was like.

"This seems strange, but I think we were meant to meet." My breathing was shallow but I knew enough about fate and life to know that everything happened for a reason.

She smiled, revealing perfect teeth, "You don't even know my name."

I smiled back. "Well then, what's your name?"

A sly look crossed her face and I knew it meant trouble. "Well," she paused, still thinking. "If we were meant to meet, and you're not from this time, let's make a game of it. Let's say that the next time I meet you, whatever time that is, then I will tell you my name."

I laughed. "Makes sense. But how will you remember?"

She winked at me, "Fate will remind me. No matter what happens, meeting you now has left a mark on me that will never fade, just like my scar. No matter what time, I won't forget you. I promise."

She put her hand in the air like a pledge before lowering it back into her lap. "For the record, a part of me really does believe you. I like to think there are still amazing and unexplainable things in this world."

"Well then, you may be the only one that does believe me. I couldn't imagine anyone else would." The conversation hit a lull as we both thought over what was just explained.

She shifted on the cushion of the couch. "Is it alright if I stay here?" She looked me in the eyes, finding a reason. "I mean besides, if you have had a seizure, you'll want me here to watch you to make sure you don't have another."

I shrugged. "Sure, I don't mind." Truthfully I wanted her to stay, not just because I liked this woman but because I was also frightened to be alone.

She shook her head with a smile. "And to think, earlier today I figured God was a fraud. I guess this is his way of proving me wrong."

I raised my eyebrows and thought about my own predicament. "Yeah, me too."

She laughed again, and it made me feel good, as though her laughter had touched my very soul. There was another couch opposite the one on which we were sitting, and I eyed it. I was sure I had a bedroom somewhere, but I desperately wanted to be close to her, to hear her sleep. After another moment of silence I made a move to get up, but she stopped me.

"You stay here." She rose from the couch and grabbed a blanket that had been thrown over the back and laid it over me, tucking the edges. She then walked over to the other couch and let herself fall into it, exhaling as her back met the cushion, dust flying everywhere.

We laid there for a moment before I heard her breathing change, and when I looked, I saw she was asleep. There were dark circles under her eyes and I could swear she looked dead, but I could understand. This woman beside me had given me all her heart, her last ounce of understanding; just as I was sure she had to everyone she'd met.

I pressed my head against the pillow, feeling lost. Why was I here? Why was I living this dream? I pinched my arm, but nothing happened. What if this was real? What if I had somehow traveled into my future, as I had longed to do for so long? I always wanted to know that there was life beyond what I knew at home, beyond the hell that was my childhood. Perhaps I had manifested it hard enough that now here I was, living it.

I shut my eyes, concentrating now on the past and the life I had known. The room began to feel cold and things around me to shook like an earthquake. I opened my eyes and looked at the woman, but she did not wake. It was then that the same feeling overcame me and my blood began to boil in my veins. I opened my mouth to scream, but before I could utter a word, I was back on the park bench with nothing but a popsicle stick in my hand and an orange stain on my khakis where it had melted.

LaVergne, TN USA
06 October 2010
199742LV00001B/44/P